LIES & LEGACY

PROJECT GENE ASSIST
BOOK THREE

ALLIE POTTS

Axil Hammer Publishing

2020

First edition
ISBN: 978-0-9968320-4-5

Allie Potts asserts the moral right to be identified as the author of this work.
Cover Image by Willyam Bradberry, courtesy of www.123rf.com

Ordering information
Special discounts are available on quantity purchases by corporations, associations, educators, and others. For details, contact the publisher.

For Tim & Ann

Who taught me there's more to family than blood

chapter one

JULIANE

Every push and pull of muscle, every articulation of bone, burnt like wildfire. Juliane had no idea how long it had taken her climb out of the metal tube or cross the raised platform housing the cryogenic cylinders—remembering her name had been difficult enough. Had it been mere minutes? It felt more like days or hours.

Her arms and chest ached where tubes once connected her to the inside of the tank. The smell of stale air, which met her upon waking, took on the scent of dirt, decay, and a hint of animal as the moments passed.

A pair of lighting fixtures dangled askew, giving her pause as she scanned her surroundings. The shadows they cast around the room made her disorientation even worse. The cavernous space should have been a familiar room. However, the image of what the area should look like in her brain directly contrasted with the reality before her.

Large blocks of stone and ceiling fragments littered the room. Pillars of steel support beams stood twisted or lay broken altogether on the ground. The floor should have been marble tile, polished to a high shine. Instead, the area could be better described as dirt-covered rubble than as a room. *A cave is a more apt description. Except a cave wouldn't have a pair of elevator doors on its far side.* That exit was blocked now.

Her heart began to race. *How do I know that?* The memory remained locked away in her brain, and the more she tried to force herself to remember, the more a sharp pain erupted from the center of her forehead.

"Get it together, Juliane," she muttered. The pain receded as quickly as it had materialized. "It's just a broken elevator shaft." Wet drops fell from her face onto the floor below. She wiped the offending moisture away. Crying would do nothing except make it more difficult to navigate her way through the room.

She inspected the ground in front of her more closely. *At least there doesn't appear to be any glass.* She gingerly took another step. She didn't yet trust her legs to keep her from falling.

She looked over her shoulder at the row of cylinders. Two lay open—the one she'd crawled from and one other. Her eyes narrowed at the second cylinder. It had to have once contained another subject like herself. *Or does it?* The throbbing in her head resumed. Though her fingers itched to pry the nearest one open to confirm her suspicion, she stopped herself. If people were contained in the other cylinders and were lying in stasis like she'd been, she might inadvertently cause irreparable harm by powering them down without the proper sequence. Her current situation was enough proof of that.

She tore her gaze from the other metal tubes and turned toward the elevator doors once more as she tried to recall why she'd agreed to go into cold sleep in the first place. There had to have been some reason. However, Juliane didn't recall being sick or having a life-threatening condition. Try as she might, her reasoning—along with the memory of the moments leading up to entering the tank—eluded her. *It doesn't matter*, she decided.

A breeze caressed her cheek. Turning toward its source, she spied another door, one she hadn't noticed before. It led to a small auxiliary room, partially blocked by a pile of boulders. Natural light shone from above, revealing a narrow tube and a dark iron emergency access ladder. The ladder's rungs were covered in clumps of dirt rather than the fine dust that covered everything else. *Had someone recently come through here?* she wondered. Whoever it was, they had left her behind.

Juliane grimaced. The walk from the dais to the ancillary room had been painful enough. Climbing a ladder would be murder on her deteriorated muscles. *What other choice do I have?*

She glanced back in the direction she'd come from. The dangling light fixtures, no longer sensing movement in the room, shut themselves off, leaving a gaping maw of infinite darkness in place of the room. It was as good as a tomb. *That settles it.* Unless she wanted to be buried down there for eternity, it was up to her to pull herself out.

Hair tucked behind her ears, she braced herself against the pain and grabbed onto the first rung, then the next. Pieces of the ladder had eroded with rust, creating pockmarks of rough patches. As much as she tried to avoid them, the narrow passage left little wiggle room. The fabric of her clothing ripped as it was caught on a ragged edge.

She cursed. She'd loved the outfit after discovering the designer years ago. Her brow wrinkled as a few memories began to return. She'd gone into the Apex building dressed to impress. There was a presentation. A door opened. *Then what?* She bit her lip in frustration. Why could she remember that much, but not the following minutes? It was like waiting for the blood to return in a leg after sitting too long.

She made a note to conduct a long follow-up discussion with the person responsible for the cryogenic tank's design.

And she'd conduct an even *longer* one with the person who crafted its safety and operating procedures when she was more fully recovered.

A pain shot down her side as her muscles cramped. The sound of fabric tearing returned her attention to the present. She grimaced both from the pain and what the sound meant. *It's only a suit*, she reminded herself as she climbed higher and higher. *You can always get another.*

Emerging at the top of the ladder, Juliane stood and turned around. She should be at the base of a building. Instead, she found herself alone on the side of a mountain of debris. Even more disconcerting, the rest of the landscape was alien in appearance. High-rises, testaments to the highest achievements of civil engineering and modern architecture, should have surrounded her. Instead, all she saw were puddles of mud, empty shells of brick and concrete, and streets devoid of humanity. Perhaps her memories were even faultier than she'd first suspected. *I can't still be in Worcester. Can I? What happened?*

A strong wind picked up, striking her face. Grit found its way into her eyes, causing them to water. *It's the wind.* She told herself. *I am not crying again.*

She scanned the ground, noting a slight path cutting into the rock. She took it as confirmation of her suspicions about the clumps of earth she'd found at the base of the ladder. Someone had come this way not too long ago.

She shielded her eyes from the sun and looked around, searching for more evidence she wasn't the only survivor of whatever cataclysm had befallen here, but found no further clues. The path proved to go no further than around the parameter of the destruction. Soon, she was back at the ladder access. She chewed her lip, debating her next step. *I guess I will have to find my own way out of this mess.*

"Wait." A muffled voice came from the access door. Juliane froze in her tracks. A pale hand reached out through the gap.

The urge to flee sent her heart racing as she looked around for a place to hide. *What are you doing?* She forced herself to remain straight and tall. *You are Juliane Faris. You don't hide.*

The hand was attached to an arm streaked with a mix of red and brown, the color of blood. "A little help here," the voice called again.

She blinked. Thoughts of panicked flight left her as memories of the voice's owner trickled into her consciousness. Her eyes widened. She rushed over to the access door and flung it open. Bending over, she pulled her onetime shopping partner and the Apex group's legal expert from the narrow opening, dragging him out until his stomach rested on the ground. "Durham! Are you okay?"

"I've been better," he answered in between panted breaths. "For a second there, I wasn't sure I was going to be able to pull myself out the rest of the way. What the hell happened?" he asked.

"I was hoping you'd tell me."

"The last thing I remember was being in the big conference room when someone ran in screaming about birds attacking the building."

"You're doing better than I am, then. I'm having difficulties remembering even that much."

"Lucky me." Durham pulled himself the rest of the way up. His forehead was streaked with sweat and dirt, making his normally short white hair appear gray. What was left of his shredded shirt was equally drenched. His arm must not have been the only part of him to have been injured. More dark streaks of dried blood lined his face like war paint.

She saw his eyes take in her appearance from head to toe. He whistled.

"I take it I won't be winning any beauty pageants any time soon, either," she said.

"Speak for yourself. Everyone knows chicks dig scars." He grinned. "I'm going to be fighting them off with a stick after this."

Juliane raised an eyebrow, wanting to laugh, but at the same time not wanting to encourage him. She'd kept her distance from Durham upon leaving the ACI and once again after learning he too had signed with Damien Knightley and the advisory board at Apex—he'd reminded her too much of . . . of . . .

"Right," he said with a chuckle. "I mean more than usual." His smile slipped looking into her eyes. "Hey," he said, reaching out. "It's going to be okay."

Juliane stiffened and pulled back. She'd let her guard down once before. She wouldn't do it again. A winged shadow danced across the remains of the sandstone office tower, reminding Juliane just how isolated they were. "We need to find you some help."

"I've had worse injuries on the field," he said as he tore a scrap of cloth off his shirt and wrapped it around his arm. "See, nothing to worry about. Though, if you are so worried about it, I'm happy to go back to your place." He winked.

"Which might have been an option if my place didn't currently look like a death trap." She nodded toward the remains of a building up ahead. "You need a doctor." Juliane held up a hand. "In fact, follow my finger." She waved a finger from side to side without breaking eye contact.

Durham laughed again. His gaze remained locked on hers. "I think I would know if I have a concussion."

"Oh, really?" she drawled. "And here I was under the impression you went to law school, not medical."

"And here *I* thought *your* title came from a Ph.D."

Juliane pressed her lips together. While he might have a point regarding her degrees, she had spent several years studying the human brain as part of her research work. She might not have a medical degree, but she was far from unqualified to diagnosis an obvious head trauma.

"Fine. I'll call up a ride." Durham's expression went vacant while he accessed the datastream. He blinked. "Um, maybe you should try. I can't seem to reach anybody."

Juliane smirked. "Are you surprised? Look around."

"I've seen worse."

"Hmm," Juliane tilted her head. She supposed whatever had turned the place into a ghost town could be limited to the immediate area. However, she doubted it. Still, to be sure she focused her thoughts and issued a command to access the datastream for herself and opened her utility apps.

A series of icons floated across her vision. Like being able to access the datastream with a thought, the augmented reality was another of Project Gene Assist's benefits. She scrolled through the list with simple eye movement, selecting the rideshare program she installed years ago, but never used. The app icon showed the program's central host was offline.

She re-routed her signal, so it appeared she was looking for a ride in Seattle and then again in Dallas. Those city's local hosts were offline too.

She toggled open her phone app, however, there were few people she could think of to call, even on a normal day, and one of them was standing next to her.

"You got nothing, too?" Durham frowned. "That can't be good. I thought the whole point of the upgrade was to ensure we never lost connection."

"I'm not sure the network is the issue."

The scream of a large bird of prey echoed from above. She glanced up at the violet-tinged sky, but the source of the sound was no longer anywhere to be seen.

"What was that?" asked Durham, who'd also looked up at the sound.

"A bird, I assume," she said, turning her attention back to the empty road ahead. "Can you walk?"

"Not a problem," said Durham. "As I said, I've played through worse injuries." His eyes twinkled. "There was this one time, back when—"

"Is this story going to end with you spraining your ankle after jumping out of a sorority girl's bedroom window the morning of the big match?"

"No," said Durham placing his hand over his heart. "It was my knee."

Juliane rolled her eyes.

Durham continued on as if he hadn't noticed. "If that bush hadn't broken my fall at just the right moment, it would have ended my season."

"That would have been an absolute shame." Juliane scanned ahead. They couldn't possibly be the only people left in the world. *Where is everyone?*

He grinned. The dirt on his face created dark wrinkles that did nothing to make him seem any less boyish. "I'm glad you agree."

The sun shone on them as they made their way down the mountain of debris and into what used to be downtown. The first sign of life, other than the bird, proved to be a wooden building, the sort that could pass for a set piece in an old-fashioned western movie. It stood where there had been empty lots before, complete with horses tied to a railing outside.

The horses shifted nervously as they approached, but appeared well-fed and otherwise used to humans. Other survivors had to be inside.

The breeze whipped grit into her eyes. A hint of coming autumn tickled her nose. *Which would mean we've been in that basement room for at least . . .* She frowned. She'd been so busy with her work, she'd barely noticed the seasons change before. However, she recalled a sea of green around the statue of Marie Curie in the park she'd gone to before making her presentation. *So at least three months.*

She rubbed her forehead. Rage bubbled up inside of her. They'd been left to die down there. *Why?* A male's voice whispered at the edge of her memories. The answer lay inside her mind, she was convinced of it, but his identity and exact words were lost like a half-forgotten nightmare. Her chest tightened. A wave of dizziness struck her, causing her to stumble.

"Whoa," said Durham, catching her arm.

She grimaced. "Sorry about that."

"What's to be sorry for? It's not your fault there's a pothole every couple of feet." His hand lingered on her arm.

"I'm fine," she said, straightening. She tested her ankle, relieved to find she hadn't damaged it like she had that night in Vegas. She noticed he was still looking at her. Her stomach fluttered. If she wasn't more careful, he was going to start mistaking her for some clumsy damsel in distress. *When did you start caring what he thinks about you?* she asked herself. He opened his mouth as if to say something. Her gaze darted elsewhere. "I don't," she muttered.

"You don't what?"

"Nothing. Just thinking out loud. Forget I said anything."

"Whatever you say, boss."

She smiled in spite of herself and turned to use his words against him, when he said, "Huh, no glass."

Following his gaze, she saw the building's only protection from the elements seemed to be a pair of worn shutters. As they got closer, she heard the distinctive clang of tableware being slapped down. The front door was cracked open. By the sound, Juliane suspected it had to be a restaurant or pub of some kind.

"What's wrong?" asked Durham, when Juliane hesitated.

"There is something about this place." She shook her head as if the physical action would counteract her body's instinct to remain out of sight. She pressed her lips together when that didn't work and issued a command to her nervous system, demanding it cease production of adrenaline or any other chemical that might get in the way of logic.

The Gene Assist serum had been developed to give people the ability to access the datastream directly from their minds instead of requiring a device like a phone or tablet. However, the team had learned it had also given them the ability to control so much more. She took a calming breath as the command took effect.

"What? Not a fan of missing windows?" asked Durham. "I wouldn't worry about it. They probably have the kind that swings open from the inside."

She tapped her lip. "It's not the lack of glass," she said, lowering her voice. "There's something else, only I can't put my finger on it." She closed her eyes and took another breath.

She opened her eyes as another wave of artificial calm swept through her system and sighed. "You're probably right. I suppose it's the result of waking up the way we did more than anything else." She turned to the door, pulling it slightly more open.

Through the crack, she spotted candles mounted to the walls which illuminated areas the sun couldn't reach. There were a few patrons, but none were seated near each other, and all were clothed in garments that hadn't received a proper cleaning in ages.

"So, are we going to just stand here?" whispered Durham.

Juliane frowned but pulled the door open the rest of the way. She expected all the eyes in the room to turn to them, but instead, everyone remained fixated on the mugs in front of them. "I'll go and talk to the bartender. Maybe he can tell us about what happened while we were asleep."

Durham nodded. "I'll find us a seat while we wait." He looked around the room. "Not that it'll be hard."

As she crossed the room, one of the other patrons rose and beat her to the bar and held his mug out for a refill. The bartender took the mug from his hand and turned to fill it. "Interesting times, Joel," said the patron in a low voice. "People are saying we're on our own again. Watch is gone. Beginning to wonder about who or what might come next."

"I did not set up shop so I could worry about a bunch of stories about things that go bump in the night. I suggest you consider doing the same."

"You've got to be the only innkeeper I've ever met who didn't trade in news on the side."

So, not just a restaurant, then. Juliane glanced back toward where Durham sat waiting. *Good to know there is a place to sleep, considering how long it is taking to get anyone's attention.* However, the last thing she wanted to do was spend the night in this place. "Excuse me," she said, turning back to the bartender. "This may sound odd, but—"

"Perhaps, but I've been in this town since the day it happened—fifteen years. I'd like to survive the next fifteen as well," replied the man behind the bar. "The way you are flapping your gums around makes me think I'd be better off collecting that credit you've run up."

"Could either of you—" said Juliane.

"Now, now, let's not say anything hasty. It's almost winter. I'll need money for salt. In fact, I was hoping you'd be willing to extend my credit based on work or some other barter . . ." The patron's voice, which had already been low, dropped significantly as he continued. "My Elyse . . ." He gestured toward the window. "She's a decent cook."

"Ahem."

He traced a finger along the surface of the bar, checking his finger for dust. "And having a woman around here . . . you'd do well by offering a few more options on the menu." The way the man said the word *options* suggested something altogether different from food.

Questions about the state of their surroundings and how they'd gotten that way fled her mind. The man at the bar couldn't possibly be trying to pay off a bar tab by selling a woman or suggesting the innkeeper do the same. She blinked as his other, earlier, comment struck her. He'd said he'd been here for fifteen years, but Juliane had never seen this place before.

"No doubt it would, but I've no interest in that sort of business," said the innkeeper. "You may, however, want to have a talk with Wally down the street. He always did have a thing for your girl. I suspect he'd be grateful enough to help you pay down some of your tab." The bartender glanced Juliane's way for the first time. "That goes for you, too."

Juliane's brow knit together. "I beg your pardon."

"We don't need any beggars here, either." He made a point of eyeing her up and down. "Or strangers who clearly aren't carrying anything to trade with other than trouble and a pretty face. Best you continue on your way."

Juliane turned on her heel and marched back to Durham. Grabbing him by the shoulder so tightly she nearly ripped his shirt, she said. "We're going."

"Did you get any answers?" He stood and followed her to the door.

"No, and I wouldn't accept help from any of these people now, even if they offered." She let the door slam behind her, startling the horses tied out front.

Durham glanced their way. "Where do you want to try next? I checked my email. Got a couple of messages from my building manager. Stuff about how he couldn't guarantee anyone's safety and how the building isn't liable for any damage. Doesn't sound like going to my place is going to be an option."

"Weren't you seeing someone who worked at the hospital? A nurse or something? Does she live nearby? What about calling her?"

He grimaced. "I doubt she'll want to hear from me . . . hold on." His eyes glazed over for a moment. "No luck. The call won't go through. Timing out. I can't even leave a voicemail. Face it. Nobody's home, at least not in Worcester."

"Hmm . . . where else should we go?" wondered Juliane, aloud.

"Well, while I was waiting for you, I did, overheard one of the guys at one of the other tables say he was heading to New York. Could be that's where most people went."

"I suppose," said Juliane, tapping her chin. "Though . . . in most post-disaster scenarios I've read about people tend to flee from the big cities, not the other way around."

"Well, interesting you say that too, because, his buddy didn't take it well. Tried to talk him out of it. Said some group runs the city now, calling themselves Sorcerers."

"Sorcerers?" The corner of Juliane's mouth turned up. "What? Do they run around in robes? Wave wands around?"

Durham grinned and shook his head. "He didn't say, but what he did say was 'Those that go there never leave Manhattan again.'"

"If Manhattan is still remotely more civilized than this place, I wouldn't want to, either."

"So, you want to head there, too?"

Juliane chewed her lip. "I'm not sure that's a good idea. I'd still like to find out what happened here."

"So, we go to where the people are and ask. You were big on me getting checked out by a doctor a while ago. Bound to be one or two."

Her eyes traced his injuries. "And just how do you suggest we get there? It's at least forty miles from Worcester, if not more."

"I might have an idea," he said with a sly grin.

"Oh? Were you able to reach a working taxi service while I stood at the bar like the invisible woman? It will take us more than a day to get to the closest one on foot."

"I didn't mean walking," he said, nudging his head to the side at the wooden railing.

"You aren't suggesting we steal these people's horses, are you?"

"You said it was like they couldn't see you."

"Yeah, well, I'm pretty sure that would change the minute either of us climbed up on one of those saddles." She placed a hand on her hip. "Besides, I don't even know how to ride a horse."

"It's not that hard once you find the rhythm." His eyes twinkled. "And I wouldn't worry about that in your case. After all, I've seen how you dance. My guess—you'll be a natural."

Heat rose to her cheeks at the reminder. She was still working with the ACI at the time. She'd had too much to drink following the success of their presentation in Las Vegas and had allowed herself to give in to the music. She'd wound up giving in to some of her baser urges too. She turned before her face gave her away. "Now I know you must have bumped your head harder than you let on." She willed the blush away and turned back. "You're nuts. What if they call the police?"

"Then at least we'd get a ride, even if it's only to jail. But in all seriousness, Juliane," Durham's voice lowered and the humor fled. "I'd be more worried about guns."

Juliane's lips twisted. "Is that supposed to convince me to agree to your plan?"

"No," he said. "This is." Without waiting for Juliane to respond, Durham jogged over to the closest animal and untied its reins. The beast looked his way but didn't protest as Durham proceeded to pull himself up into the saddle.

Juliane stood in place, stunned, as Durham directed the horse away from the inn. She strained her ears for any indication that the patrons inside had noticed the animal being led away. However, the only sound was that of the odious man from the bar announcing to the group that his Elyse would be joining the inn's staff.

Juliane's gaze fell upon the horse. With any luck, it belonged to the man bragging about his Elyse. She imagined him coming outside and finding it missing. Her lips twitched. Perhaps, whoever Elyse was, she, too, would be gone before he returned home. She would be doing Elyse, or any other Elyses unfortunate enough to be tied to these men, a favor by delaying the horse owner's return.

"I can't believe I am doing this," she muttered to herself as she untied the second set of reins. The animal snorted and pulled away. Juliane wrinkled her nose at the animal. "I'm as excited as you are." A shout came from the direction of the inn. The horse shook its head as if to say, "Hurry up."

"Don't get an attitude with me. I'm trying," muttered Juliane under her breath as she pulled herself up on its back and set off after Durham.

chapter two

STEPHEN

Stephen lay on his back, looking up at the pink-tinged sky. His eyes itched like they'd been left out too long in the desert, but every time they closed, he saw his foster-mother's cold dead face staring back at him. Except it was different—the way she looked at him—it was as if she saw all his flaws in death in a way she never could in life. A buzzing by his ear provided the much-needed distraction from his thoughts. He slapped his arm where a mosquito landed. "I'm pretty sure I've lost enough blood, thank you very much," he muttered.

"Did you say something?" The girl lying next to him asked.

"Nothing," he answered. "Just talking to myself."

Bean smiled and reached out her hand. He took it, entwining her fingers with his own. Another insect buzzed near his forehead. His eyes closed by instinct, and his foster-mother's withered expression jumped in to fill the void. It wasn't the Helen he remembered. *I mean Nadia*, he corrected himself. His guardians may have lied to him his entire life about their true identities, but learning they had other names didn't bother Stephen at all.

Ed or Chad, Helen or Nadia—they could have called themselves whatever they wanted. A number of the people he'd met since leaving the farmhouse changed names like clothing. However, in all his nineteen years, he'd never once questioned that Chad and Nadia loved him. Only there was no love the face he saw now when he thought of Nadia—only hurt and accusation.

Stephen deserved every bit of it. Nadia died because of a touch. His touch. He'd been injured, barely on the warm side of death. His body had pulled at her energy on instinct. Robbing her of her life force. Draining her dry before he even comprehended what he was doing. It might have been an accident, but his foster-mother was no less dead. All because of him.

Bean's hand was warm in his, the exact opposite of his foster-mother's. It was full of life. Energy. It sang to him like a siren of myth, calling to him with a sweet potency more addictive than any sugary treat. All he had to do was let it pour in. Opening himself up to its rush was the easy part.

Stopping the flow, on the other hand, was the problem. He yanked his hand away from hers before whatever lurked inside him took advantage of the situation. *Don't even think it.*

The smile fell from her lips.

His brain hadn't allowed him to fully process what he'd done to Nadia at the moment—it had been too busy working on how to keep both he and Bean alive. In his mind's eye, he relived the race through the maze of hallways. He saw, all too clearly, the beastman's fist connect with Bean's jaw. His ears rang with the sickening crack followed by the thud of her body hitting the floor. There had been no time for guilt or grief in those adrenaline-fueled minutes. But now? He chewed his lip until the wave of emotions passed. Bean was all he had left in the world. She needed him to be strong. What would she think if he suddenly became a blubbering mess? He pretended to swat at the air with the hand that had held hers a moment ago.

"These bugs are driving me crazy," he said. "Good thing the weather is changing. A cold snap will take care of them."

Deep down, he knew Bean would understand if he told her what was going through his mind. All he had to do was say the words. After all, a similar event had happened to her, back when she was a little girl. The victim had been her sister.

But just because she would understand didn't mean he wanted her to. He'd seen the look in Bean's eyes when he'd told her she wasn't a monster, before battle erupted. If he told her about the swirling mix of self-doubts filling his brain in the hours that followed—if he told her what he might do— she might start thinking his second thoughts were about her, too. He couldn't, *wouldn't* risk that.

Though her sister's death had been accidental, Bean's parents had given her to Dr. Lambda and the Watch to experiment on. She hadn't told him all they'd done to her, but he'd seen how she'd looked at Dr. Lambda the second before the doctor's life ended. Bean might say a person's past mistakes didn't matter, but some mistakes were harder to forgive than others.

At least the Watch and its leader, Dr. Lambda wouldn't be terrorizing anyone anymore. *Focus on the future. You can't change the past,* he told himself.

He turned on his side and centered his thoughts. The world around him was replaced with a digital construction— the datasphere. Though he lay on the ground in the real world, he stood in the middle of a grassy field in the digital one. A large button floated approximately three feet off the artificial ground. Stephen pressed it, and another figure materialized.

"You rang?" the newcomer asked. It was a young man, aged somewhere in his late teens or early twenties. He realized he'd never asked his friend what his age was before. Now, he supposed, it didn't matter. His best friend was dead now, too. All that was left of him was an avatar programmed with his memories and personality who'd made the datasphere his new home.

"So, this lady with all the answers. Where are we supposed to find her, anyway?"

Wes cocked his head as if listening to the wind, which was ridiculous as there was no wind in the digital world. Not even a breeze, but that was just the sort of thing that made Wes, Wes. "Her calendar says her last known appointment was a presentation to the advisory board at Apex in Worcester."

That information gave Stephen reason to pause. He'd seen first-hand what the Apex building looked like now. "Yeah, well, I'm pretty sure that she's no longer worried about any advisory board."

If the woman they sought had been inside when the bombs first went off, then she was either dead or far from that place. *Then again*, thought Stephen, *maybe there's a third option. He and Bean had* found a survivor, of sorts, buried in the basement of that building. *Alan.* He'd also been at Apex that day and had found his way into a cryogenic tank while the rest of the world descended into chaos. There had been more than one of those tubes lying around. If he got into one, perhaps others did, too.

His body shook, bringing his attention back to the real world. "Time to get up," said Bean.

The digital field was replaced once more by real trees, dirt, and bugs. His head throbbed and his body ached as he stood up. "We have to go back to Worcester."

"Um, you wanna tell me why? They aren't exactly going to throw out the welcome mat for us after that." She gestured behind them at the blackened husk that had served as the Watch's headquarters. Stephen had turned it into a giant lightning rod to save himself and Bean, taking out a number of the Watch's members in the process. It didn't help that the energy surge had also killed several genetically modified former athletes, Stephen called beastmen, who also happened to be there at the time, rebelling against the Watch, or that those same beastmen previously called Worcester home.

He rubbed his eyes. More deaths. All because of him. "Because of the woman I told you about. The one who my birth mother said would have answers. She was there when it happened. Must have gone into one of those tube thingies."

"But your father said—"

"We may share some genes, but he's not my father."

"That wasn't what—"

"I know what he said, but that doesn't mean it was the truth. He's good at lies, remember. So good, he even convinces himself it's the truth. Or had you forgotten how I got here in the first place." Alan had tricked him into going with Dr. Lambda and the Watch. He'd thought they could help him. Instead, he'd learned they'd had been only interested in his blood and didn't care if he was a willing donor.

Stephen's shoulders slumped. "Sorry, I didn't mean to sound like I was taking that out on you." He issued a command and a digital map unfurled across his vision. A pulsating dot appeared.

He focused in on Worcester and Apex's location on the map. He didn't need to do the math to recognize it would take days to get back to where it had all begun. They also didn't have nearly enough supplies. If only they had transportation like what the Watch had used.

"Vans."

"Is that supposed to be some sort of farm boy curse?"

"The Watch still has at least one working van. At least it did when they brought me here."

"Okay . . ."

"So, we take it."

"Right, we just walk back inside and pick their pockets until we find a set of keys. Great idea."

"It's better than going on foot."

"No doubt, but do you even know how to drive?" Bean asked.

"Do you?" Stephen might have spent his childhood hiding from the plague and chaos in the middle of nowhere, but was good with machines. He'd rebuilt a computer from spare parts without training. He could figure out how to drive a van. It wasn't as if there were a lot of other cars on the road.

"I'm just saying we might have to worry about you driving us into a tree. We can go there on horseback. Then we wouldn't have to worry about running out of fuel. And I just happen to know where some might be."

Stephen had forgotten that Bean had arrived in town on horseback with the Sorcerers. Wes's face popped into his thoughts. Wes had as much as admitted to coming up with the name for the group. Stephen shook his head. Wes's sense of humor was an odd one. The term was technically accurate, even if it was a terrible play on the term, source code.

The Sorcerers were people who were able to access digital information that passed through the network known as the datastream or visit the virtual world called the datasphere with their minds. It gave them a sort of telepathy. They also had the ability to alter and control their bodies—though it required skill and some had more talent for it than others. Bean was one of them. If it hadn't been for the Watch, bringing them together, he might never have learned he shared those same abilities too.

"That'd work. Where did you leave them?"

"There's a park or former campground. Not too far from the Watchtower. We believed it would be a safe enough place."

"Do you think they are still there?"

"After that storm the other night," her lips twisted. "I honestly don't know. Probably bolted, but it's worth checking to see."

Stephen pressed his lips together. He'd seen the park when he was connected to the Watchtower's sensors. Bean was right; it wasn't far, but going there would also mean turning around and going back the way they came. He scratched his head. Still, only an idiot would pass up the chance for faster transportation.

He caught Bean's eye. She may have turned calling him an idiot into a term of endearment, but it didn't mean he had to give her reason to think it true. "Guess we're going to have to go back, then."

Her eyes twinkled in the morning light. "And *I* guess that makes me the leader."

Stephen snorted. "Don't let it go to your head."

"Like it did yours?" She ran ahead before Stephen reacted.

"Hey, I can't help it that I am a natural-born leader." He cupped his mouth and shouted.

"Oh, is that what you are telling yourself now?" She shouted back.

"It's the truth," he said, picking up his stride. He assumed Bean rolled her eyes, but she allowed him to catch up. As soon as he did, Stephen pulled her into his arms, forgetting for a moment about his worries. "Otherwise, why would such a strong, capable, woman want to hang out with the likes of me?"

Bean's voice deepened as he lowered his face to hers. "I *suppose* you have a point." She reached up and touched his cheek. "However, you forgot to say gorgeous, too."

He inhaled her scent. It was a mix of earth and the smell of the sort of crisp static immediately following a thunderstorm. Bits of dried blood colored her clothing and dark red-and-purple bruises still marred her skin. She might have meant the comment as a joke, but as far as Stephen was concerned, she spoke no greater truth. He leaned in.

Their lips touched—hers pressing into his with the same hungry intensity he felt as well. He pulled her closer, threading his fingers through her hair. He closed his eyes, savoring the taste of her on his tongue.

Nadia appeared in his mind without warning. The expression on his foster-mother's dead face was no longer just one of accusation, but disappointment, too. Stephen opened his eyes in a panic, breaking off their kiss. *How had he forgotten?* Arousal fled from his body. He turned away, but not fast enough to miss seeing the look of confusion on her face.

"We'd better hurry. If the horses didn't bolt from the storm, the beastmen might find them before we do."

Bean's forehead knit. "You saw how fast those guys were. They made it here all the way from Worcester in the time it took us to arrive from the tower. I highly doubt they need them."

"Maybe not for transportation . . ."

Bean's lip curled in disgust. "Okay, so that's another good point." Her jade eyes shone in the morning sun.

"Huh. That's now two in the same day," he said.

She snorted. "We should write this day down. Probably a record."

"Har har. Just stay sharp. They might have left the Watchtower when we did, but I didn't get the impression they were going far."

"You say that like it's a bad thing," Bean wiggled her fingers, allowing purple-white arcs of lightning to jump from tip to tip. She held her hands close together, though did not let them touch. The sparks arced faster and faster from palm to palm until the space between was filled by electric light. She clapped her hands together, then released them and the electricity in a sudden motion. A branch in front of her tumbled to the ground. "I, for one, am looking forward to showing Jeremy what I can *really* do."

Stephen's stomach turned over at the mention of Jeremy. The man leading the beastmen's attack on the Watchtower might have looked like the former general manager. He might have sounded like him, too, but Stephen was fairly certain the real Jeremy had never left the stadium in Worcester.

It brought his thoughts back to Alan—his biological father—the person who'd abandoned him at age four. He was also the person who'd created the so-called upgrade in the first place. Stephen balled his hand into a fist. There were so many deaths on Stephen's conscience already, but he supposed he would welcome one more.

chapter three

JULIANE

urham raised his hand in the air. "We should stop here for the night." While they'd ridden, Juliane had searched for answers in the datastream. Five media outlets detailed the destruction of the Apex building, but the facts in each report were so different and so fanciful Juliane couldn't trust any one of them to have reported the story right. One even suggested aliens were to blame. Juliane had dismissed them all as nothing more than sensationalized click-bait.

Archived headlines from more reputable news outlets beyond Worcester mentioned things like mass layoffs and the rise of a mysterious illness occurring shortly after the closure of the ACI and the collapse of her office building, but there was no single news story announcing anything she would have considered to be a world-ending cataclysmic event. Then the news stories simply stopped. She'd turned the feed off hours ago.

"When you say here, you don't mean here, here, do you?" asked Juliane gesturing around them. The buildings surrounding them should have been marked with caution tape and slated for demolition years ago. It made the tavern they'd left seem bustling in comparison.

He led his horse to a grassy patch in front of an abandoned storefront and slid from his saddle. "Yeah, unfortunately, I do." He came over to her side and stretched out his hand.

She looked at his hand, but didn't let go of the reins. "There's got to be a better option. Maybe we can go just a couple more miles?"

He pointed to the sky, which was in the process of transitioning from red to purple. "As much as I want to sleep in a real bed, it's getting hard to see the road, which would be dangerous enough if it were in good condition, but we both know how bad it is. So, unless we want our rides to break their legs in the dark, this is going to have to be it." He shrugged. "It'll be like summer camp, but without the marshmallows."

Juliane pursed her lips. "I wouldn't know the first thing about summer camp."

"No? What about camping in general? Didn't your family ever do that?"

"My parents weren't exactly the family-vacationing type." She sighed but had to concede Durham's assessment was correct. She stretched in the saddle and massaged the small of her back. "I suppose I could use a break, too, though I'm still having a difficult time processing it's been fifteen years. Or longer. I mean, weren't they talking about having to widen this road to accommodate all the traffic just yesterday?"

Durham chuckled. "Yeah, I heard that on the news, too. The whole controversy about how we needed to preserve historic properties." He nodded at their surroundings. "Guess someone got their wish. No one's developing around here now."

"Lucky them." She lowered herself from the horse's back. It raised its tail and released several round balls of excrement onto the cracked and broken pavement. *Lovely.*

Durham walked over to the store's entrance. The panes of glass on either side were gray-brown with dirt. He pushed on the door. It didn't budge. He frowned. He looked at the ground and then back at Juliane. "Do you see anything large or heavy?"

Juliane glanced around "There's a bit of brick lying over there." She pointed to the side of the adjacent building.

Durham grabbed the brick and flung it into the storefront. Glass shattered as it fell to the ground.

Juliane frowned. "First you steal a horse, now you're breaking and entering."

"Admit it, this is the most fun you've had since Vegas," he said with a toothy grin.

"That was a long time ago," said Juliane. Her cheeks pulled at the corners of her lips. *Don't encourage him. Even if he's right.* Durham had met her on the flight to the conference. They'd made a bet, to pass the time. He'd lost. As a result, he had spent most of the day as her personal errand boy. "All I am saying is for a former lawyer, you've been remarkably quick to start a crime spree since waking up." She'd meant the comment as a joke. Then she recalled blows to the head. Concussions had been known to alter a personality, and the comment was no longer as funny as she'd intended. "You *are* feeling okay, aren't you?"

"Like I said, I've been in worse scrapes. Besides, it's not a crime if you know how to defend yourself." Durham's eyes twinkled like the stars multiplying in the sky above.

"I'm pretty sure it still is."

"You'd be surprised. For example, there was this one time—"

"That's okay."

"It's a great story."

"Oh, I don't doubt that in the least, but aren't you concerned at all someone might have heard that noise and will come to investigate?"

"What? That?" He pointed at the ground littered in glass shards. "It was like that when we got here."

"No one in their right mind would believe that," said Juliane, shaking her head. "And that's not what I meant. We have no idea what sort of people might be around here."

"What people? Besides, if there are others nearby, they probably hear things crumbling and falling apart all the time." He gestured to the pile of loose brick. "What's one more broken window? Doubt anyone gives it a thought."

He reached through the opening he'd created in the storefront and twisted the lock on the other side of the door. Unlocked, he pulled the door open, revealing nothing but a blackness within.

His shoes crunched over the broken glass as he made his way inside. Juliane's legs ached as she found a spot near Durham's to secure her mount. She wrinkled her nose. She bent down to locate the saddle's strap and touched the animal's stomach. It whinnied and shied away. "Settle down, you are supposed to want me to remove this thing." She tried again, but the poor lighting made her effort futile.

She turned over her hand so the palm was facing up and issued a command to her cells instructing her body to produce luciferin and luciferase. A yellow-green glow, much like the light of a firefly, expanded over her palm's surface.

Durham's head emerged from the open door. "Ah, Juliane?" he asked. "Should I be concerned you're green?"

She arched an eyebrow. "This method is less likely to ignite any lingering gases stuck in there than starting a fire might."

He looked back over his shoulder into the shop and back at her. "That's genius."

"No. Simple biology."

"Well, I wouldn't have ever come up with it."

Juliane smiled, accepting the truth of his words as the compliment he intended. Conversation with Durham was proving to be refreshingly uncomplicated. She didn't have to worry about one-upmanship with him or what his ulterior motive might be. She almost regretted keeping her distance. Perhaps if things had played out differently before, they might even have been friends.

Her smile evaporated. *You do remember who else he was friends with, don't you?* a voice in the back of her mind whispered. *Louis.* Her throat tightened. How could she have forgotten about him? *Louis betrayed me first,* she told herself. *I have every right to finally move on.* Moisture filled her eyes. She took a breath and instructed her central nervous system to flood her system with calming enzymes until she was once again in control. "Have you found anything useful in there?"

"Not yet, but since you're now the human nightlight, I might have better luck finding something we can eat."

She pursed her lips. "I suspect anything remotely edible or potable is long gone."

"You're probably right," he said. "But there's always the chance we'll get lucky."

Juliane looked at her mount and held up a finger. "Stay." The horse ignored her and bent its head to nibble on some stray grass.

Together they inspected the abandoned store. The green glow of her skin cast on the rows of empty shelves reminded Juliane of alien encounters depicted by Hollywood. Near the back, Juliane found a rack of cotton shirts. She thumbed through the meager selection. While the oversized tees were hardly her style, there was a chance they were in better condition than her ruined clothing. A shirt fell off the hanger and onto the floor. Juliane picked it up and saw large holes in the cloth. *Or not.* Mice must have found it first. She threw the shirt over the top of the rack and moved on. "See anything?"

Durham shook his head. "Nope. Guess we're going to have to find dinner the old-fashioned way."

"As in hunt? And have you ever done that before?"

"I'll figure it out. People used to do it all the time. Aren't you hungry?"

"Actually, I hadn't given it much thought," said Juliane. The ceiling panels caught her attention. The panels were no longer a factory-new brilliant white, but they were the same sort she'd insisted on having installed in her office years ago, which meant nano power supplies were embedded in the materials. All she had to do was redirect the current.

A dark shape ran along the bottom of her peripheral vision, breaking her concentration. Instinctively, she jumped backward, bumping into the clothing rack and the exposed hanger.

"What happened?" Within an instant, Durham had come to her side. "Did you see something?"

"It's nothing." Her cheeks warmed. "I suspect it was nothing more than a rodent. No reason for me to react like a child. I saw larger ones in the labs at the ACI," said Juliane, grateful for both the poor lighting and another dose of artificial calm.

He touched her chin, forcing her face up until her eyes met his own. "You know, you don't have to pretend with me."

Juliane wrinkled her forehead. "Pretend what?"

"Pretend you're cool with all this."

Her heart slowed as the chemicals in her system took effect. The muscles of her face relaxed as cool logic took back over. Durham let his hand drop away. She was surprised to find her skin mourned the loss of contact.

"I'm not," she said. "But I've learned not to get emotional about things outside of my control. Media outlets have a field day with that sort of nonsense."

"If you haven't noticed, the tabloids don't exist anymore," he said. He searched her face. He must not have liked what he saw as his jaw tightened. "Sorry, I shouldn't have brought them up."

She straightened her spine and broke eye contact. Her gaze found the scrap of fabric on the floor. "See," she said. "There's something positive to come from all of this."

He raised his hand once more, as if reaching for her, only to let it drop back to his side. "You know," he said with a quiet voice, "had things gone differently." She looked up. There was a strange expression she'd never seen on his face before—both earnest and sincere. "I would have never forced you to go through any of that. At least, not go through that alone."

Pressure built up behind her eyes. She turned away, suddenly keenly aware of the lack of space between them. While part of her reveled what his words implied, she needed to stop the conversation before she allowed herself to feel something more for him than she already did. Her time with Louis had taught her what would happen if she allowed herself to open her heart, or worse, lose her focus.

Besides, she told herself, *its Durham*. While they hadn't spent all that much time together, she knew that he'd practiced talking women into his bed far longer, and far better, than he'd ever practiced law. He knew the words to say. He probably even believed them, but once he'd gotten what he wanted, they'd go their separate ways. It's what he did.

She decided no good would come from talking about the past. Nor could she trust her feelings at the moment either. She told herself, her swirling emotions and desire to lean into his touch were nothing more than a biological response to being placed in a stressful situation. If they were going to survive in this new world, she needed to remain focused on reaching New York. They couldn't afford the complication.

Her brain understood. Her hormones, however, would take further convincing. *Shut him down.* Juliane stepped back before her body could betray her. "But you did," she said in a voice more bitter than intended. She looked at him through narrow eyes. "All that time we worked together. You never said anything." She couldn't remember the last few days, but recalled all too well the day she'd entered the room and seen him after being introduced to the rest of Apex's advisory board by Damien Knightley.

There'd been no signs of recognition on his face. Nothing to indicate he remembered their time together. His lack of response had baffled Juliane. She'd considered the conference one of the best times in her life. To then be treated with less regard than one might a footnote—it was crushing. "You acted like you'd never met me before."

Durham searched her eyes with a pained look. He held his hands up. "That was a mistake. But in my defense, I'd assumed, after everything, that's what you wanted."

His defense gave her pause. His assumption at the time might have been well-founded. She'd even welcomed his reaction, eventually—after the initial shock faded. It had been an improvement compared to the looks she'd gotten from most people she worked with at the ACI. People like her research assistant, Chad, or her peer, Betty, back before Betty had made it official with Alan and became the other half of the Doctors Dronigh. The other people in her life couldn't stop pitying her. Every time they looked at her, she saw it. Poor Juliane. Even worse, it was because of a man.

The fact that Juliane had nearly sacrificed her entire career for that same man—Louis—hadn't helped. Their pitying looks became a reason Juliane found excuses not to attend Betty's get-togethers or check in on Chad's new work assignments.

His earnest expression pulled at her like gravity. The space between them, at once, seemed as narrow as a blade of grass, and yet, as wide as the ocean. *No more mistakes.* "So, you think you know me, then?" She crossed her arms over her chest. "Just because we spent one day together?" She laughed without humor. "It was a great day. I'll give you that, but one day is hardly long enough to get to know a person." *Don't let him know how much he hurt you. It will only give him the power to do it again.* "Besides, I'm not the same person I was back then. I was naïve. I let my hormones get the best of me." Her lips twisted. "You should know, I won't make the same mistake again."

Durham broke into a grin.

Juliane blinked; it wasn't the reaction she'd expected. She hadn't wanted to hurt him, but it was still a rejection. However, there was nothing about him that indicated he was anything but overjoyed at her statement. *It's because it's just a game to him. He's a flirt. That's what he does. He doesn't mean any of it.* Once again, she was glad her skin was colored by bioluminescence so it couldn't show her blush. *Just as well.*

"Are you sure I can't convince you otherwise?" His eyes sparkled as he gestured toward his chest and biceps.

The corner of her mouth twitched. His eyes twinkled.

He continued, "I've had plenty of experience with women who made noises along the lines of making a mistake but were quick to make an entirely different sound once we got started."

"Is that so." She'd intended the reply to be condescending, but instead it rolled off her tongue. "I guess it's too bad, then, that I'm not like those other women."

Durham snorted. He took a step until only inches separated them. As much as the logic in her brain screamed against it, Juliane wanted his arms to wrap around her waist. Instead, he rested his fists on his hips. He leaned forward. A warmth spread through Juliane's body. *Damnit. What's wrong with me?* She knew better. There was no reason for her to act like a teenager. She looked up, meeting the challenge in his eyes with her own. She considered sending a command to silence the surge of desire she hadn't felt for anyone other than Louis in years.

Thinking about Louis was like jumping into an icy shower and more effective than any artificial endocrinal command. Durham must have seen the change in her eyes as he backed away. "I know you're not," he said softly. "That's why I—"

Her former lover appeared in her mind's eye, standing next to the woman he'd married without so much as a courtesy break-up call. They stood in *her* lab—minimizing *her* involvement in the serum's development or the Gene Assist upgrade procedure. She synthesized a surge of gamma-aminobutyric acid, building a wall around the synapses in her brain, preventing them from processing feelings that only lead to pain. Her body relaxed as the chemical took effect.

She looked back at Durham. He had the same odd questioning expression on his face as he'd had outside of the inn, but the artificial blocker numbed her to it. "Why you did what?" she said. Now that her hormones were silenced, she found herself more willing to spend the evening in conversation.

"Ah, right. Well, you see . . ."

It wasn't like Durham to be tongue-tied. She gave him a once-over from head to toe. As much as he claimed his injuries were no big deal, Durham clearly had suffered a more serious trauma than he was willing to let on.

"Never mind. It can wait," he said, looking away.

"Are you sure?"

"Yeah, guess I've got food on the brain. Can't think straight," he said, shaking his head. The look that spoke of deeper conversation vanished from his face, replaced by the expression of casual indifference she'd grown accustomed to. It would seem she wasn't the only one able to mask what was going on inside her head. "Too bad we're going to need those horses. Otherwise, I'd consider eating one."

"That's barbaric." Juliane wrinkled her nose. While she wasn't hungry, Juliane wouldn't have minded a steaming cup of coffee or a cold glass of ice water right now.

"Yeah, well, hopefully it won't come to that." He turned and left before Juliane said another word.

She sighed. When he got back, she would give him the opportunity to talk about whatever it was that was on his mind, but first, she'd try explaining energy transfer. She didn't have high hopes Durham would be interested in the science behind it, but at least they wouldn't have to worry about where their next meal would come from. Juliane faced the nanobots and pulled. Energy stored in their battery cells surged through her veins like a wave.

Alert and satisfied, she canceled the feed and issued another command, redirecting the leftover power to the lighting system. A pair of large square panels began to glow with a warm white light. Juliane frowned when the other lighting panels remained dark. *Their circuitry must be damaged.* Her body tingled as the two working panels began to transmit performance data back and forth. The data was so basic, Juliane was surprised she was even aware of it. The sensation was akin to hearing crickets on an otherwise still night.

She went about looking for a space where they might be able to pass the night. Jagged shards from Durham's break-in shimmered on the floor by the door, ruling that area out. A black electronic box mounted to the side of the front entrance caught Juliane's eye. *An electronic lock.* She shook her head. If Durham had only bothered to give her a second, she might have located and hacked it, sparing her now from worries about getting cut to ribbons. Her gaze fell on black mold.

That does it. There's got to be a better place to sleep than this. She exited the store. Durham's horse was gone. *So much for not risking the horses at night.* Unfortunately, it did mean she'd have to wait until he got back to inform him they'd be moving on.

A pungent odor Juliane couldn't quite place filled the night. Her mare pulled at her tethers; eyes wide.

"I don't like that smell either, but there's nothing we can do," she told the mare. *It's probably something rotting in the store. Yet another reason we should find a different place to sleep tonight.* Her horse pulled again, jerking Juliane's arm. Its hooves echoed as they struck the concrete.

A shadow covered the moon. Juliane ducked her head out of pure instinct as the air changed in pressure. A gust scented by death and dung assailed her senses. A call like a mix of chicken and seagull came from behind. She risked a glance over her shoulder.

A dark shape stood between Juliane and the storefront door. Its sudden appearance silenced Juliane mid-curse. She spun on her heel, in the process damaging the same ankle she'd weakened earlier. Whatever it was, it walked on two legs and was the size of a tall human, but moved like an animal. It had massive shoulders and a head set low in its body. The effect somehow reminded Juliane of a football player in full pads.

It took a step. The light from inside the store outlined its silhouette, showing it had a bald head with dark feathers jutting from the base of its neck like a wrapped boa. It shifted. Wings as wide as tractor-trailers stretched out before her. She'd never seen a bird so huge. Her pulse quickened, while her legs seemed rooted to the spot.

She pinged the datastream to help her identify the creature blocking her return, but none of the results of her query matched what she saw in front of her. It resembled a California condor, but the size was all wrong. *California condors happen to be extinct, too.* In terms of wingspan, it was closer to descriptions of the so-called thunderbird, but that creature was nothing more than a myth.

A large rodent, likely a rat, and possibly the same shadow she'd seen earlier, bolted from the store toward Juliane. A second bird—smaller than the first, but still larger than any avian Juliane had ever seen—fell from the sky and joined its mate. The smaller bird, which Juliane assumed to be the female of the pair, extended its neck as it tracked the rodent's movement. The creature cawed as if asking the first a question.

Its mate answered with a cackle-like sound.

The female then stuck the rat with a beak that looked like a scythe. It pulled back from the rodent but did not stand fully upright. It lowered its head again, slower this time, probing the unfortunate creature with its beak. The rodent lay motionless on the ground. The first bird cackled again.

Is it dead? Why did they kill it, if they aren't going to eat it? wondered Juliane, her scientific curiosity overtaking her fear. In her experience, beasts, unlike humankind, rarely killed unless out of necessity. Her hand stretched out of its own accord. The first bird swung its head in her direction. Moonlight reflected off its eye. The bird blinked. *Then again, biology was never my area of expertise.* Juliane pulled back her hand. *It might have been better not to have captured its attention.*

The male bird clucked.

The female stopped its investigation, returning to its full standing height. It curved its neck closer to that of the first and repeated the same caw as before. The male tucked its head into the ring of neck feathers. It extended its wings again. A large band of white feathers stretched across its body from wingtip to wingtip. It flapped its wings, producing a sound like a clap of thunder as it launched itself into the air.

Its companion followed. Juliane looked up to see the pair circling in the moonlit sky. One of the birds began to descend directly toward her. A primal urge to move shattered Juliane's artificial calm.

She launched into an erratic run away from the birds, weaving herself between buildings in hope the narrow space would be harder for the bird and its large wingspan to navigate. The creature screeched as it broke out of its dive and swooped back up into the skies.

She zigged.

The male's call was answered by the female.

Juliane zagged.

She didn't have to look up to know she'd be trapped between the circling raptors. Another sound filled her ears—wild, like a thing long broken. Juliane realized she was laughing hysterically.

The toe of her shoe found a crack in the broken pavement, breaking her stride, and sending her the ground. She bit her lip and tasted blood. She scrambled to rise. The thunderbirds' calls rattled in the sky. The air pressure changed.

They are going to dive again. Juliane's ankle, strained further, throbbed. Her lungs burned with each breath. However, she kept going. In her fall, she'd seen a cellar door up ahead, partially covered by weeds. She hoped the door was unlocked.

Adrenaline fueled her forward. Her legs and lungs protested each step of the way. Before going into the cryogenic tank, a day of strenuous activity consisted of a brisk walk from her parked car to her office. Now, her muscles screamed in agony. She refused to listen to their complaint.

The air pressure surrounding her changed. The scent of excrement filled her nostrils. She dropped to the ground next to the door. Her head jerked to the side as a large clump of hair was torn from her scalp followed by a thunderclap.

The beast misjudged, landing on the ground at least a yard away. Not nearly as agile on the land as it was in the air, the male waddled as it turned to face her. The birds called out again, producing a sound Juliane knew would haunt her nightmares.

She grabbed at the latch. The female, still in the air, called out, increasing its pitch as if sensing their prey had found an escape. Juliane focused on her goal. Hinges long since rusted protested as she pulled upward, but the door was otherwise unlocked. A narrow gap opened, exposing nothing but darkness. Juliane wedged her fingers into the space. Splinters of wood bore into her palms. The smell of death intensified. *I'm running out of time.*

She shifted her weight and pulled again. The gap widened. Sweat dripped from her brow. *It had to be birds.* Juliane cursed out loud. Images of dark feathers and flying above the clouds in pursuit of an animal stirred in her brain—she'd accidentally taken over the mind of one of the Project Gene Assist's early test subjects, a raven, when she'd first undergone the upgrade procedure.

The hair on the back of her neck rose. *Focus, Juliane.* The door moved an inch. *I just need two more minutes.* The bird on the ground chortled as the air pressure changed once more. "Go away," she shouted toward the night sky as she adjusted her hold on the door one more time.

The rusted hinges gave up their hold on the cellar door with a final scream. Juliane opened it just enough to squeeze inside before slamming the door behind her. A weight slammed into it from the other side.

She hadn't found cover a moment too soon. The creature called out in its frustration. Then a portion of the wooden board cracked. She drew back as a wicked beak pierced through the aging wood. The beak disappeared, then reappeared. She looked over her shoulder, but it was too dark to see if there was anywhere she might be able to hide if the beast found its way in. If anything, she would be trapped further. The beak struck again like an ax.

A memory of being trapped in a back room surrounded by empty cages as men fought to make their way to her sprang unbidden in her mind. They'd been after her for reasons she'd hadn't understood then and understood even less now. What had she done to get away? Her memory remained foggy. She cursed at the bird. If it would only give her a moment's peace, she might be able to cobble together another portion of her missing days.

The bird's call changed. It gave a short deep cry, as if it was answering her. Juliane fought a wave of vertigo. *Not now.*

Another call cried out on the other side of the door. *Of course,* Juliane thought, *the bird isn't talking to me. It is coordinating with its partner.* The scientist in her couldn't help appreciating the show of intelligence on display before her, while the less-rational part of her mind screamed to find a deeper, less-accessible hole to crawl into. She wondered how the creatures hadn't been discovered before. *Unless they weren't discovered,* she told herself, *but made in a lab.*

I wonder. In the case of the raven, it had just sort of happened immediately following her initial injection. She'd simply accessed the bird's senses without knowing what she was doing or how she was doing it.

She reached out with her mind. The bird redoubled its attack, slamming its body into the door. Light cut the darkness of the cellar as the gap in the wood grew larger. *Experiments can wait until later.*

Death and rot filled her senses as a pair of talons curled their way into the space. Juliane ran down the stairs. There had to be something she could use to defend herself, but she was blind in the darkness. Her body took on the pale green glow she'd used to find her way around the service station.

The bird screamed and tore.

She dismissed the light as quickly as she'd summoned it. It hadn't revealed anything useful she might use as a weapon. All she had illuminated was an empty cellar. The light also made her even more of a target. Even worse, she was blinder than she had been a moment before. *That was a mistake.* She grimaced. *I hope I live long enough to make another one.*

chapter four

STEPHEN

A narrow creek cut through the forest, framed by a sloping bank. Stephen knelt down and splashed its cool water on his face. Droplets of red, brown, and black splattered his clothing. He cupped his hands and filled them again. He wondered how long it had been since he'd bathed, regretting he hadn't taken advantage of the running water back at the Sorcerers' apartment building.

Stephen hadn't kept track of time since he and Bean first fled from members of the Watch, but he guessed they'd been on their own for three or four weeks by now. *It feels like a lifetime, though.*

He caught his reflection in the water and barely recognized the person he'd become. He scratched at the line of hair growing on his chin. The lack of a razor in their supplies was the least of his concerns. *Hope Bean digs beards.*

"There is a fenced-in area just on the other side of this hill," said Bean. "Should be a few water bottles lying around, too. Come on." She waved. "Or are you going to make me carry you the rest of the way?"

"I was wondering when you were going to pay me back for that little favor," joked Stephen. "However, I should point out I carried you for five miles. While I was injured. At night."

"Oh, is that all. I'm guessing all uphill, too?"

"Maybe . . ." He knelt down and scooped up more water with both hands.

Bean's eyes narrowed as Stephen stood. "What are you doing with that? I just said there should be water bottles ahead."

"Have I mentioned how hot you look?"

Bean took a step back. "You wouldn't dare."

Stephen flung the handful of water, watching the droplets fly through the air toward Bean. She jumped out of its path with ease. "You think you're a funny guy. Don't you?"

"It's crossed my mind once or twice, yes."

The corner of Bean's mouth turned up. Her jade eyes sparkled. Stephen realized her intention too late as Bean charged into him, knocking Stephen onto his backside and into the creek. Water splashed her as well, darkening her clothing and causing the fabric to cling to her curves as she used her body to hold him in place.

"Who's funny now?" she asked as she closed her eyes and raised her face to his. Stephen shivered, and he shifted out from under her weight. Bean's eyes snapped open. "Oh," she said. Her cheeks turning a charming shade of rose. "I shouldn't have done that." She scanned his body. "I didn't hurt you, did I?"

Stephen shook his head. "Nah. I'll be fine. But this water is freezing."

Bean frowned. "Are you sure I didn't hurt you?" She placed a finger in the water. "It's warm enough to me."

"That's because you aren't the one still sitting in it."

A man coughed.

Bean spun into action like a cat as Stephen jumped up. A large dark-skinned man with muscular arms stood under the branches of a nearby tree. Bean reacted first, balling up her fists.

"Electricity and water don't mix. Even a person like me knows that." His voice was like sandpaper and cracked from underuse.

Bean narrowed her eyes but released her clenched hands.

"We aren't looking for trouble," said Stephen before Bean might say or do anything that would ensure trouble found them whether they were looking for it or not. She gave him a look through the corner of her eyes but remained silent.

Stephen released a breath he hadn't realized he was holding. They'd met the man, named Ahman, before in Worcester. From the outside, he didn't appear to be different than an average human, albeit an average man with muscles larger than Stephen's head, but that didn't mean he hadn't been altered beneath the surface. All the beastmen were in some way—and not just the former professional athletes—coaches, like Ahman, had too.

They'd done it to make themselves more competitive. Some had undergone artificial muscle transplants, giving them catlike speed. Others had skin as tough as rhino leather. The league hadn't minded. It wasn't cheating if everyone did it. With every tweak, they'd become more animal than man. They'd been teams before, but now . . . now they were a pack.

Bean's jaw tightened. She took a step forward, planting her feet on the solid dry ground. Her fingers twitched. Stephen squared his shoulders and joined her her side.

"Before you do something you'll regret," said Ahman, "I wasn't part of the fight at the Watchtower."

Stephen frowned, sharing another look with Bean. She shrugged.

"Expected you hours ago. Forgot how slow regs are," said the beastman, unsmiling.

"What do you mean, you expected us?" asked Stephen. "We didn't even know we were coming back here until this morning."

"Obvious. Horses."

"You found them."

Ahman nodded.

"Look. All we need is two of them. Just two. You can have the rest."

Ahman's laugh was just as grating to the ears as it was the first time Stephen and Bean heard it.

"Boy, you can have your pick. Take them all if you want. Come with me."

This has to be a trick. Jeremy, or more accurately Alan, impersonating the beastmen's leader, might have let them walk away following the battle, but that didn't mean the rest of the group was as forgiving. Stephen glanced around. Ahman had snuck up on them without a sound, which meant any number of his teammates were likely hiding behind the surrounding trees. He should never have let his guard down.

Another thought struck him. He turned his gaze to the canopy above. With their modifications, beastmen could easily be hiding in the upper branches like jungle cats. All Ahman had to do was issue a signal to make more appear from all directions. Stephen braced himself for battle.

"What if we say no?" asked Bean.

This time it was Stephen's turn to shoot her a look.

"That'd be a mistake."

"Oh, really," She shifted, turning her body to the side. Her eyes flashed like emeralds, making her pale skin appear as if she'd been sculpted out of marble. "Mine or yours?"

One side of Ahman's lips turned up. "Yours."

Stephen's stomach grumbled loud enough to be heard over the running water of the creek. Both Ahman and Bean turned to look his way.

"Seriously?" Bean asked. "How can you possibly be hungry right now?"

Ahman laughed and raised his hands, palms out. "I have food, too. Come."

Stephen pressed his lips together. Hanging out in the datastream all night, speeding the body's healing process, communicating mind-to-mind, or, Bean's favorite, generating an electric spark in the palm of one's hand intense enough to take out a threat with a touch required massive amounts of energy. Stephen had learned those same abilities would kill them if they didn't pay attention to the warning sides. He must now be near the end of his reserves.

His shoulders loosened. It was likely why Bean's lifeforce sung so strongly to him the other night. It was another warning sign. Maybe if he got a good meal in him, the craving would stop. He smiled as his mind jumped to all the other things he would like to do with Bean if he no longer feared losing control in the process. "Sure. Why not? What'cha cooking?"

Bean shook her head, grumbling loud enough for Stephen to hear. "If that stomach of yours leads us into an ambush, so help me."

"We need those horses. Besides, he's the one that needs to be worried," said Stephen. "Unless that thing you did with the branch was just showing off."

Bean chewed his comment over. "I suppose you have a point."

"That's three times you've said that now," he said with a grin. "I must not be as big an idiot as you thought after all."

Bean grinned back. "Oh, you are. Trust me. I just must be rubbing off on you."

"Have I mentioned how I love it when you talk dirty?"

Bean's face puzzled at Stephen's statement. Then her eyes opened wide and her cheeks blazed in color as understanding dawned.

Ahman made a gagging grunting sound. Turning without further instruction or looking to see if they followed, he disappeared into the forest, forcing Stephen and Bean to run to catch up.

Ahman handed Stephen a piece of blackened meat which Stephen bit into with enthusiasm. "War is coming."

The meat seared Stephen's throat as he choked it down. "War? But haven't enough people died already?"

"Most wars aren't fought over people." He poked at the cookfire with a stick. "I didn't mind the Watch. They were corrupt power-hungry bastards, but I understood where they were coming from." He placed another skewer of meat on the flames. "Reason with them, too." He looked to Stephen and pointed at the cooking meat with a question in his eyes.

Stephen nodded. Ahman returned to his cooking. Stephen was beginning to wonder if that was the end of the conversation for the night.

The beastman pulled the meat from the flames and handed it to him. Only then did he continue. "With them gone . . . See, there's a vacuum."

"So, what?" asked Bean. "It wasn't like the Watch was *really* in charge. We just let them think they were."

"That so? I've known a few people who would have said differently." He poked at the flames. "If they were still alive."

"They would've been wrong," Bean straightened her back. "Look at me, for example. I was able to find my way around them. Twice."

"You were lucky."

"Luck had nothing to do with it." A shadow crossed over Bean's expression.

Stephen reached out to squeeze her hand. She flinched at his touch. Her eyes widened apologetically, and she gingerly met his fingers and entwined them around her own. It felt good to have her warmth in his hand once more. It was even better than a stomach full of hot food.

Stephen bit into the meat skewer while they remained sitting by the fire, hand in hand. He wished the moment would last all night, but he knew only too well that the hunger would return. Releasing his hold, he turned back to Ahman. "So, what makes you sure war is coming?"

"Jeremy," Ahman said. "He's not himself. I used to think Jeremy never had more than half a playbook. Meaning he only played defense. Now, suddenly he is leading an attack?" He shook his head. "People don't change like that." He frowned. "Doesn't smell right. Hasn't since the day you arrived."

Stephen cringed. The real Jeremy wouldn't be hidden away in a dark corner of the team's former stadium if Stephen hadn't brought Alan to their gates.

"So?" said Bean, standing up. She walked to the fire and stared into its flames, putting her profile in sharp relief. Stephen wondered what she saw. She took a step back and rubbed her eye. "Why should you care? You're one of them—don't you want to win?"

Ahman grunted. "There are no winners in a war. Only a side with fewer losers."

"We had nothing to do with it," said Stephen, holding his hands up.

Ahman's eyes narrowed. "I didn't say you did."

"Then why are you telling us all this?" asked Stephen in an attempt to distance himself from the comment before Ahman started asking questions he didn't know the answers to. "Are you saying we should run away? Fine. We weren't planning on sticking around anyway."

"No, I'm asking you to help me stop it."

"Stop a war. Us?" Stephen shook his head. "And here I was coming around to the belief you weren't as crazy as the others." He stood up and patted his stomach. "Listen, thanks for the meal, but we've got a mission of our own." He turned to Bean. "You ready?"

"*I've* been ready to go since before we got here."

Stephen turned to Ahman. "Where are the horses? You said we could take them."

Ahman chuckled. The sound was no more pleasant than it was before. "Sure can. You just have to catch 'em first. I freed 'em hours ago."

Bean clenched her fists. "You had no right."

"You didn't have the right to tie them up in the first place," said Ahman with a shrug.

Stephen touched her wrist. "We'll figure out another way to get there."

"The city is the last place you want to go, if that's where you're headed," said Ahman. "Weren't you listening before? Jeremy's building an army. I suspect *your* kind are, too."

Bean's nostrils flared.

"Or will be, once they realize what happened back there. You go there, you'll be in danger." A log on the campfire popped as the heat of the flames penetrated its center.

"Sorry, but you're wrong about where we are going. And you're wrong about us."

"Prove it."

"We're not leaving town because we're afraid." Bean gave him a look. "We're on a mission." Bean shook her head.

What? Stephen sent the question to Bean via a datastream chat program.

You did hear yourself, right? Her voice echoed in his mind as she replied.

It's true, though.

The corner of Ahman's mouth twitched. "This mission more important than stopping a war?"

Stephen hesitated, not sure how much he wanted to share with the man. "There's a woman—"

Ahman glanced at Bean and chuckled. "There usually is. Though from where I'm sitting, you already have more than you can handle."

"Not like that. She's—"

"I had a daughter once." The smile slipped from Ahman's features. "She was killed . . . murdered . . . simply because she was in the wrong place at the wrong time. Now, there's going to be others. Regular people, just like her, who have no clue what's coming. Is one woman so much more important than all of their lives?"

"She might be," said Stephen. She was one of the originals. She was one of the people who created the upgrade. She knows how to . . . how to . . ." *How to stop people like Finn.*

Stephen bit his tongue before the words exited his lips. He didn't need to share all of their secrets.

Finn was who'd sent him on a quest to retrieve a piece of lost technology–the Wand. He had dangled Bean in front of Stephen like bait. The Wand proved able to alter a modified person's DNA, restoring their youth. Stephen learned Finn intended to use the device for a form of devil's bargain. Those that sided with him would be given immortality. However, Finn demanded more than loyalty oaths from his followers.

Unfortunately, fealty meant giving Finn control of your mind and body, with deadly consequences for disobeying. There was also the drain to consider. A side effect stemming from being too far away from a power source and the reason Stephen had taken Ahman up on his offer of food. A large portion of the remaining population would die if Finn had his way. Only those who recognized the warning signs would realize what was happening and why. For the rest, it would be the plague all over again. Finn didn't care. He considered it the survival of the fittest.

Alan had the Wand now, and as much as Stephen hated him, it was likely better off with him. From what Stephen understood, Alan enjoyed manipulating people into doing what he wanted. Giving them no choice in the matter would take his fun away.

"Are you talking about Juliane Faris?" Ahman sighed. "I can save you a trip. Woman's dead."

"She's not."

"Listen, you don't want to mix yourself up with those people. See, my baby girl's momma was *there*—Gena. She was applying for a job at Apex when this whole rush of people run out the door yelling about a swarm of birds hitting the window upstairs. Got most of the people outside, but not my Gena."

The corner of Ahman's mouth twitched. "She thought it was a test to see how she handled emergencies. Not as crazy as it sounds. The stories we'd heard about people who worked there made it sound—well, let's say we'd heard they only hired the best." His mouth twitched again.

"But then Louis Evans came in." He reached into his pocket, pulled out a flask, and took a swig from it. "And before you say anything, I do mean as in *the* Louis Evans. Gena had been obsessed with him for years. Super rich guy. Used to say she'd leave me for him if the Sharks kept losing." He took another sip from the flask.

"Gena starts thinking this might be her chance to introduce herself, but then this other lady, Dr. Juliane Faris, shows up outta nowhere. Gena recognized her, too. Apparently those two, Louis and Juliane I mean, used to date back in the day, or so my Gena liked to tell me. Was always showing up in the tabloids. Guess it didn't end well, cause the way he looked at her . . . Gena'd seen that look enough to recognize something bad's going to go down. She decides the people who freaked out over the birds had the right idea and starts heading out of there, but these other dudes are now blocking the exits."

Stephen's hopes started to crumble. Had Alan been telling the truth about the contents of the other cylinders after all? Was he really the only person to have survived the Apex bombing down there?

"Ah, Gena." He shook his head. "My woman was a fighter," Ahman continued, lost now in his memories. "Especially when she was riled up, but she's still outnumbered. She hasn't quite broken free when the whole building shakes and the doors to one of the elevators puckers out. The same elevator she'd seen her Mr. Perfect drag his ex into. Then there's this smell, she says."

He returned the flask to his pocket. "The way she described it, it was a mix of smoked metal and burnt meat. Then more explosions. Only this time, they are everywhere. The first one is in the elevator, and the guys guarding the front door don't expect that. Gives Gena the chance to get away." His voice softened. "She told me afterward she learned what hell smelled like."

Stephen and Bean exchanged a glance.

You have to admit, it doesn't sound good. Stephen heard Bean say in his mind.

Remember what Alan told us about that day? He knew Louis was in the elevator. How would he know that if it hadn't made it all the way down?

So now you're ready to trust something Alan said?

Out loud, Stephen said, "You're probably right, but there was a lot of confusion that day. Gena got away. If there's even a chance Juliane managed to get away, too, we have to try to find her."

"Sure, Gena survived the initial panic, but she was murdered in the days that followed trying to save our little girl. And for what?" Ahman sighed. "I know you know more than you're saying. Don't deny it. Even if I couldn't smell a lie, I can see it in your face. I also know you're chasing a ghost. Wouldn't you rather save the living?" Ahman pressed his lips together and looked away before saying, "You know, like that guy I saw you with outside the hospital."

Stephen's lips tightened at the mention of Ed. *No, not Ed. His real name is Chad. Think of them by their real names, remember?* Jeremy's true identity was on the tip of his tongue. All he had to do was tell Ahman where to find the body, and Alan's ruse would be over. The beastmen would tear the imposter apart, just like they would if he or Bean walked into their camp, and the war would end before it started. But then there would be no one left to challenge Finn if they failed to find Juliane or a way to stop the drain.

"And how do you expect us to do that?" asked Bean. "Are we supposed to go door-to-door shouting 'The beastmen are coming! The beastmen are coming!'"

Ahman frowned. "Beastmen?"

Bean nodded at him. "It fits a whole lot better than Sharks. I've seen the team. Didn't see a single fin."

Ahman cocked his head. "And what do you call your side?"

"We're not on either side," interrupted Stephen. "Which is exactly where we want to stay."

Ahman's gaze swept Stephen from head to toe. "You might not have a choice, you know."

Stephen turned and stared into the flames. "You always have a choice." He muttered.

chapter five

JULIANE

Juliane faced the door and grimaced at the small protection it offered. A booming sound echoed as the beast on the other side continued to pound away at the puny barrier. She reached out and touched the walls. Her only hope sprung from the fact the narrow room would not allow the creature to move comfortably. It was far too large, and she'd seen how it walked above ground. There was also the matter of its companion. *One problem at a time,* she thought.

She took a step back. There wasn't much room for her to maneuver. *If I stay near the ground . . .* She shook her head. That hadn't worked for the rat and worse, would slow her further. However, the creature did seem startled when she'd flashed the light. Perhaps, she could use light blindness and the narrow passage to her advantage. She braced herself, ready to launch her body the moment the creature was fully inside.

She didn't have to wait long. The remaining fragments holding the cellar door together snapped. The remains of the door and their meager protection were yanked off its hinges and tossed into the night. A dark silhouette filled the space where it had once been. Juliane tensed. The two birds screamed in unison. Then, suddenly, the shape blocking her exit launched itself into the air. Juliane was still trying to process what was happening and how she might use it to her advantage when flames appeared in the opening.

"What are you waiting for?" A woman's voice asked from outside.

Juliane ran up the stairs leading to the surface. "Are they gone?" she asked her would-be rescuer. However, when she looked around, all she saw was a floating fireball hovering at her eye level.

First giant killer birds, and now this. I'm losing my mind. She issued a command for her body to conduct a full scan. *Although, if my mind is going, can I really trust the results?* She canceled the scan and instead synthesized another dose of artificial calm. Ice cascaded through her veins as the effect took hold.

"I realize how this must look," said the ball of flame. The air under it shimmered and warped, revealing a figure wrapped in dark cloth from head to foot. The figure then reached up with its free hand and pulled a mask away, revealing a woman's face. The flames proved to be connected to a torch. "I can explain later," said the new arrival, "but right now, we don't want to be here when those birds decide to try to pick you off again."

Juliane glanced over her shoulder into the night sky. Clouds had rolled in, blocking much of the moon's light. The giant birds could be circling up there, even now, and she'd have no way of knowing.

Juliane nodded for the woman to lead the way. She followed the woman to a brick building on the other side of the street. From the outside, it appeared more structurally sound than many of the other buildings she and Durham had passed along the way, but far from what she would have considered habitable before today.

Durham. She stopped short. *He's still out there.* She glanced at the door. *But so are those creatures,* the cold voice of logic reminded her. Another wave of ice chilled her blood. *You're going to need to slow down,* she thought. *Your memory is already faulty. Too many inhibitors, and it will only get worse.*

The woman latched the door before she could run back outside. Dark threadbare curtains hung from the walls, though there were few other furnishings. The woman carried her torch into another room. Juliane heard a snap, then the light disappeared, leaving only the trace smell of smoke. Juliane found a light switch and toggled it. However, the switch didn't do anything. She attempted to connect to the building's nanobots but found nothing.

She then realized that she had no access to the datastream either. *This place must have been a historic preservation site.* She frowned, then shuddered. Hospitals used similar signal-blocking technology. It meant that even if their phone apps were working, she wouldn't be able to reach out to Durham to tell him what had happened to her. It also made her skin crawl.

However, the technology only blocked outgoing signals. She still had command of her cells. Juliane's body took on the bioluminescent glow to take a better look around. The woman ran from the other room.

"Turn it off," she said, closing the curtains with a snap.

"Why?" asked Juliane as the room was plunged back into darkness. "Oh, does the light attract the birds?" She waved at the curtains. That would explain why they targeted the store.

"It attracts them," the woman nodded, "but it'll also attract the attention of the sort of people you don't want to meet at night. You're lucky I'm the one who saw you first. What were you thinking?"

"I was thinking I was about to become dinner and was looking for something to protect myself with." She held her chin high. "What is that thing you're wearing, anyway?" asked Juliane, gesturing with sweeping arms at the woman's outfit.

"Pretty neat, isn't it?" she said with a toothy grin bright enough to be seen even in the poor light. "It's a stealth suit, though I like to think of it as an invisibility cloak. Bends light so you see what's behind it, even if you are looking straight at it. No idea what it's made from. Some sort of fiber optic thread or something. Apparently, Finn had some military connections back in the day."

"I'm familiar with the technology." Juliane glanced in the direction of the stairwell. "And is Finn here, too?"

"Finn? Here?" The woman laughed. "No. He doesn't ever leave Manhattan." Her tone hardened. "Actually, he'd prefer most people didn't."

"Most people," Juliane latched on to the words. "I take it, not you."

"He knows I can't stay away long." The woman's tone made it clear that she would prefer not to elaborate on the subject further.

"I can't stay here either. My . . ." How should she describe Durham? "My colleague is hurt." She pointed to the windows. "I'll need to go back to where I last saw him."

The woman sucked in her lip. "You're not from around here, are you?"

Juliane tilted her head. "No. Simply passing through. We were heading to New York, until those things—"

The woman rubbed the back of her neck. "Lucky for you then, I'm on my way back there too. You can travel with me, but we're not going anywhere tonight. The birds aren't the only threats out there, especially not for a woman. You might as well hang a sign around your neck saying Open for Business."

"I can handle myself."

"I don't mean to imply you can't." The woman sighed. "Most people who have survived this long can. You just don't need to put yourself at risk if you don't have to."

Juliane realized the woman standing before her offered the opportunity to learn more details about what had happened to the world since she'd been buried under a pile of rubble, however, those questions would need to wait. Durham was her more pressing concern. "I need to find him."

"Is he like us?"

"Us?" Juliane asked.

Light flashed for a moment across the woman's fingers.

"Oh, you're asking if he's undergone the Gene Assist procedure." Juliane nodded. "Yes, of course. We all did." She pressed her lips together. Her rescuer clearly had some biases, if she cared about something as inconsequential as a person's upgrade status, but Juliane would exploit them for all it was worth if it was the difference between going back for Durham tonight versus waiting until morning.

"Fine," said the woman, walking over to the door. "I'll go and check it out. But not you. You stay here and wait for us to come back."

Juliane crossed her arms and shook her head. "If it is dangerous for me to be out there, then it is just as dangerous for you." The brief arc of electricity jumping between the woman's features unlocked another memory. She'd seen someone do something similar before. *Do not let yourself get distracted, Juliane.*

The woman smirked. "I wouldn't be so sure about that."

"I'm going with you."

"No, you aren't," she said. "And before you waste more time arguing, I have two reasons. One, I don't want to leave my safehouse unguarded, and two, unlike you," she picked at the fabric of her stealth suit, "I have an invisibility cloak."

A memory tickled her mind, but remained just out of reach. "So, let me borrow it." Juliane reached out. "Trust me, I'll bring it back. This place is far better than where we were going to have to spend the night."

"So you can bleed all over it?" said the woman, hugging the material close to her chest. "That isn't going to happen."

Juliane glanced down and saw her arms were covered in deep scratches clotted by dirt. As if on cue, her ankle throbbed, reminding her that Durham wasn't the only one in need of medical attention. She glanced at the door again. If only there was a signal in this place. She could figure out what was wrong with the phone app or send Durham a message.

She ground her toe into the floor. For the life of her, she would never understand why some people actually preferred living in places like this. Looking back up, she pressed her lips together and gave a reluctant nod. "You'll want to look for the most stubborn horse you've ever seen tied up outside," she began.

chapter six

STEPHEN

Bean lay on the ground next to him, breathing with the soft rhythm of sleep. He wished he could do the same. Like the evening before, Nadia's face appeared the minute his eyes were closed. However, this evening, Chad's face also joined hers in his mind's eye, looking equally judgmental. Abandoning sleep, he accessed the datasphere.

Wes, or more accurately, Wes's replica, joined him in an instant. His feet hovered inches above the ground, allowing the grass to move freely underneath him. He appeared tall and muscular, albeit with muscles defined by a series of skin-colored triangles rather than from working in a field or lifting weights.

It was the go-to avatar he'd regularly chosen back when they used to meet up to play *Colony Defenders II*. It was a far cry from the skinny teen with glasses Stephen met in real life, and even further from how he'd appeared during those last minutes on the train.

"Did I make a mistake?" asked Stephen, forcing himself to look away before he started dwelling on Wes's final moments. It was risky to let your thoughts stray in the digital world. Your deepest secrets could be made visible for all the world to see. He'd also learned you could get trapped in a loop if you weren't careful, which is what had happened to the real Jeremy, and what had allowed Alan to assume his identity without threat of being caught.

He focused on his feet. Unlike Wes, he'd chosen to appear like his regular self, though his shoes were covered with a lot less mud. The legs of his pants contained far fewer stains, too. If only the blood on his hands was as easy to wash away in the real world. *Get it together Stephen,* he told himself.

"Knowing you?" said Wes. "Probably." He laughed, not unkindly. "But about what?"

Before, Stephen might have attempted to tease Wes back, but he didn't have a witty comeback. "There's a war coming." He looked down again. "People are going to get hurt." Neither he or Wes cast a shadow in this place. The light came from everywhere and yet nowhere. Stephen frowned. The effect was somewhat off-putting.

He looked up toward the sky. A digital sun bloomed into existence. Stephen turned his attention back to his friend. While the light was still not as bright as the sun outside of the datasphere, it was enough to cause silhouettes to expand out under their feet like growing puddles of water.

Wes cocked his head to the side. His eyes glanced down to the shadows by Stephen's feet. "And you feel bad because you're doing the smart thing by getting as far away as possible?" His body broke apart into pixels for a moment, and when they condensed again, his appearance was that of the boy he'd met in Manhattan, rather than the gaming character he'd met online.

Stephen became sadder from the transformation. "What if I could stop it?"

"You?" Wes shook his head. "I hate to break it to you, man, but as much as I like you, you aren't some sort of mystical chosen one."

Stephen's temper flared. It was sort of thing the real Wes would have said, but it wasn't his friend saying it. It was a computer program. The most advanced software he'd ever seen, sure, but Wes, the real Wes, was never coming back. All because of him. He slapped the palm of his hand with his fist. "This isn't a game."

Wes's avatar wilted before Stephen's eyes. "I'm sorry. I went too far."

Stephen sighed. Wes didn't deserve his anger. "No, I'm sorry. I shouldn't have lashed out at you," said Stephen. "You can't help how you were programmed." Wes shrank even further. "What?" asked Stephen. "Ah, don't feel bad about it. Wes, I mean the real Wes, was brilliant in the best possible ways, unlike some people I know. It's clear he wanted you to be happy."

"Not just me," said Wes. The beginnings of a smile returned to his face.

Stephen turned away and looked into the distance. "Yeah, well, that's not your fault either." The unnatural lighting surrounding them dimmed. He sighed. "I guess, deep down, I know what I need to do. I'll go back. Tell Ahman about Jeremy. With any luck, the other beastmen won't be so willing to follow orders when they see their so-called leader is a liar. Doubt it, but it might be better than doing nothing."

"Dude, I don't have a clue what you're talking about, but that reminds me, I got a lead on Juliane Faris."

"Oh yeah, that's another thing. She's dead. The guy we met today, Ahman, he told us what happened inside Apex. So, you don't have to keep searching for her for me." Stephen described Gena's account in a thickened voice. "Guess I am going to have to find something else to do with my life."

Wes frowned. "Did this witness say she saw her die?"

"She didn't," said Stephen. He pressed his lips together. "But from what she saw up until that moment, it's pretty likely."

Wes frowned. "No, that can't be right. I've spotted code since we last talked. I'm sure of it."

"Code?"

"Yeah, code." He gestured at the landscape. "Take this, for example. You see us standing in a field, but I don't see us standing anywhere at all—it's all just code." His arms fell to his sides. "After a while, you start to recognize certain strings, like recognizing a person's handwriting. I've learned to recognize what's hers."

"So?"

"So, I've detected a new string. Which means she's accessed the datastream. As in recently."

Stephen froze as if struck. "Where is she?"

"She tried to use a rideshare program in Worcester, if you'd believe it," said Wes. "It's safe to say she isn't still waiting around for a lift, but it's a start."

Stephen searched his friend's face, looking for any sign of lie or prank. "Worcester? Recently?" He slammed his fist into his hand. She must have been in one of those tubes after all. But who freed her? Not Alan. *Unless . . . what if it's a trap?*

All he had was Ahman's word he was trying to stop Alan from starting a war. But what if he wasn't? What if Ahman was simply following Alan's orders? They'd told Ahman they were trying to locate Juliane, and Worcester was beastman headquarters. He could have easily passed that information along to Alan the same way that he and Bean were able to communicate via the datastream, mind-to-mind. This whole thing could be a set-up to get them back to the beastman's home turf. "How long?"

Wes sighed. "There've been a couple more pings since then. Too fast and encrypted for me to get a read on their location, but that's another reason I know they're hers."

"I meant *when* did she ping the datastream in Worcester?" Stephen's breath bottled in his chest.

"Yesterday? Today?" Wes looked to the ground. "Sorry, it's hard to tell how much time passes anymore."

Stephen rubbed his face as if he might wipe his guilt away. Wes might have achieved a form of immortality in this place, but it didn't take a genius to see all he wanted was to be a real person again. "So, still a wild goose chase, then?"

Wes's face snapped up, though his expression remained somber. "Hey, the thing about wild geese is, sometimes they get caught. We'll find her. I promise."

"Yeah, and sometimes all the person chasing after them finds is a pile of shit at the end," said Stephen to himself. He looked toward the horizon. Wes no longer had to worry about the passage of time, but it had to be close to morning by now. He was no more convinced continuing to pursue Juliane was the right decision, versus going back to Ahman, than he was when he'd first entered the datastream. "Play me the recording again."

"I might be just code, but I still have feelings, you know."

Stephen sighed. "Would you play the recording, *please*?"

"Much better." Wes dissolved into the landscape, and the image of a brown-haired woman took his place—his birth mother, Betty Dronigh. Aside from the recording, the most he knew about her was she'd died while he was still a small child.

Betty held up a picture of Juliane. "Find her," his mother said. The recording stopped.

Find her. The woman before him claimed to love him before asking him to find Juliane. The recording had left it vague exactly why he was supposed to find her, but Stephen was sure it involved the drain. After all, Juliane had created the upgrade and was supposed to be brilliant. She'd be able to find a way to patch the code and halt the drain's effects. Not just for him, but for everyone trapped on the island with Finn.

Chasing after Juliane had seemed like a great idea immediately following the battle at the Watchtower. Then again, he hadn't been thinking straight. His initial cold acceptance of Nadia's death proved it. But now that he'd had more time to think about honoring a dead woman's command, it seemed more and more like the opposite.

It wasn't like he remembered the woman who'd given him life. She could be just as much a liar as his biological father. She'd married him after all. And yet, hearing that there was still a chance to return to a normal life, he found he couldn't walk away. The image faded, and for a while, Stephen did nothing but stared at the grassy hills that undulated before him.

Wes reemerged from behind him. "You okay?"

Stephen pulled his gaze away from the horizon. "Yeah."

"Anytime you want to talk," said Wes. He reached out, like he was about to place his hand on Stephen's shoulder. "About anything. I'm always here."

Yeah, because of me. Someone pulled on Stephen's arm in reality. "Gotta run," he said. Exiting the datasphere, he opened his eyes and saw Bean hovering over him.

"You were out cold," she whispered. Her eyes darted around. She moved to give him space but kept her body tucked into a crouch.

What is it? What's wrong? he projected.

We're not alone. she answered.

He heard the sound, too. Something or someone with heavy footsteps was approaching. He glanced in the direction of the other campsite. The smell of their cookfire still floated on the pre-dawn air. *Do you think it's Ahman?*

Maybe, said her voice. Bean shook her head. *But it's coming from the wrong direction.*

Stephen listening more closely. *We should warn him.* Stephen didn't need the light of day to know that Bean scowled. "I need to tell him the truth about Jeremy."

The noise shifted. Bean covered his mouth with her finger. *Are you trying to let whoever that is know where we are?*

It slipped out.

Good thing you have me to save you from yourself.

Yeah, but who's going to save Ahman?

Bean shrugged. *He seems like someone who can handle himself. He'll be fine.* She grabbed their meager belongings. *We should go while whoever that is, is distracted.*

Stephen stood. *I wouldn't have expected you to want to run from a fight.*

Bean stopped in her tracks. Stephen didn't need daylight to sense her glare. *Let's get two things straight: it's not our fight, and I'm so not running, but if you are determined to be an idiot about it, by all means, let's go and risk our lives for that guy. I'm sure he absolutely would have done the same for us.*

She threaded her way through the trees back toward Ahman's campsite like a silent shadow. As Stephen followed her into the darkness, he wondered if another face would be joining Nadia's when he next attempted to find sleep.

chapter seven

JULIANE

Juliane sat up in the antique chair with a jolt. She'd found it while she waited for the woman to return with Durham and must have nodded off. She stood and stretched her back. The chair must have been worth a fortune at some point for someone, but had clearly seen better days and was far from what Juliane would consider comfortable.

She wiggled her foot. Her ankle no longer gave her pain. The scratches on her arms, too, had knit closed while she slept. *Thank you, Gene Assist upgrade. Better yet, thank me.* She paced around the room and peered through a crack in the curtains. The rose blush of dawn colored the sky. Dread settled into the pit of Juliane's stomach. She must have passed more of the night in the wooden chair than she'd intended, and still there was no sign of the woman, who'd left without ever giving Juliane her name.

That's it. I've waited long enough, thought Juliane, *I'm going myself.* Birds chirped all around, but they were the songs Juliane was used to—normal-sized bird songs. Even more promising, the air no longer contained the scent of death that Juliane now associated with their larger, murderous brethren.

The streets looked different in the light of the day. Juliane realized that finding her way back to the store might prove somewhat difficult. She hadn't been exactly paying attention to road signs, nor had she run in a straight line in her efforts to avoid becoming dinner.

She attempted to access the datastream, but the signal blocker ensuring the historical address remained a digital-free zone extended out to the immediate street front as well. Juliane looked for the rising sun. *That must be east.* She shielded her eyes. *Which would mean, north should be* . . . she looked to the left. *That way.*

"I found your friend," said the woman, emerging from the house behind her.

Juliane hadn't heard any sound indicating another was inside. She turned to face her. "You should have woken me as soon as you got back."

"I decided the news could wait." The woman's expression took on a look that Juliane hated more than anything—pity. She reached out her hand, but then let it drop back to her side. "I'm sorry."

"What are you saying? Sorry, as in, you couldn't find him?" The woman's silence filled the room. "Or sorry, as in . . ." Juliane pressed her lips together and searched the woman's face for some indication that her comment didn't mean what it sounded like. "You're saying he's dead?" She shook her head. "You're wrong. It has to be someone else." Juliane cursed the technology that prevented her from being able to ping Durham. She's just seen him—they'd just been joking around. He couldn't be dead.

The woman's head dropped. She picked up something from inside the house. It proved to be a large bloody strip of cloth. "You recognize this, don't you?" She held the swath up higher. The fabric resembled the cloth that had once covered Durham's torso, though it was difficult to tell for sure. The red stain swayed in the breeze. She lowered her arm. "There was more, much more, but . . ." She sighed. "He's gone."

"Show me. I need to see him for myself."

She gave a small shake of her head. "I buried what was left of him. I didn't think you'd want him to be left out like that for the animals to find him. Like I said, I'm so, so sorry."

The woman had said it again as if her apology might somehow summon her colleague, no her . . . her . . . Juliane blinked. *Friend? Had he really become that? Or had he already become more?* Juliane clenched her fists at the unbidden thoughts swirling around her head. She'd rejected him—pushed him away—like she had everyone else, and with good reason.

However, her lower lip still trembled. She clenched her jaw. It would serve no purpose to break down in front of a relative stranger, other than to make her look weak or not in control. She flooded her system with every enzyme or biological compound known to numb the sudden ache in her heart over what might have been.

She then turned toward creating longer-lasting mental walls around her thoughts—a skill she'd mastered long before undergoing the gene assist procedure. However, her natural techniques weren't nearly as perfect. With her defenses in place, she dismissed thoughts of Durham. It was easier . . . no, she corrected herself, it made more logical sense to focus on next steps rather than what-ifs.

Besides, as her former research partner, Betty, was once so quick to point out, Juliane didn't need friends. She didn't need anyone. She steeled her shoulders. *Never had,* she reminded herself. Friends only served as a demand on her time and another form of distraction. She'd continue on to New York like she'd already planned. That idea, at least, still made sense—where else did she have to go? Her life in

Worcester lay in ruins. It was pointless to turn back. Once there, she'd seek out this Finn person, if he truly was in charge, and offer her assistance. Society might have descended into chaos while she slept, but it didn't have to stay that way. She'd changed how the world worked once. She would change it again.

Juliane glanced back toward the north. "Tell me more about this group of yours."

The highway stretched out before them, as eerily quiet and devoid of life as it had been the day before. The sight was hard to process. The last time she'd traveled it, the roadway had been packed as far as the eye could see with bumper-to-bumper traffic. Even the skies had been filled with passing vehicles.

In her mind's eye, helicopters should be hovering overhead, reporting on the scene below, while a constant stream of larger aircraft made their way to the nearby airports. The roar of engines, blaring horns, and shouts from drivers with short tempers should be filling her ears—not this unnatural quiet.

"We're almost there," said Morgan and pulled on the reins. She'd named herself shortly after they'd departed.

While she hadn't brought back Durham's remains, Morgan had managed to locate Juliane's stubborn, skittish mare. Juliane's lip curled. *Why it should survive when Durham hadn't . . .* She pushed the complaint down, fixating instead on her distaste for the animal. More than once, she'd debated whether they would have been better off leaving it tied outside of the store, but Morgan insisted they would make better progress on horseback, even if they had to share the saddle of this beast.

"Then why are we stopping?" asked Juliane as the mare slowed its gait.

"Because we aren't quite close enough to make it there before dark, and this old girl has carried us far enough for one day."

Juliane slid off the horse's back and rubbed her legs while Morgan rummaged through one of the saddlebags. She pulled out a large canteen. "The bad news is, this is the last of it," said Morgan, throwing the container at Juliane. "But the good news is, there's a group of cars up ahead." Morgan pointed at an exit ramp. "So, no more horseback riding today."

"Working cars? As in we can ditch this creature? Because that would be good news."

Morgan glanced at her with a frown. "The only working cars belong to the Watch."

"The who?"

"Where have you been living for the last ten . . . fifteen years?" She closed her eyes in a wince and shook her head. "Never mind, doesn't matter now anyway. I'll just need you to wait for me by the cars. Okay?"

"Why? Where are you going?"

"There's a place near here, but the thing is, the people who live there can be a little . . . ah . . . nervous around strangers. So, I'm going to see if they'll be okay with us staying over. Don't worry, though. Worst case, we can camp in the cars."

"You're not suggesting we sleep in a junkyard?"

"Would you prefer to sleep on the ground again?"

Juliane raised an eyebrow. A night without insects buzzing around her ears or the threat of late-night storm would be a nice change of pace after the last several days. "Fine."

A rusted blue minivan lay at the bottom of the highway ramp next to a small yellow hatchback-style sedan. The gas panels on both vehicles were open. A police cruiser rested on its side on the other side of the roadway. Juliane assumed any gas in the cruiser had long since been siphoned off. The entire scene screamed tetanus risk. "I'm starting to wonder if the ground might not be the better option."

Morgan chuckled. "This is another reason most don't leave the city very often. Now, I'm guessing it might be difficult, but try not to get too comfortable."

The minivan's third row had been replaced by a mattress. However, she didn't need to access its sensors to determine it was crawling with insects, or worse. A large yellow-brown circle marked one end. Juliane refused to even contemplate potential sources for the stain other than rainwater. The window above it was cracked, and the entire interior reeked of mold.

She eyeballed a folded blanket lying next to the stain and curled her lip. While leaves on the surrounding trees had taken on the golden tones of autumn, evening wouldn't be nearly cold enough for Juliane to use it in the event Morgan's friends turned them away.

Grimacing, Juliane exited the van, and leaned against its side while she waited for Morgan's return. She had seen the towering skyscrapers in the distance, but even if she hadn't, she would have known it was close by. Though a number of New York's high-risers in the distance were pockmarked by large swaths of broken glass, exposed sides, and even a few burn scars, she sensed the pulse of streaming data. Each packet was like a wave of soothing water on her skin.

As they'd traveled down the highway, each step closer to the city had only strengthened the sensation. She'd felt more like her former self by the minute. More importantly, the data served as confirmation she'd made the right decision in continuing on to New York, even if it was without Durham. Her breath caught in her throat.

She reminded herself that the signal meant there were other people. Other survivors. Once there, it would simply be a matter of identifying the brightest minds available and pooling their resources. She'd fix her missing memories. She'd fix everything. She bit her lip as the image of Durham's bloody shirt waving in the early morning light sprung to mind. Or at least she'd fix what she could. She stared at the skyscrapers and the future they promised. The only thing that could improve upon her plans was a hot shower. Durham's dirt-covered face and toothy white grin appeared unbidden. *Not the only thing.*

She pressed her lips together, banishing the depressing thought before it could undo her. An idle mind was risky. To pass the time, she expanded her consciousness and intercepted a random transmission passing through a nearby node. The level of security protecting the data seemed overkill considering how few people they'd encountered.

As she'd done more than once already, she pinged the datastream for any sign of Durham before she could stop herself. Like those other times, the results of her query came back empty. *Why do I keep doing this to myself?* She bit her lip. The walls she'd erected in her brain weren't doing the trick. She was going to have to do something more.

"We're in luck," said Morgan stepping back into view. "They're feeling more welcoming than usual." A young man with sun-streaked, bushy brown hair stood next to her. He had the sort of bronze complexion that came from working long hours outside. "This is my . . . This is Lyall." Morgan shifted nervously. "Lyall, this is Juliane."

"Nice to meet you," said Lyall. He leaned back on his heels with a grin. "You picked the right day to pass by. It's Mags's birthday." He took their horse by its reins. He waved for Juliane to come closer but didn't take his eyes off Morgan. "If we leave right now, there's even time for some dancing."

Juliane took a breath as the memory of the night in the Vegas nightclub sprung to mind. The three of them had gone there after the convention—she, Durham, and their boss, Louis. Durham had even danced with her for a time, but then he'd found other partners and she'd . . . she'd made one of the worst mistakes of her life. She'd left the club with Louis.

"You ready?"

Juliane blinked. "Sorry, yes. I was just trying to remember how long it has been since I attended a party. Sounds fantastic."

Lyall continued to chatter while he led their horse down a narrow dirt-and-gravel trail. While he made sure to keep pace with both of them and to include Juliane in the conversation as much as Morgan, he walked closer to Morgan than was required by the width of the path. His fingers also twitched by his side whenever Morgan's hand strayed too close, like it was itching to grab hers.

Juliane caught the sound of a drumbeat first. Guitar music filled her ears next. The notes were delivered without particular technique or finesse, but were nonetheless followed by enthusiastic applause and laughter. Whoever the musicians were, they were providing quite the performance.

Lyall grinned, pushing a branch out of the way. "Here we are. Home sweet home." A large wall appeared up ahead. The wall itself consisted of a mix of wooden boards. Most were gray and splintered, though some appeared to have once been painted brown. Lyall placed his hand on Morgan's shoulder. "I'll be back in a second." His teeth gleamed before he turned and disappeared into the growing night.

"There's something I need to tell you," said Morgan.

"That Lyall has feelings for you? Yes, that's pretty obvious."

Though the sun had almost completely set, there was enough light to see Morgan's cheeks redden. "It's not that. The people here—" Morgan pointed at the wall. "They're not like us. They're Analogs."

"Analogs?" Juliane's brow knit. "Oh, you mean they haven't undergone the Gene Assist procedure." She relaxed. "Well, that's inconvenient for them, I suppose." She shook her head and waved the comment away. "But I don't see any reason why that should cause you or I any concern."

It still wasn't clear to her what exactly had happened to the world in the time since she entered the cryogenic tank. Her questions to Morgan as they'd made their way down the empty highway had largely gone unanswered except in the most general terms. Morgan, apparently, had been too young when it happened to truly understand what was going on.

She curled her knuckles, rolling the news reports she'd read around in her head again. Bombings. Mass layoffs. Pandemic. Each of those things were serious, but independently none of them should have been enough to have caused civilization to collapse. However, combined, she now understood they'd transformed the world into the post-apocalyptic landscape it was today.

Still, it hadn't needed to be that way. The world's greatest minds should have banded together to find a solution, a cure, or a common purpose the population could rally behind. *Minds like hers.* However—her nails dug into her palms—short-sighted individuals with more ambition than brains had taken over instead.

Now, knowing what to look for, she'd dived further into reports online. The masses had left the major metropolitan areas all at once. The rural communities they'd fled to—with their limited resources and smaller understaffed hospitals, hadn't been equipped to handle the demand. She ground her teeth. The situation had spiraled out of control from there, as more people either succumbed to the illness or became victims of unchecked violence.

With every insight she gained, Juliane became more convinced the entire situation could have been prevented. If only she'd been awake and not trapped inside a tin can. She clenched her fist tighter. She might have been able to do something. She forced herself to relax her hand before her nails broke the skin. *Why did I go in that tube? If I'd only known. If I'd only been awake* . . . More and more of her memories had come back to her, but that one remained stubbornly absent. She needed time to reflect and relax, but thus far, the road had provided too many distractions. *It will be better once I'm back in the city.*

Lyall appeared behind them. "We're all set." He waved at them to follow.

A roaring bonfire held the evening at bay. Juliane counted at least twenty people mingling in its light. The growing darkness wasn't the only thing the fire held back. The burning logs also masked the scent of livestock. Dancing flames illuminated a goat loitering near the enclosure's edge. A chicken pecked the ground in front of Juliane's foot. She scanned the area for any sign of pens, but instead only spotted a large wooden table. "Please say you don't actually eat out here," she said.

"Where else would we eat?" said Lyall.

"Inside, of course." She pointed at the table. "That's not sanitary."

"What doesn't kill you . . ." said Lyall with a laugh.

"It still might," Juliane muttered. However empty space was all that remained next to her. She turned to address Morgan, but found the woman, too, had vanished.

Juliane spotted the pair a moment later, silhouetted by the bonfire. Lyall appeared to be pleading with Morgan. Morgan shook her head. Whatever the disagreement was about, it was short-lived, as Lyall then reached out and twirled Morgan.

"I haven't seen you around here before," said a broad-shouldered man, coming to stand by her. "But I am wishing I had. Would you like to dance?"

Juliane looked toward the flames. She'd lost track of her companions among the other revelers. She glanced back at the stranger. His smile shone in the darkness, reminding her of Durham. She took a breath, holding it like a dam against waves of emotion. How had that man worked his way into to her psyche so completely? She reminded herself of all the reasons his loss shouldn't affect her so.

He was a womanizer, a jock, and even worse, a proven liar. If they hadn't worked together, they wouldn't have had anything in common at all. In fact, there was nothing about him that should have appealed to her, and yet for some reason, she didn't seem to be able to get over the fact that he was gone.

Understanding her feelings for Durham was like trying to solve a jigsaw puzzle, knowing full well a piece was missing. "Maybe in a little bit," she said before the silence grew awkward, "but I've been walking for days, and right now, I just want to stay back and listen."

She expected him to return to the party, but instead he remained by her side. "You've come a long way, then?"

She nodded. "I must have driven this route at least a hundred times. The funny thing is, it never seemed like a long distance before."

"We took a lot for granted back then," said the man in a tone that spoke volumes.

"You say that like it's a bad thing," said Juliane in an attempt to lighten the mood and escape her own thoughts. She reached down and massaged her calf muscle.

"Isn't it?" asked the man, extending his hand. "I'm Sam, by the way."

"Juliane," She straightened while taking his offered hand. "I just meant that I, for one, wouldn't mind going back to a time we had the luxury of taking things for granted."

"Ah." Sam nodded. "Yeah—" A scream cut off whatever he was about to say next, and the music came to a screeching halt. Juliane looked toward its source where the firelight revealed a woman bent over, clutching her abdomen. Sam's eyes grew wide. "Rebecca," he said, releasing Juliane's hand. He gave her an apologetic look and ran toward the others while Morgan came running back.

The woman cried out again. The others rushed her inside the nearest building. "This isn't good. Rebecca's pregnant," explained Morgan. "But it's early—too early for her to be going into labor. It's not going to end well. We should leave while they're occupied."

"Why? They aren't going to blame us. We just got here. If anything, they should blame the livestock. Who knows what sort of bacteria they're carrying?" The goat swished its tail as if aware of Juliane's comment. "Also, you saw how fast everyone leapt into action. Everyone taking on a job. This can't be their first delivery." She pointed at the goat, noting its sagging belly. "For example, their pet lawnmower looks like she's given birth once or twice," she said. "It's just another baby. People have them all the time."

Morgan's eyes bored into Juliane's. "No," she said. "They don't."

"Of course they do." Juliane pressed. "The government might've collapsed, but I'm pretty sure people are still having sex." Juliane scanned their rustic surroundings. "In fact, considering what little else there is to do around here, I suspect they're having it more often."

Morgan turned her face to the ground and mumbled something too softly for Juliane to hear.

"Sex is nothing to be embarrassed about," said Juliane.

"Maybe it wasn't when you were growing up—"

The laboring woman screamed again, cutting off the conversation before Juliane pressed further. Juliane cocked her head toward the sound and pressed her lips together. She had little experience with pregnant women, but even to her untrained ears, it didn't sound like the woman's delivery was progressing normally. "Hmm, you might have a point."

One of the doors to the house opened, and a man stumbled out. His gaze settled on them. "You two," he shouted. "Don't just stand there. We need boiling water, and something hard for Rebecca to bite down on."

Juliane glanced at Morgan.

"She's going to die," said Morgan loud enough for only Juliane to hear. "They both are." Her lips twisted. "There's a reason I don't stay here often. These people have certain opinions about people like us. We will get blamed for this. We should leave."

Juliane squared her shoulders and looked toward the house. "It wouldn't be the first time I was blamed for something outside of my control. I doubt it will be the last. Go, if you're so worried about it. I, however, am staying." She looked around. Her forehead wrinkled. "Now, if you were a bucket, where would you be?"

Morgan glanced toward the gate to the compound. Her shoulders slumped. "Try looking over by the chicken coop," she said after a moment.

Fantastic. Juliane took a deep breath. *More birds.* "Right. Well, then, let's get on with it."

Juliane entered the house clutching a metal bucket she'd found outside. Water sloshed as she followed the screams to the room where the laboring woman had been relocated. The poor woman lay on a bed. The others hovered around her, looking just as lost as Juliane felt. The pregnant woman cried out again.

A man, standing by the woman's feet, placed his hands between her legs. "Becky, you have to stop. It's too soon," he said. "Try not to push just yet."

Juliane started and straightened her back. While she might not have medical training and no experience with childbirth, his advice sounded terrible.

The woman on the bed cried. "I'm trying, but I can't help it."

"You have to try harder." The man attending the woman looked to one of the other men in the room. The man nodded and raced out of the room.

"You don't understand. It's coming. I know it is." The laboring woman cried out between panted breaths.

"Calm yourself," said the man. "It's not good for you . . . or our baby."

"Something's wrong with it. I can feel it," she screamed.

"Sssh, just try not to push."

"Are you insane?" Juliane dropped the bucket of water by the footboard with a thud, not caring if water sloshed from its rim as she came to the woman's side. "It doesn't take a genius to see that this baby is coming."

"Who's this?" The man shouted at the others in the room.

"I saw her standing around outside," said one of the men. "Thought everyone should be helping."

"Her name is Juliane," said Sam. Juliane hadn't noticed him among the others.

The laboring woman groaned. Tears streamed from her eyes. "I'm sorry," she said to the man at her feet. The woman's voice was fainter than it had been a second before.

Juliane bent down and touched the woman's shoulder as a mad idea sprang into her mind. "I'm a doctor," she said.

"You are?" There was relief in the man's voice, though it was mixed in equal parts with distrust.

"I am," said Juliane, daring anyone with a glare to disagree. "Now, stand over there so I can better understand the situation we are dealing with here." She rubbed her hands together. "Better yet, please find another place for the others to wait. There are far too many people in this room."

The first man frowned and looked like he wasn't going anywhere.

The laboring woman moaned. "Please, Rob," she whispered. The woman's eyes squeezed shut.

"We've never seen this person before," he said.

"Please," the woman repeated. Her skin appeared paler than it had even a moment ago.

Sam called out from the other side of the room. "Let her help, man."

Rob's lips narrowed to a fine line, but he nodded. "I'll be in the hall." He shot Juliane a pointed look. "We all will." Juliane shot him the same look back.

As the others filed out of the room, Juliane accessed the datastream. The signal was weaker than what she'd detected outside, but strong enough that soon, data and digital images augmented her vision. She moved until she stood in front of the woman's legs. Blood and bodily fluids were everywhere.

Juliane hesitated. This was going to be more difficult than she imagined. She looked at her hands. They were covered in dirt from the road, and no doubt, now played host to civilizations-worth of bacteria. She glanced down at the bucket and shook her head. While the water appeared clear, it could contain any sort of bug larvae. She sent a query into the datastream. A research study appeared on the healing effects of plasma-activated water. The woman moaned again. Juliane hated that her theory relied on so little supporting information, but she didn't see much other choice.

She held her hands apart and issued the command to her cells. Electricity sparked from finger to finger as her cells took on the properties of an eel. She concentrated, and the intensity increased. As soon as the sparks were strong enough to jump from one hand to the next, she plunged her hands into the water.

Juliane's hands tingled as the power she'd generated passed through the liquid. The bucket and its contents glowed with a purple-tinged light, bright enough to illuminate the room. Juliane waited a heartbeat before releasing the lightning from her hands. She then returned to the woman.

The woman drew her legs back. "I saw what you did," she said with a whimper. "I know what you are. You're one of them."

Juliane raised an eyebrow. "Which, incidentally, makes me your best friend at the moment." Information scrolled across her vision. "It's Rebecca, right? Let's see what we're working with." She placed a hand on the woman's knee. The woman shuddered. Juliane's lips twisted. "Please," she said. "I want to help you, but I will not force you."

Rebecca looked anywhere except at Juliane, but parted her legs.

Juliane glanced down. It took all her resolve not to allow her true emotions to show on her face at the sight. "The baby is crowning," she said, grateful at the moment to have never been cursed with the desire for children of her own. "When I count to three, I want you to give me a good strong push."

"I'm not supposed to push." The woman cried. "Rob said so. It's too early."

"Rob doesn't have another whole human being inside him," said Juliane. "One . . . Two . . . Three . . . Push."

The woman clenched her fists and closed her eyes. However, tears continued to escape.

"That's good," said Juliane focusing on the baby. "On my count, do it again."

"I . . . can't," said Rebecca between panted breaths. Her eyes rolled back in her sockets.

"You have to," said Juliane. "Three."

The woman's body tightened as she bore down, then relaxed.

Juliane pressed her lips together. The baby's position had hardly changed. She softened her tone. "I get it. You're scared, and what I'm asking you to do is hard, but you are going to have to try harder," she said.

"I can't." The woman's voice was barely more than a whisper.

Juliane tapped the woman on her knee. "Look at me," said Juliane. The woman's tear-filled eyes opened. "The timing might be less than ideal, but this baby wants to be born. Don't give up on it before it has even had a chance. Now, push."

Rebecca took a breath and nodded. Her body tightened, though this time, she did not call out as the baby's head emerged.

"That's it," said Juliane. "One more."

The rest of the baby's body followed next as Juliane scooped up the child in her hands. Juliane frowned as she wiped away blood and fluid and looked upon its face. The child was pale and silent. *Aren't newborns supposed to cry?* The mother's body lay equally limp on the bed. Juliane sent another query to the datastream, unsure of what to do next. She opened the child's mouth with a finger as more data and diagrams appeared over the top of her vision.

The baby remained silent, though its motionlessness worried Juliane more than its lack of cries. Not sure what else she could do without access to a hospital or more advanced medical equipment, Juliane stared at the umbilical cord connecting mother to child. *There's so much blood.* She glanced at the baby in her arms and back at Rebecca. She'd given it her best, but it hadn't been enough. Still, thought Juliane, the woman deserved to meet her child at least once. "It's a girl," she said, laying the child on the woman's chest.

"A daughter," said Rebecca. Somehow, she gathered the strength to raise an arm and cradled the infant between her breasts.

Juliane looked away. Sounds of tiny breaths came from the bed. Juliane looked back. The child's eyes fluttered as she tested out her lungs with great volume. The door flung open, and Rob returned to the room. He ran to the bedside and dropped to his knees. "It's a . . . It's a . . ." he said.

Rebecca looked at him. Love radiated from her face as her fingers gingerly touched the child's hair. "It's a girl."

Rob beamed. "A girl." He encircled the pair with his arm.

Juliane frowned at the man. "Congratulations." While the baby had found its voice, her mother's voice remained far too weak. Juliane didn't need to see the dark stain at the foot of the bed to know the mother wasn't out of danger. "Now, step aside." She plunged her hands back in the bucket of water. "We're in for a long night."

chapter eight

STEPHEN

Embers twinkled like stars in the darkness, and the scent of charred meat still lingered in the air, but otherwise, there was no other sign of Ahman. Purple-white light arced across Bean's fingers as she stood in the center of the clearing. She cocked her head, listening for sounds that might give away the position of whoever or whatever else crept through the woods. Stephen followed suit.

A twig snapped. Bean dropped into a defensive pose, but all that emerged from the underbrush was the shadowed outline of a small fox, which quickly ran off back into the night.

Are we too late? wondered Stephen as he returned to where they'd shared a dinner. Ahman was nowhere in sight, and there were even fewer clues to suggest where he'd gone.

Bean's fingers quit sparking as she crouched down near the remains of the fire. The remaining coals winked out of existence as they were smothered by a handful of dirt. *There hasn't been anyone here for hours,* her voice said in his mind. Her shadowed outline straightened and returned to his side. *It must have been him we heard out there. Probably was trying to catch a peek of us together. Pervert.*

Stephen's lips twisted. As much as he wanted to argue, the woods had grown quiet. If there had been someone else in the woods with them other than Ahman, they'd figured out how to move in it as Bean did.

"So, what do you want to do now?" asked Bean. She stretched. An owl hooted. "Because if I have a vote, I say try to get a few more hours of sleep." She turned and swept the clearing with her gaze. "Just not here." She rubbed her arms. "Way too exposed."

Stephen reluctantly nodded and followed Bean back the way they'd come.

A rock dug into his back. He shifted, only for his back to find another. For the millionth time, Stephen envied the easy way Bean drifted into a deep sleep. He listened to her calm breathing and closed his eyes. The hair on his arm tingled. His fingers found a bug crawling across his skin. He flicked it away and tried to force himself to sleep again.

The darkness behind his eyes transformed into the familiar tall grass of home. The windmill that powered the well's pump, as well as their overworked generator, turned lazily in the breeze. Stephen broke into a grin as he ran through the wall of grass protecting the farmhouse from casual view. *Finally, a dream that isn't a nightmare.*

The door to the house squeaked as rusty hinges stretched open. A woman stepped out onto the front stoop. She raised her hand to her forehead, shielding her eyes from the sun and hiding her face from view, but Stephen recognized her at once. "Mom," he called out. "Nadia." Strands of grass slapped his face and cut the skin of his exposed arms. He didn't care. "I'm home."

Nadia lowered her hand. "Nadia? Who told you my name was—where have you been? We've been worried sick." She tucked a strand of hair behind her ear and looked over her shoulder, back at the house. "Don't you dare ask me if you can go out on another supply run anytime soon."

"It's okay, Nadia. You and Chad don't have to use secret identities anymore." Stephen laughed. Clearing the last of the field, he ran up the steps. He picked her up and swung her around in an embrace. "I've missed you so much," he said. "I'll never ask to leave you again."

The corner of Nadia's lip turned up. She squeezed him back once. "What's gotten into you? All you've ever wanted was a chance to get away."

"I was wrong."

Nadia shook out of his embrace. "Well, enough about that. Now that you're back you can help with chores. Chad's gotten it into his head that we need to upgrade our entire filtration system. He's been in and under the house all day. Who knows what he's broken by now?"

Stephen chuckled and took a step back from the stairs. "I'll see if I can find him."

Nadia's smile broadened. "When you do, tell him he better not come inside without leaving his boots at the door. I've already had to clean up after him twice this morning."

Stephen nodded and wandered around to the side of the building, where a chipped wooden door marked the entrance to the crawl space under the farmhouse. He pulled the latch and opened the door but saw only darkness on the other side.

He poked his head in. "Chad?" he called out. "Are you down there?" He listened for any sound that would indicate the man who'd helped raise him was hard at work. "Nadia said you're fixing the filter. Said you could use some help?" He frowned. Maybe it had been so long that anyone called him by his real name, his foster father had forgotten to respond to it. "Dad?"

The wind picked up, which caused the windmill to creak and moan as it spun around. Watching it, Stephen felt a pulling sensation, and then, it was as if he'd been sucked away, though he remained exactly where he stood.

"Ah, this must be where you grew up." Alan stood at the windmill's base. "What a lovely place," he said looking around. "It's so . . . so . . . simple."

"Get out of my dream," said Stephen, tightening his jaw.

"Is that any way to speak to your *real* father?" Alan opened his arms. "Especially after what I've done for you."

"What you've done for me? Sure, let's talk about all the things you've done for me." Stephen waved his hands about. "First, you abandoned me. Then you sold me out to the Watch." He tapped his chin. "Oh, yeah, and there is that other minor thing." He glared at Alan. "You being responsible for millions of people dying while you slept through it all."

Alan dropped his arms to his sides and cocked his head. "You were injured and in need of medical care. How was I to guess what that woman intended? I've been in stasis for the last fifteen years."

"Don't act like you didn't suspect something," said Stephen. "You had to." He crossed his arms over his chest. "Unless you aren't the genius you like to claim you are."

The smile left Alan's face. "Being a genius doesn't mean you have the ability to anticipate another person's *every* action. Take Albert Einstein, for example. On one hand," he flipped the palm of one hand up, "I imagine he never expected others to use his early work to create the atomic bomb, let alone use it." He flipped his other hand over. "But if they hadn't, it is highly probable that neither you nor I would exist today." He shook his head and let his hands drop back to his sides. "Sometimes, bad things happen, no matter how many years you spend planning. However, it doesn't mean some good can't still come from them."

"She tried to bleed me dry," said Stephen. "I could've died."

"But you didn't, and now she's not in a position to hurt anyone else ever again."

Stephen's eyes narrowed. "The beastmen are going to figure out who you really are. You thought about that yet?"

Alan shrugged. "Oh, I'm sure that a number of them already suspect, but I'm not worried."

"They will rip you in two."

"I doubt that very much."

"You willing to bet on it? Because I sure wouldn't, if I were you."

Alan shook his head. "Have you always been this angry?"

"What can I say. You bring out the best in me."

"That's probably true," said Alan. He examined his fingernails. "But I appreciate your concern. For what it is worth, though, while I can't say I can anticipate everyone's reaction, history has proven time and time again that people are willing to turn a blind eye to an unpleasant truth, provided you are giving them what they want most of all. It's not my fault that it happens to be revenge. Especially, now that the Wand has given them all their youthful energy back."

"So, you *are* starting a war," said Stephen.

Alan tutted. "Who exactly have you been talking to?" The corners of his lips turned up. "No, I'm not starting a war. Sure, there might be a skirmish or two. There's unfinished business, after all. But from my perspective, it's simply a change in management structure." He shrugged. "Happens all the time."

"Except people are going to die. Lots of people." Stephen shook his head and glanced back at the farmhouse. Its windows were dark and as devoid of life as a grave. "You didn't do a good enough job destroying the world the first time around, you need to do it again?"

"Destroy it?" Alan's eyes widened. "Is that what's gotten you so upset?" He shook his head. "One of these days, you'll realize I'm not the bad guy you've convinced yourself I am. I've only ever wanted to save it."

"Could've fooled me."

"That's because you keep allowing yourself to be fooled," said Alan. "If you would have only listened to me—"

"I've listened to you long enough." Stephen turned away.

"It doesn't have to be this way between us. I can help you."

"I seriously doubt it."

"Son, you and I are connected. You might not want to accept it, but it is true, and not just because we share the same blood. We're bonded in the datasphere too. I can sense you out there. Not with pinpoint accuracy mind you—you're too far away—but enough to give me a general idea of where you're standing right now. Or sitting. Look, I don't know what you've done, but I do know you are losing control."

"I don't need your help."

"But you do," he pressed. "That's what I've been trying to tell you. The man who sent you to find the Wand—he gave you something, didn't he?"

"Some supplies." Stephen shrugged. "I assumed because, unlike some people, he actually wanted me to live."

"No, I mean a file. Something over the datastream?"

An uneasy feeling settled in Stephen's stomach. "A map."

"Ah," said Alan. "A map. Clever. Then again, Damien always has been."

Damien? wondered Stephen. *Who's Damien? No, don't give him the satisfaction of asking. He must mean Finn. Just yet another person using a fake name.* "So, are we done then?"

"The map was a Trojan horse. A virus."

"And how would you know that?"

"Because he and I go way back," said Alan. A wistful expression crossed his features for a moment before being replaced with one of regret. "I can assure you, Damien Knightley doesn't do well with anyone potentially upsetting his plans or challenging his authority. Hence the situation we find ourselves in today." He gestured absently at Stephen. "I'm sure he saw you, and that *endearing* stubborn streak of yours, as a threat the minute you crossed his threshold . . . maybe even before. The virus, therefore, was likely designed to be his insurance policy. Something he could trigger if you ever got out of line. Which, unsurprisingly, you obviously have."

"If you know him so well, fix it."

Alan's mouth twisted as if he'd bitten into something unpleasant. "If it was that easy, I would've already," he said after a pause. "You'll need to come to me. In person."

All he had to go on was Wes's ardent belief Juliane was alive and well, but even if they somehow managed to find her, there was no guarantee she'd be able to fix the drain. On the other hand, trusting Alan was a terrible idea. "Call off the attack."

"What attack?"

"The attack on Manhattan. Or whatever it is you plan to do as part of your whole management-change thing."

Alan snorted. "Does this mean you accept I'm telling you the truth?"

Stephen fought to keep his expression neutral.

After a moment, Alan shook his head and sighed. "I'm relieved you're willing to give me a chance. However, unfortunately, events have been put into motion. There's not much I can do."

Stephen scowled. What Alan was really saying was he'd allowed the situation to get out of his control. *Why am I surprised?*

"But I can stall them. I can give you time to get here, but I suggest you do so within the week. Alone, I should add. I'm afraid my offer does not extend to your friend. Which reminds me. She can't learn about our talk, and before you cross your fingers and promise not to say anything, I'll remind you, we're connected, whether or not you want to admit it. I'll know."

Stephen's eyes narrowed. "Why not?"

"It's not that I don't like her. The opposite, actually, but she's . . . compromised." He picked at his sleeve as though there was a speck of dirt. "I can't have her giving away our advantage."

"Which would be what exactly?"

"The element of surprise, for one. Damien might decide he needs to attack us first, and then where will we be?

"Bean wouldn't tell him anything." He jutted his chest out. "She picked me. Not them."

Alan smirked. "I don't mean to imply she'd do it intentionally, but if you and I are linked, can you really trust that Damien, or Finn if you prefer, and Bean aren't also?" Alan shrugged. "Unfortunately, there's no real way for us to find out one way or another. You can't ask her about it. She'll either lie about it or, like you, have no idea."

"You're nuts."

"Am I?" Alan tapped his temple. "Think about it. She's not suffering to the same extent you are. Sure, she needs the occasional boost, but I don't recall her complaining about being hungry all the time like you are." He pointed at Stephen's stomach. "Have you ever asked yourself why that is? Because I have, and I've come to the conclusion it can only mean Damien didn't feel compelled to put the same insurance policy in her head as he does yours. Which means he either has reason to trust her more implicitly than I've known him to trust anyone, or he is controlling her through other means."

Stephen clenched his fists. It was true that Bean didn't seem to be as affected by the drain as he was, but he'd assumed it was because she'd lived with it longer. Alan couldn't be right. He couldn't.

"I'm sorry, but I simply can't risk it. At least, not at this stage in the game." He shot Stephen a pointed look. "More importantly, though, *you* don't want to risk it." Alan paced. "Assuming your friend is an unwitting participant, she's a fighter. You tell her that she's carrying around a stowaway in her mind—she'll try to break free or force him out, and Damien won't like that." Alan shrugged. "She's a tough woman. Might even succeed in the short term, but Damien has an army at his command. In the end, you both will lose. That is, unless I . . . we stop him before he grows any stronger."

Stephen's stomach twisted. Had Finn or Damien or whatever the hell he wanted to call himself been watching him through Bean's eyes this whole time? Had he made her stay with him after the attack on the Watchtower? *No*, he told himself. Alan was just messing with his head. What they had . . . that couldn't be faked. It was just another one of Alan's manipulations.

He ground his teeth. Alan didn't want him to find Juliane, otherwise why lie about no one else being in the cylinders. *Why?* Stephen's brow furrowed. Because if they found Juliane, he wouldn't be the smartest person alive. *Don't get your hopes up. She might be just as terrible as he is,* the small voice in the back of his mind whispered.

As if sensing his thoughts, Alan stopped his pacing and turned back toward Stephen. "I can see the wheels spinning around in your head. So, here's another reason you two should go your separate ways. Perhaps this is even the more important one. We both know what will happen if you don't leave her side sooner rather than later. Maybe not today. Maybe not tomorrow. But it *will* happen."

Alan gestured toward the farmhouse where Stephen last saw Nadia. "I told you I like her. I'm offering to save her as much as I am offering to save you." He held up a finger. "One week. After that, it may be out of my hands . . ." His lips twisted, and his eyes narrowed. "Now, I've talked too long, and you've spent long enough in this place. Your body needs sleep."

"I am asleep. Or at least, I *was* until someone decided to pull me into the datastream."

Alan waved the comment away. "I encourage you to hurry. For both of your sakes." He dissolved into pixels before disappearing entirely.

Sleep. Stephen turned back to the farmhouse. Alan made sleep sound so easy. Pressure built behind his eyes staring at the structure. Movement in the window caught his attention. "Wes? Is that you?" The door swung open and instead of Wes, Nadia appeared in its frame. "Mom?"

"What is it, honey?"

"Nothing," said Stephen, smiling. How he'd found his way back into the dream was as much a mystery to him as how he'd been pulled out of it, but if she was back, that's where he must be. "Just wanted to make sure you were still there."

Nadia laughed. "Where else would I be?"

Stephen ran to the stairs and hugged her.

"Are you sure you are feeling all right today?" Nadia asked.

"No," said Stephen. He looked into her eyes a minute longer in an attempt to banish the image that haunted him during the daytime with the one before him. "But I'm trying." He released his hold.

"Well, that's good," said Nadia. "Because you have company." She gestured toward the table where Bean sat dressed in clean clothing and sipping on a mug of something spiced, by the way its scent tickled his nose. Nadia poked his chest. "You've got some explaining to do, mister." Her face took on a stern expression, though warmth still radiated from underneath. "Don't you dare think you are going to be leaving again anytime soon."

Stephen's face broke into a smile from ear to ear. His concerns about their options and his worsening condition faded away as he soaked in their presence. "I wouldn't dream of it."

chapter nine

JULIANE

The animals in the yard were still asleep, except for the goat, who continued to chop at surrounding grasses with barely a notice of Juliane's presence. The large wooden gate enclosing the yard swung open. A red-faced man ran in and panted as he made his way toward her. "I came as fast as I could." His upper lip was covered with a bushy mustache that would have made him resemble a walrus if his skin weren't so gaunt and loose around his frame.

She narrowed her eyes. "I know you," she said, though she couldn't recall how or exactly where.

"Do you?" he asked, tilting his head to the side.

Juliane pursed her lips, struggling to connect his face with a name or where they'd met before. "Ah, upon second thought, I may have been mistaken."

"Perhaps I have one of those faces."

"Perhaps," Juliane agreed, though the idea this was not their first meeting continued to nag at her thoughts. "They're stable now," she said.

The man did a double-take at her words. "They?"

"Yes, the mother and the baby. Morgan told me she'd called for the doctor earlier when Rebecca first went into labor." *Took him long enough to get here.* "I assume the reason you are coming here in a run is because that's you."

He blinked and wiped his forehead. "Thank God. I left as soon as I got Morgan's message, but it was already so dark outside . . ."

She placed her hands on her hips. "You can thank me as well."

The man's hand returned to his side. "You assisted with the birth, then."

Assisted. Juliane's nose wrinkled at the word. She crossed her arms over her chest. Rob telling his poor suffering wife to wait to give birth, as if she had a choice when she was that far along. She clenched her jaw. Both mother and child would have died if she hadn't taken charge of the situation. However, her face relaxed as she realized the doctor likely meant the term with regards to the laboring mother, rather than the way the term had been used during her academic years.

She nodded, relaxing her arms. She gestured for the doctor to follow her. "Rebecca's lost quite a lot of blood, but I'm confident the worst is over. They're resting now." The doctor followed her inside. "In here."

Opening the door to the small bedroom, Juliane found the new family in much the same position she'd left them. Rob sat in a chair by the side of the bed. His head was bowed in sleep. Rebecca was also asleep, though her child lay nestled in her arms.

Rob jerked awake as they crossed through the entryway, though his eyes remained bloodshot. Juliane turned to the newcomer. "I suppose I should leave them with you, then?"

"Who's this?" asked Rob.

"Just a second opinion," said the doctor, approaching the bedside. "No need to worry. I can see that congratulations are in order. I'm so glad."

Juliane closed the bedroom door behind her to give the family some privacy. Only then did she finally allow herself to revel in the fact that she had been able to save a life. *Durham.* Her colleague's bruised and battered face popped into her mind. If she'd stayed near the shop instead of being more concerned about saving her own life, would she have been able to save him, too?

She accessed the datastream and drafted a message to Durham while she made her way back to the gated yard. He might not ever be able to receive it, let alone read it, but it felt cathartic to compose it all the same.

"I don't know where you are now, but I'm in some little community called Woodspring. It's not far from New York, or at least, what's left of New York, but there are people here. You would have enjoyed the party they were throwing when we arrived. Supposedly, there is an even larger group in the city.

"You teased me about my degree, but guess what? I delivered a baby last night." The corners of her lips turned up. "Although, after seeing what I've seen, I'll never understand why some women want to go natural. Nature is so poorly designed." Her smile slipped. "I don't know why I'm telling you all this. I don't suspect this means anything to you anymore. But I just want to say—" She pressed her lips together. Her mental eye hovered over the delete key. *If only thoughts were as easy to control.* She added the words "I miss you," and hit send before she could change her mind.

"Did I hear you tell the other guy they're going to be okay?"

Juliane jumped at Lyall's question. She must be more tired than she realized not to notice he'd been the one to open the gate for the doctor. She dismissed the datastream connection.

"Yes," said Juliane with a smile. "I am happy to say that they are all resting comfortably." Rob's exhausted expression sprang to mind. "At least, the mother and child are."

"How can we repay you?" Lyall's eyes shone in the morning light. "I don't know how you managed it, but thank you."

"I did what I could," said Juliane. She looked at the gate. On the other side lay woods and the abandoned cars-turned-campsite. As much as she was looking forward to the idea of reaching the city, and starting to work on restoring society, her body craved rest. She yawned. "I don't suppose there is a room around here I could sleep in?"

"Of course there is," he said, placing his hand on her shoulder. "After what you managed to do here, no one is going to turn you away. Mine's the one right next door." He pointed. "But erm . . . have you seen Morgan?"

Juliane yawned. "Not recently. The last I saw her, she was going that way." She gestured at the gate. "The doctor," she nodded in the direction Lyall had pointed moments ago, "I mean the *other* doctor—she called him. He might know where she is. Now, which room is yours? That one?" She pointed.

He nodded. "It's unlocked."

"Thanks. Oh, and by the way, when you do see her, make sure that you tell her that I told her there was nothing to worry about."

Lyall spun on his heel so fast, he left a hole in the dirt by the open gate. She sighed watching him go. The boy had it for Morgan bad. Juliane had thought that's what she had with Louis, years ago. *You wound up better off,* she told herself, blinking away the moisture which threatened to fill her eyes before anyone could see. *Imagine what might have happened if he had stuck around.* Louis's wife, the woman he'd left Juliane for, had died in an automotive accident. A drunken Louis had been behind the wheel. *He did you a favor.* She tried to steel her shoulders but swayed where she stood instead. She needed to find someplace to lay down.

Juliane barely noticed the details of Lyall's home as she made her way inside. All she cared to find was a room with an empty bed. She found one in the first room on her right. The bed inside was narrow and covered with a thick faded quilt. It was beautiful. Juliane pulled the coverings over her head to block out the sunlight and soon was asleep.

She woke to the sound of a creaky door opening. Birds chirped outside, but it had to still be early morning. She expecting to see Lyall or even Morgan. Instead, Juliane was taken aback to find the doctor instead. She sat up.

The man held up a dingy pink dress and some underthings. "I've brought you a change of clothes," he said with a whisper. "Take them. It'll make you less easy to spot on the road."

Juliane frowned at his offering but took it all the same. "Um, thank you?" She had no idea what he was talking about but arguing would delay her ability to go back to sleep.

The man looked at her expectedly.

She frowned. *What, does he think I am going to get changed with him in the room?* She held up the bundle. "Thank you," she repeated, hoping he would take the hint to exit.

"You need to leave."

"I wasn't planning on staying. Just passing through."

He clenched his jaw and nodded toward the door. "I mean now. You need to leave now."

Still clutching the pink dress in her hand, Juliane crossed her arms under her breasts. As much as she wanted nothing more than to get out of the rags that covered her body, she wasn't ready to leave the comfort of her bed, nor did she appreciate being bossed around. "No," said Juliane. "I've been up all night doing *your* job. I need a chance to rest."

"I don't think you comprehend the situation—"

Juliane flicked her fingers and rolled her eyes. "I *comprehend* a lot more than you think I do."

The man glanced over his shoulder and back at Juliane. "Perhaps I'm going about this the wrong way. I'll start over. I'm Doctor Thomas." He offered his hand. "You were right, before. We've met. I treated a friend of yours—fifteen years ago."

He said it like that should mean something. "My memory hasn't been its best recently," she said, forcing a smile on her lips. "Doctor." She ignored the extended hand and looked him square in the eyes. A query to the datastream matched the name and his image with one of the physicians working at a hospital not far from her office in Worcester. It was all she could do to keep the smile plastered on her face. Durham would still be alive if that facility were open.

Her vision blurred, reducing the doctor to a brown-and-peach blob, though his name remained clear. She shook her head, and her vision was once again clear.

"I know you're tired," He said. "You've no doubt been through a lot, but it's time to go. Here, I'll help." He swooped her out of the bed in a single rushing movement before Juliane registered what he was doing. Juliane tried to twist herself out of his grip, but her exhausted body was no match for the strength of his arms as he carried her out into the hallway.

"Um. What do you think you're doing?" She kicked. "Put me down." Juliane curled the fingers of her free hand and jabbed upward. The base of her palm connected with his chin. It wasn't a solid hit, but enough to catch him by surprise all the same. He loosened his grip. She tumbled to the floor. She rolled to her feet and tried to run, but he grabbed her arm before she could move an inch.

"You don't understand," the doctor panted.

"You're right. I don't. Because you're obviously crazy," she replied.

"I didn't want to have to do this," he said. He reached into his pocket and pulled out a syringe.

Juliane's eyes widened. She attempted to pull back, but his grip wouldn't break. She willed her cells to redirect the light in order to make herself invisible, much like how Morgan's stealth suit operated, but the process took more than a heartbeat. She was still translucent when he pulled her back toward him.

Juliane attempted to pry his hand off her arm, but his grip was too tight. He raised the syringe. She kneed him in the crotch. Her assailant doubled over for a moment but did not let go. Juliane raised her leg again. He shifted, protecting his groin area as he returned upright. Juliane's foot connected with his ankle.

"Stop it," he said. He struck her with the syringe. Its needle pierced her flesh. A sensation like the burn of ice filled her veins as its contents entered her system. He released his hold and took a step back. "I'm sorry it had to be this way, but I'm trying to do what I wasn't able to do for your friend," he answered.

The empty syringe fell to the ground. Juliane touched her neck where the needle had entered. Blood smeared her finger. "What did you do?" Adrenaline battled with whatever he'd injected her with in her system. The drug proved stronger. Her thoughts grew sluggish. Her fingers appeared to sparkle and leave a trail as they moved. She closed one eye, hoping to stop a wave of nausea. Her stomach flip-flopped. Arms scooped her up.

A beating heart sounded next to her ear, bringing back the memory of Louis carrying her to his car after she'd twisted her ankle dancing. The same night, they'd allowed the boundary between boss and employee to blur. Her great mistake. "Louis," she said, cuddling into the sound. As much as she'd convinced herself it was the worst decision of her life, deep down, she knew she'd do it all over again. But he was gone, just like Durham was now, too.

"Shh now. Don't fight it."

Don't fight it. Someone else had used those words. *Alan*, she recalled. He'd used that same phrase after injecting her with the gene assist serum. He'd hidden the risk from her until it was too late. It wasn't the only thing he'd hidden . . . Her adrenaline spiked with her anger. She tried to move her head, but it was like a lead ball. Another needle flashed across her mind's eye. The doctor's needle had struck like a serpent's bite. This one, however, descended slowly enough for her brain to capture every detail as it came closer to her forehead. A voice—not Alan's—whispered in her ear. There was something she needed to remember. She tried to focus on what the whispered voice was saying.

"Trust me," said the doctor, breaking her concentration. "I'm saving your life."

chapter ten

STEPHEN

Rose-gray light from the rising sun colored Bean's features. A soft smile, begging to be kissed, graced her lips. Stephen was inclined to give them what they wanted. "Hold that thought," she said with a husky chuckle. "I'll be right back." She walked away, no doubt to take care of the needs of a demanding bladder. Stephen would need to do the same—eventually. He appreciated the view of her backside until she vanished into the forest. After she was gone, he crossed his arms behind his head and lay back down. He might not have slept long, but at least his dreams were finally getting better.

A stick snapped, and not from the direction where Bean had disappeared. He turned over onto his stomach. Thoughts of Bean, and what he'd like to do with her when she returned, ceased. Another twig snapped. This time much, much closer. Leaves shook, and Stephen saw a flash of blue. Whoever had been in the woods with them the night before must have returned. The leaves parted, and a man stepped into view. His clothing, torn in several places, hung from his frame. He carried a sack draped across his shoulders.

Stephen tensed. He accessed the datastream in search of Bean's signature. He needed to warn her to stay put. He blinked as his stomach lurched. The evening spent in the digital world had drained the little energy he'd gained eating the skewers of meat the night before. The race to Ahman's campsite and the hike back out in the pitch of night must have taken a larger toll than he'd expected. He blinked, leaving the datastream without informing Bean of their visitor.

He tensed and readied himself to fight or flee. The old man took a step closer. *Does he see me?* Stephen wondered. The man took another step. Stephen pressed his lips together. His stomach rumbled loudly enough that even Bean should have been able to hear it. He cursed under his breath.

"Who are you?" growled the old man. "You shouldn't be here. This is my land."

Standing, Stephen held up his hands. "Sorry, I didn't know anyone lived around here. I'll be on my way." The man didn't need to know about Bean.

"You knew this land belonged to someone," said the man. He pointed to a sign nailed into a tree that read, "Private Property. Trespassers will be shot."

Stephen took a step back. "Look, I didn't see that last night. It was too dark, and I'm just passing through. You want me to go. Fine. I'll go." Stephen bent and threw their meager possessions into the blanket. Grabbing the bundle, he turned to leave.

But the man had crossed the distances between them while he worked and grabbed Stephen's shoulder. "Compensation is in order," he said gesturing at Stephen's makeshift sack.

Stephen tried to shrug the man's hand away, but his grip remained tight. "Let go of me."

"Not until you pay me."

The man's energy, in such close proximity, became impossible to ignore. All he had to do was open himself to absorb it. *You don't have to take it all,* the voice in his head whispered. *Alan's wrong. You're still in control. Just take a little, then stop.* Stephen's stomach cramped. The clearing began to spin as a wave of hunger struck. *Besides, it's self-defense.* Nadia's face flashed in his mind. Gone was the warmth from the night's dream. Her eyes were once again vacant orbs that saw nothing and yet seemed to drill right through to his soul.

Stephen's legs wobbled. Another wave of hunger-induced lightheadedness threatened to send him back to the forest floor. "Let. Go. Of. Me," he said between clenched teeth.

The man's fingers dug into the meat of his shoulder like a claw, unaware of the danger he was putting himself in. "Hand over the blanket."

Stephen's eyes tightened. He turned his face. His instincts took over. Waves of energy crested over the flimsy wall of self-control he'd constructed, flooding his senses. The pressure on his arm abated, though the man still hadn't broken contact. The part of Stephen not reveling in the euphoria that came with the energy surge wondered if the man could get away from him at this point if he tried.

Pressure built, begging for release. Emotions like fright and guilt fell by the wayside. Only the promise of joy remained. *Bean.* Flush with power as he was, he could touch her without putting her in danger. *I can do more than touch her.* He extended his senses, connecting his brain with sensors embedded in the surrounding trees back when people still worried about monitoring the health of the forest. If he could only find where she'd disappeared to before the old man had arrived.

The old man. The thought was a cold shower on his brain. Stephen opened his eyes and grabbed the man's hand. It was stiff and cold. Stephen uncurled the man's fingers as gently as he could. He winced as one knuckle cracked anyway. The sound was all too clear with his heightened hearing. The man crumpled to the ground the second he let go.

Leaves crunched behind him. Stephen spun to find Bean on the other side of the clearing. She looked at the form at the base of Stephen's feet. Stephen reached out to her, not knowing whether he wanted her to take his hand or if he was trying to warn her away. "I . . . I . . ." he began. Alan's offer in the middle of the night came back to him.

His shoulders slumped. Even if Alan lied about having a cure, he told the truth when he said that joining him would keep Bean safe from the out-of-control monster he'd become. Stephen wanted to explain what had happened, to offer an excuse, but it was as if his tongue were solid lead.

Bean looked at him with eyes like stone. "You did what you had to," she said after what seemed like an eternity.

Stephen used his enhanced senses to analyze her face. He captured every twitch of her mouth and every blink of her eyes, memorizing every inch of her. He also couldn't help noticing that, though nothing in her features gave her away, she hadn't stepped toward him either. He dropped his gaze. While he appreciated her words, he knew the truth. He could have run. He could have generated the bolt Bean was so fond of and subdued him with a touch. The man hadn't needed to die.

"I don't know how he snuck past me," she said, breaking the agonizing silence that followed. "There's a trailer parked not too far from here. I'm guessing it's his."

Stephen kept his gaze locked on the body at his feet. The sensible thing would be to take Alan up on his offer before it expired, but that meant leaving Bean without telling her why. *I'll find a reason to go off by myself. Worst case, she'll worry I got myself lost for a while, but eventually, she'll give up and move on. Best case, she'll be safe. And if Alan's cure does work, I can always find her again—assuming the war doesn't find me first.* "He might have a family. I should go there and tell them what happened."

"He doesn't." Bean shook her head. "I peeked in the window. At the trailer." She pressed her lips together. "I saw . . ." She clenched her jaw. She nodded at the body on the ground. "Trust me. No one is going to miss him."

"Still, I should bury him. You go on ahead. I'll catch up."

She was next to Stephen in a matter of steps, taking the bundled supplies from him. "We don't have a shovel, and we've got a lot of walking to do."

Stephen gestured at the body. "But it doesn't seem right to leave him lying here."

Bean turned and walked away without replying.

Stephen made a move to follow her. Then he stopped. *Now's your chance*, he told himself. *Let her walk away.*

However, as much as he knew he should turn and go in the other direction, his legs wouldn't budge. Bean's parents had left her with Dr. Lambda and the Watch when she was a child following her sister's death, as if she'd caused the girl's death intentionally. They'd abandoned her, knowing she would be experimented upon without an explanation or even a goodbye. *Cowards.* No, he decided. As much as he knew it was the right thing to do, he couldn't make her go through that again. All he had to do was keep his distance a little while longer. He jogged after her, leaving the body of the old man on the forest floor.

chapter eleven

JULIANE

Juliane's body hadn't needed much incentive to drift back into sleep after the grueling night before. However, her mind wasn't inclined to be carried off so easily, even if the sedative working its way through her veins continued to make her thoughts sluggish. Even worse, there was little she could think of to stop the drug's progress, short of stopping her heart from beating. *Filter. I can't stop it, but I can filter it.*

While the rest of her body lay limp in the doctor's arms, she issued a command to her liver, prioritizing its breakdown of the drugs in her system. Her mind grew sharper by the second. She continued to keep still, so as not to alert her kidnapper until she was sure she would be able to get away without risking another injection, or worse.

Despite her intention, her fingers twitched of their own accord. Dr. Thomas paused. *He noticed.* Juliane readied herself to fight.

"Morgan," he said. "I can explain."

Juliane resisted the urge to sigh in relief. She'd been rescued.

"Can you, now?" Morgan asked.

"I found her this way, by the wall. Obviously overcome with exhaustion and probably dehydration, too. I'm just carrying her to a more comfortable accommodation."

"Well, that's considerate of you. Although I am rather surprised you've left the new mother's side. She could have died. Still might."

"Both mother and baby are resting comfortably," said the doctor. "I thought their savior deserved to do so, too."

"I agree, which is why I was surprised to find Lyall's room empty after he told me that's where he'd sent her."

Juliane risked opening her eyes a sliver. The scene in front of her rippled as if she were viewing it from underwater.

"Do you want to tell me what you are really doing?" asked Morgan.

The doctor took a step back. "You know as well as I do what will happen to her if *he* gets his hands on her."

Morgan's features twisted, and a strange expression came over her face. Juliane fought to keep the contents of her stomach down. "Do I?"

The doctor took a step back. "No—"

"I'm starting to think you aren't committed." The words came from Morgan's mouth, but the voice was all wrong. The dark memory fluttered at the edge of recognition. Juliane tried to fixate on it, but it was like attempting to catch smoke with a butterfly net.

"I took an oath," said the doctor.

"So, you're fond of saying." Morgan inched closer. "I don't see, then, why it's so difficult for you to take another."

"I can't be a part of this."

Part of what? Juliane wondered. Colors swirled. The goat appeared next to Morgan. Its limbs stretched and twisted until it became the size of the mare. *I'm hallucinating.* The drug, it seemed, had not yet been fully expunged from her system.

"I don't recall you having an issue when you begged us to take your family in."

"That was before."

Morgan shook her head. The movement left trails across Juliane's vision. "Your son knew what would happen if he left the city. You both did."

I'm going to be sick. Juliane closed her eyes and stopped trying to make sense of the conversation.

"He did it for me," the man muttered. "He left a note. Only way for us to be free."

"You know what this means."

Juliane risked peeking again after the wave of nauseousness went away. This time, there was no sign of the goat and her vision was clear. *Finally*, thought Juliane.

She twisted in the doctor's arms. She expected him to tighten his hold or fight her, but instead, he turned and lowered her feet to the ground behind him.

A single tear rolled down his face. "I was only trying to protect you," he whispered.

"Protect me from what?" Juliane touched the sore spot where the needle had entered her bloodstream. "A good night's sleep? What is wrong with you?"

"It's going to be alright Juliane," said Morgan coming to Juliane's side. Juliane couldn't help noticing her voice sounded normal. The change Juliane had heard in its timbre, must have been as real as the horse-sized goat she'd seen.

"Alright? Alright! He tried to kidnap me. Injected me with who knows what."

"You'll survive."

Juliane glared at Morgan. "Why are you so calm about this? He. Drugged. Me."

"Because I know you don't have anything to worry about." Morgan shot Dr. Thomas a look. "Isn't that right, doctor?" The doctor nodded meekly.

"Forgive me if I'm not convinced," said Juliane, taking satisfaction in the purple bruise blooming across the doctor's face from where she'd hit him.

"You should be."

"And why is that?" Juliane clenched and unclenched her fist as she fought the urge to give him another one.

"He's not a bad person." Morgan held up a hand before Juliane could protest. "Really. He's not . . . but . . . um . . . well you see, Dr. Thomas lost his son recently," said Morgan as if that explained everything. "I'd hoped being part of a birth might help give him a purpose. Obviously, I made a huge mistake. If anyone is at fault, it's me. I'm sure now that he's had a second to realize what he's done, he's appalled."

Dr. Thomas nodded his head eagerly.

"I don't care if he is the reincarnation of Mother Teresa," said Juliane, glaring at the man. "He needs to be locked up."

Morgan sighed. "Yeah, well, unfortunately, it's complicated. He's the only doctor in a fifty-mile radius."

Juliane pressed her lips together. The conversation she'd overheard back at the tavern came back to her—men, speaking freely about selling a woman to settle a bar tab, with no fear of retribution. Those that lived in the tower must be so desperate for medical knowledge, they were willing to turn a blind eye to the man's obvious mental unbalance, too. Justice, it would seem, was another victim of the global catastrophe. Rage bubbled under her skin, burning more of the drug away. However, she didn't act on it. Morgan's words had made it clear lashing out would do nothing in this new world order except further exhaust her.

Morgan glanced at Juliane through the corner of her eye. "Then again, he *was* . . ."

Lyall burst into the hallway. "Oh, good," he said spotting Juliane. "You found her. I thought for sure you'd be asleep until lunchtime, but if you're still up, um . . . Rebecca's asking for you. I told her that you needed your rest, but . . ." His expression was like a beaten dog. "Sorry, I hate to ask, but do you mind staying up a little longer?"

The doctor tensed and lurched toward Lyall and the doorway. "Did something happen while I was gone?" he asked.

Juliane took advantage of the Lyall's appearance to put more distance between herself and the mustached man. However, her movement was still sluggish as her body continued to filter the last of the drug out of her system. Pressure built in her lower abdomen. She would need to relieve herself sooner rather than later to make sure whatever he had injected her with, was fully gone. "I think you've helped here enough," said Juliane. She touched the spot on her neck again. "Don't you?"

Dr. Thomas hung his head.

Either not reading the body language in the room or choosing to ignore it, Lyall answered, "Rebecca's asking for Juliane, here. Don't worry. She's okay. Said it was a women's thing."

"I'll be right there," said Juliane, straightening her back. She would show these people they had other options. She would show everyone. She shared a look with Morgan and nodded. They didn't need to put more patients at risk by allowing people like Dr. Thomas to continue to walk free. Not when anyone who'd been upgraded could access medical information the same way she did. However, when she tried to take a step, she stumbled. She bit back a curse. *There goes my grand exit.*

Lyall came running to her side. "Oh, wow, you've got to be exhausted. Are you sure? I can still go back and tell her you were asleep when I found you."

"I can manage a while longer," said Juliane. It wasn't like she would risk sleep again until she was sure Dr. Thomas was as far away from her as possible.

"Lyall," said Morgan, "Why don't you go with Juliane? Just to make sure she gets there alright, while I escort the doctor back to the bridge."

Lyall pursed his lips. "Are you sure he shouldn't stick around a little bit longer? I mean, just in case?"

"There's nothing he can do at this point she can't," said Morgan, pointing at Juliane.

The doctor looked like he was going to argue but then slumped his shoulders in defeat. "She's right," he said. He turned to Morgan. "And there are several lives still counting on me back in the city. I'll be good." His eyes shimmered. "Plenty of work to go around."

"Okay, then," said Lyall. "But you're staying a little longer though, right, Morg?"

A myriad of emotions flickered across Morgan's face. "I'll stay as long as I can," she said, "but—" She clenched her jaw, cutting off whatever she was about to say next and addressed Juliane and Lyall instead. "Go and see what Rebecca needs." Her gaze shifted to the side as if listening to someone whisper in her ear. Her mouth twisted in a frown for a moment, but she nodded. "I'll come back as soon as I can."

chapter twelve

STEPHEN

ean walked ahead of him. She usually preferred a brisk pace, but she moved at a faster clip than he was used to. As the distance between them seemed intentional, he hadn't attempted to keep up. He didn't blame her for wanting to be as far away from him as possible; he disgusted himself, too. An image of Nadia's accusing face flashed across his mind. His stomach turned, and for once, he didn't feel hungry.

He looked toward the horizon. The sky would be taking on the golden shade of evening before much longer, forcing them to stop for the night. Although they'd kept to back roads, it was getting harder to avoid formerly urban areas. While Stephen expected the various highway stops along the way to be abandoned, the man they'd encountered in the woods was proof they weren't entirely empty. They'd have to be more careful when they camped tonight. He didn't want to add more ghosts to his dreams.

Thoughts of the old man turned in his head. How had the man managed to approach their campsite without alerting either of them? He'd nearly been on top of them. He shuddered, thinking of what might have happened had they not awakened with the dawn.

Bean might be a warrior when alert, but she was just as helpless as anyone else while she slept. They both were. *It's a good thing, then, you don't sleep much anymore*, said the voice in Stephen's head. He steeled his jaw. *At least the main roads have better sensors.*

A bird's eye view of their location appeared in front of his vision, representing their location as a pulsating dot. The satellite image was at least fifteen years old but good enough to give him a basic idea of how to get back onto the road without straying too far from their current route to Worcester. He smiled. A small creek not far ahead would provide them with needed freshwater and might give him a chance to wash away the stink of death clinging to him. "There's water up ahead," Stephen called out, grateful for an excuse to break the silence between them.

"Okay," Bean answered in reply.

Stephen mentally begged her to say something, anything else, but nothing more came. "If we turn left at the creek," said Stephen after the silence became too much, "we might even reach the next town before night."

She paused but continued to look forward as if searching for the creek. "Um . . . do you really think that's a good idea?"

So, she doesn't trust you around other people anymore either. Good. A sour taste filled his mouth. *She just hasn't realized that also means her, too.* He straightened and took a breath. *Talk to her.* He might not be able to tell her where he was going, but he could at least tell her about what was going on inside his head. He'd explain why they needed to go their separate ways.

Bean looked back. Her green eyes pulled at his soul. The minute the truth left his mouth would likely be the last time he'd ever see them.

His resolve evaporated. His chest ached. He spit on the ground. "Bug got into my mouth," he said.

Bean's forehead wrinkled, and for a moment, she looked at him like she had the day they met.

Stephen clung to the expression on her face like a life raft. Now that the silence was broken, he wouldn't allow it to take back control. "Should we stop and try to find something to eat?" asked Stephen, forcing his features into a smile while burying his other thoughts. They still needed to talk, but maybe, just maybe, they could have one more night together before they did.

Bean's brow smoothed. "Oh, right this way. We have a lovely selection tonight. Your choice, weeds with a side of weeds, or grubs."

"Oh, had I realized that bug was an appetizer, I wouldn't have been so quick to spit it out."

Bean snorted and allowed Stephen to catch up, but turned her gaze forward. "So, towns. You're sure?"

She was close now. Stephen knew that if she turned in that moment and looked at him like she had by the river the night before they'd reached New York, it would be over. He would have no choice but to confess everything, from his spiraling loss of control to how he spent his evenings in the virtual world instead of sleeping. The tall grass to their left rustled, shattering the moment.

Bean's shoulders tensed as she dropped to a crouch. More grass shifted. Whatever was causing the noise was big and coming closer by the second. She glanced at Stephen and gestured for him to duck out of view as her palms flared with purple lightning. The grass parted, and out of the brush, a man on horseback appeared.

He was shirtless and covered in dirt. Long scratches crisscrossed his torso. What remaining clothing he had on was in tatters. Close cropped hair, more silver than yellow, did nothing to hide a large bruise on his head. The man groaned and swayed in his saddle. The purple light surrounding Bean's fist blinked out. She caught the man as he slid head-first from the saddle.

Be careful, said Stephen with his mind. *He might be dangerous.*

Bean looked over her shoulder at Stephen and raised an eyebrow. *Please. Just look at him,* her voice answered in his mind. *He looks about as dangerous as you were when we first met.*

Stephen pursed his lips but did not argue further. Coming to Bean's side, he helped to lower the man to the ground. *So now what? Dangerous or not, we can't help. We don't have enough supplies for ourselves.*

We don't, but he might. She gestured toward his mount.

The horse, relieved of its burden, had dropped its head and was nibbling the grass. Stephen approached it from its side, careful not to startle it or cause it to break into a run. As Bean had pointed out, a pair of saddlebags hung from its withers. Stephen lifted the flap on the bag closest to him and rummaged through its contents.

"Well?" Bean asked out loud.

"Not much," answered Stephen. "No, wait." His hand grabbed a long cylindrical object wrapped in plastic. "Jerky," he said pulling the bit of meat out. "Guess dinner's on me after all."

Bean laughed. "Aw, you cooked."

The man groaned. Stephen's triumph morphed into shame at the realization that without a second thought, he was ready to take advantage of a man who had done him no wrong—an injured man at that. His smile slipped. His parents would never recognize the person he'd become.

It's not just about your survival, the voice inside him said. *Think about Bean. You want one more night together, then you'll have to eat. You won't be able to control the hunger on grubs alone. Better yet, say goodbye now. That's all you have to do. Say goodbye.*

"Jule… Juliane?"

Stephen froze. His eyes narrowed on the injured man. "What did you say?" *Juliane's not that unusual of a name. There is no way he's asking for the same person as the woman we are looking for.*

"Must have bumped his head pretty hard to mistake you for a person with a name like that," said Bean with a shrug.

"Need to find Juliane."

"Sorry, but no Juliane here," said Bean, standing up. "But we really do appreciate this very fine horse you are giving us."

Stephen closed his eyes. What would Nadia and Chad say if they saw him now? "We can't leave him lying there."

"Why not?" asked Bean. "Look at him. He's pretty much dead already, and you said it yourself, we don't have enough supplies."

Stephen looked at the wrapped piece of meat in his hand, shining bright with the reflection of the sun. He steeled his shoulders. What had he told Chad before leaving the house the night of that disastrous supply run? He wanted to have a life that was more than mere survival. He ripped the jerky's wrapper open and crouched on his heels beside the man. This was his chance to prove he wasn't a complete monster. At least, not yet. "Here," he said, holding the jerky next to the man's lips.

"That's supposed to be our dinner," said Bean.

"I felt a jar when I was fishing around in the saddlebag. Could be more to eat in there."

"And if there isn't?"

"Then you can take it to the creek and bring back enough water for the three of us."

"Oh, can I?" asked Bean her voice dripping with sarcasm.

"Bean, be reasonable."

"I am," she said. "You're the one who seems to have lost his mind."

"Please."

"Fine," said Bean. She reached into the bag and pulled out a canteen much like the one they'd lost back before the battle of the Watchtower. Then she turned on her heel and raced off in the direction of the stream.

At first, Stephen assumed she'd run out of annoyance at him, but after she'd disappeared, he began to wonder if she ran because she was more afraid of what he might do to the man while she was gone. The sour taste returned to his mouth as he realized she didn't see him as a hero in either scenario.

Stephen eyeballed the man. He was filthy and bloodied, but then again, so was Stephen. However, the man's chest was twice as wide as Stephen's, and he had a square jaw and an athletic frame. "I bet you never had these sorts of problems with women when you were my age," Stephen muttered.

The man on the ground chuckled. "You have no idea, kid."

Stephen jumped back. "You heard all that."

"As you were so kind to point out, I'm not dead yet." The other man rubbed his forehead before trying to roll to his side. "Though your girl seemed ready to write me off."

"She does what she has to do." Stephen bit his tongue before answering. "We both do."

The man sighed. "I know her type. Reminds me of my missing friend."

"Juliane."

"Yeah . . . Juliane." The injured man looked at the horse. "I hate to ask after you so kindly pulled me down from that nightmare on four feet, but would you mind helping me stand back up?"

Stephen hesitated, not wanting to place a hand on the man's exposed skin. "I don't think you should be moving around too much right now. That bump on your head looks nasty."

The man touched his head. "Suspect it looks worse than it feels."

"You would have landed on your skull if we weren't around. Pretty sure that's a bad thing."

The man laughed. "Yeah, well . . . sorry about the dramatics, but when you two appeared out of nowhere, I thought it best if I played possum. Figured you were more likely to leave me alone if I wasn't a threat."

"You played possum." It was a statement as much as a question.

"Well, yeah. I used to play more than a few sports back in the day. Could have gone pro if I'd kept at it instead of listening to my parents. I've been known to make an injury work for me."

"You mean all that was an act?" asked Stephen in disbelief. "Then why are you asking me to help stand you back up?"

"Because it's not entirely an act. More like an exaggeration. Also, I've been on that horse for god-knows-how-long, and my legs cramped up."

Stephen glanced in the direction he'd sent Bean to collect water from the creek. She was going to call him worse than an idiot when she returned and learned how much Stephen had been duped. Stephen's stomach rumbled, reminding him that Bean's anger was the lesser threat to the stranger's general health and safety at the moment. "If you aren't dying, you should leave before she gets back." Stephen took another step away. He bit into the jerky stick and had swallowed before its spicy taste registered on his tongue.

"Leave? But I just told you, my muscles are cramped."

"She's not going to care about your muscles." An image of Bean fighting a beastman beneath the remains of the Apex building flashed in his mind. She'd taken out the man and his surgically enhanced frame before they'd learned the beastman had been sent to the underground chamber to help rescue them from the Watch. No, Bean wouldn't care about the stranger's muscles at all.

The man smiled. "In my experience, when it comes to the ladies, I've found the opposite to be true."

Stephen looked at the stranger, then at the horse. "I'm serious. Take your horse and get as far away from here as possible." The loss of the mount would mean they'd have to continue their journey on foot, but at least Stephen wouldn't have another death on his conscience.

The man sat up with a groan and extended his hand. "Nice to meet you, Serious. I'm Durham."

Stephen stared at Durham's hand. His stomach growled again, reminding him that a bit of dried meat wouldn't sustain him long. He took another step back, crossing one arm over his chest while he took a second enormous bite out of the jerky stick.

"So, dinner is on again, I see," said Bean, returning with the canteen in hand.

She glanced down at Durham and back at Stephen. Her lips narrowed. Durham dropped his hand and started to stand. Bean tensed.

"I wouldn't make any sudden movements if I were you," said Stephen.

Durham sat back and raised his hands with his palms out. "Wouldn't dream of it. I'd hate to get another bump on the head to match the first one," he said pointing at the injury.

Stephen shook his head. "She's capable of giving you more than a bump."

Bean's gaze shifted back to Stephen. Her eyes narrowed as she cocked her head. *What?* He projected the question her way via the datastream. *It's true, isn't it?*

Durham laughed. "Of that, I have no doubt."

The corner of Bean's mouth inched upward while she handed the canteen to Durham. "Here, drink something before I regret leaving this one on his own for so long." *We'll talk about this later,* Bean's voice said in his brain.

Durham took a long sip, causing water to run down his chin. He made a face, scratching at the beginnings of a beard. He looked at Stephen. "You don't happen to have a razor, do you?"

Stephen fought the urge to touch his own face. Though they'd been in the wilderness for days, his facial hair could hardly be described as a beard. "How old are you?" he blurted out.

"Older by the second," replied Durham. "I take it that's a no."

"So, are we camping here?" said Bean. "Or did you still want to try to make it into town?"

"You don't want to go that way," said Durham, pointing in the direction he'd come. "There's nothing but ghost towns, monster birds, and friendly people who are under the impression giving a person a concussion is a nice way to say hello." He touched his head with a wince.

Bean snorted. "Some of that's the same this way, too."

Durham sighed. "And here I thought the adventurous life was behind me after leaving the ACI."

The humor left Bean's face, and her body tensed. "You were with the ACI," she said in a voice cold enough to freeze a waterfall.

What is the ACI again? Stephen asked her with his mind.

How do you not know? Bean replied. *Oh, that's right, you grew up in the middle of nowhere. They're only the people responsible for ending the world.* An image of a widescreen television hung on an apartment wall flashed in his mind. Graphs with plummeting lines floated above a banner of scrolling text. ACI repeated over and over again. Random other initials would appear afterward, followed by bright red numbers. A stack of children's books and a pair of dolls lay on the floor of the apartment. Then the image was gone.

"Officially, yes ... as Louis's personal counsel," continued Durham, unaware of their exchange online. "But in reality, the law had very little to do with what I did. Mostly, all I was expected to do was to make sure he was sober enough to attend interviews and to make sure the girls we met on our travels were ... ah ... well, taken care of." His eyes sparkled. "For example, there was this one time—we went cruising on Lake Como, just outside of Milan. Louis spots these women drinking espresso and—wait, that story ended with us *both* in front of a judge."

Durham held up a hand. "Okay, better example. There was this other time in Prague. We were out celebrating closing on a brand-new location when this model comes up to us and . . ." He glanced at Bean. "Er, you're older than eighteen, right? I mean, I am guessing that's not a thing anymore, but old habits . . ."

"Such a tough life you must have led before," said Bean, rolling her eyes.

The grin slipped from Durham's face. "Yeah, it sounds bad now, I'm not like that any—I mean I quit after Louis—er . . . when he . . . we were just kids with more money than sense back then. That is to say, it was a long time ago."

Bean turned to Stephen. "I'm voting we skip town tonight." She gestured toward Durham. "There could be more winners like this guy."

"So, Juliane," interrupted Stephen. "That's the name you called out when you were pretending to be dying." The name had been nothing but a coincidence. *But what if it isn't?* Was she close by after all? If so, he wouldn't have to go into the beastmen's camp—wouldn't have to trust Alan. Even better, he wouldn't have to leave Bean. His nostrils flared with hope's breath. "What's her last name?"

"Faris," replied Durham. He took another sip from the canteen. "Dr. Juliane Faris." Durham looked up when both Stephen and Bean fell silent. "I take it you've heard of her. Not sure how she'll feel about that."

Don't say a word, Bean's voice said in his head.

But you heard him; he's looking for her, too. Bet they were traveling together and got split up.

Or she ditched him on purpose. We've only heard his version of the story. We have no way of knowing why they split up. What if they weren't traveling together by choice? He's the admitted womanizing friend of a terrorist, after all. If it was up to me, I'd probably ditch him the first chance I got, too.

You're being paranoid.

No, I'm being sensible. You should try it sometime.

"So, what's the verdict?" Durham asked. "I know that look. I assume you were talking about what to do with me."

"He's a smart one," said Bean

"I'm funny too," Durham said with a smile. "Or so I've been told."

"I bet," said Bean. "So, Mr. Funny Guy, give us one reason why we shouldn't take that horse," she gestured toward the animal that was grazing on shoots of grass, "and leave you here."

"I'll give you two. One, because a cold front is rolling in, and unless you're considering changing your mind about going into town, you'll want to take this time to build a fire. Otherwise, it's going to be a long, long night. And two, because you won't get very far. Take a look at Silver over there. She's done. You push her any more tonight, and she'll drop. Do you really want to be on top of her when that happens?"

Stephen examined the mare. Now that Durham pointed it out, he noticed white froth on the animal's withers. Its nostrils flared.

"Silver?" asked Bean.

"I had to call her something. Especially when I was cursing at her for not listening to a word I said. Sounded like a horsey name."

"And the cold front?" Bean placed her hands on her hips. "How can you be so sure about that?"

"I can't seem to be able to make a call, or even send a note." Durham touched the bruise on his temple. "Must have gotten banged up harder than I thought, but my inbox still works. I get a data dump from the weather bots. Always liked to make my own forecast."

Stephen glanced up. Not a cloud marked the sky. "Yeah, well, at least there shouldn't be any rain tonight." He'd had enough of the rain. The bits of his clothes not covered in dirt were black and green from mold.

"I like you, kid," said Durham. "Such the optimist."

"Quit calling me that. I'm not a kid."

"Sure, but since you haven't bothered to introduce yourself, I decided I'd give you a name—like Silver over there." The horse twitched its ears. "Really?" Durham asked it. "Now you listen to me. Why couldn't you do that two days ago, when I still had a chance of catching up with Jules?"

The horse swished her tail.

"Right. Right, you got a point. When we catch up to her, don't tell her I called her that. Makes her all sorts of crazy."

He's lost his mind, Bean's voice said in Stephen's head.

Maybe, replied Stephen, *or he's really lonely.*

That's equally uncomforting. A gust of wind caused the grass to sway like ocean waves and sent a cold shiver down Stephen's spine.

"Guess we're sleeping outdoors again, then," said Stephen out loud.

"Hooray." Bean turned and walked in the direction of the creek. "Oh, by the way, I saw some dead wood we can use for a fire not far from here," she said. "Made me think of you." She shot Durham a pointed look before disappearing to the sound of his laughter.

"You poor bastard," Durham said after his laughter died down. "You didn't stand a chance, did you?"

"Stand a chance against what?" Stephen asked.

Durham laughed harder. He raised his hand. "So, now that you two have decided not to kill me, will you please help me up? I was serious when I said my entire body is locked up. I feel worse than I did after a three-day bender in São Paulo."

Stephen took Durham's arm and helped to steady him as he rose. "Have you really traveled all over the world?"

"More than once," Durham said. "How about you? Ever gone anywhere interesting?"

"I took a train ride once," mumbled Stephen.

"The train," Durham said with a twinkle in his eyes. "Ah, that brings back some memories. I haven't taken a train ride in years. You like it?"

Stephen thought of Wes. "It was . . . memorable." Wes had insisted they take the electric train car he'd rebuilt in secret to Worcester. He'd wanted to help them get there faster. He took a breath. Wes had died on that train. If Stephen had only refused Wes's offer—told Wes to stay behind . . . Stephen's eye twitched, and he turned away, looking about the field and picking up bits of dried grass. "This will make good kindling," he said holding the bits in his hand.

"I trust your judgment," offered Durham. While a smile remained plastered on his face, it no longer reflected in his eyes."

That's one of us. "Yeah . . . well, alright then," Stephen flailed, not knowing how to respond to Durham's comment. Bean's return couldn't have come at a better moment. Soon long flames cackled, which was a good thing, as Durham proved to be right about the change in the weather.

Bean settled into the crook of his arms as the night grew long. However, Stephen made a point to pull down his sleeve so their flesh wouldn't make direct contact. Crickets played their song, though sleep avoided Stephen yet again. *I'm not going to access the datastream tonight,* he told himself. *I'm not.* But before he realized what he was doing, his avatar was looking out across a foreign cityscape, the likes of which he'd never seen and would never see in the real world. A gentle breeze ruffled his hair. His heart ached at the beauty that lay before him. *If only you were here, Bean.*

Fingers wove their way between his. Bean stood to his side. Her white-blonde hair floated in the virtual breeze. She tucked a lock behind her ear. "It's beautiful," she said.

"How'd you find me?"

"You didn't exactly make it easy." She turned back toward the vista. "You should have told me."

His heart skipped a beat as her fingers tightened around his own. "I'm sorry," he said. "I've been having a hard time falling asleep ever since—"

Bean turned to him. "I know," she said. Her normally jade-green eyes took on a dark deeper tone under the purple-red light of the twilight sky. Stephen's breath caught in his lungs at the sight. The knowledge that the sight in front of them was nothing more than a digital construct made it all the more heart-breaking. She turned away. "That's what I came here to talk to you about. I tried before . . . um . . . I thought if I—"

He sighed. "Yeah, I need to talk to you, too." He struggled to come up with words, wanting to tell her about all the things going on in his head, but at the same time, there was nothing he wanted more than to savor the moment. *Tomorrow*, he decided. *I'll tell her tomorrow.* He pulled her closer, wrapping his arms around her. Her body seemed to melt into his. "But not yet. Right now, I'm just glad you're here."

"Okay. Later then." She looked up at him. "What do you want to do until then?" The corners of her lips slid up ever so slightly in a smile that was both promise and an invitation.

Thoughts of conversation vanished as he lowered his mouth to hers. She broke from their kiss for a moment. A look flashed across her face as if there was something more she needed to say, but then she moved her lips to the base of his neck. It was as if she'd thrown gasoline onto a match. He tightened his hold around her waist. She moaned and wrapped a leg around his. His hand slipped to her thigh. Her moan grew louder, more insistent. His gaze darted around, locating a nearby wall. He released her waist, only to grab her buttocks. She wrapped her other leg around him, laughing with a throaty chuckle. It was all the encouragement he needed.

Turning, he carried her toward the building. She nibbled on his ear. Blood rushed from his brain to his groin. Using the wall as leverage, he explored her body with his lips and his hands. His chest was bare. He didn't remember removing his shirt. The fabric of her sweater offended him. He frowned, pulling at its hem.

She giggled before capturing his mouth with hers once again. The offensive garment transformed into the thinnest silk. Stephen growled as he twisted the fabric in his hand. The need to be rid of any barriers between them became primal. The bit of cloth in his hand transformed again. Cool silk became sheer lace. He broke from their kiss only long enough to see the new garment left little to the imagination, while at the same time hinted at the stuff that dreams were made of.

Her smile deepened. She reached up and caressed the back of his neck, sending shivers up and down his spine. It was almost enough to undo him.

"Bean," he said between panted breaths. "I . . . I . . ."

Her hand slid down his cheek. "I know," she said, dragging a finger across his lips.

The sheer fabric shielding her body transformed again until it was nothing at all, and Stephen was only too eager to follow her every command.

Stephen grinned from ear to ear, though his eyes remained closed. It had been the first decent night's sleep since he'd met Bean. Thoughts of Bean and what they'd done together in the digital world the night before roused him in more ways than one. He turned on his side and opened his eyes. Bean's eyes were still closed, too, but he saw the corner of her lip curve up as if she knew she was being watched. He shifted, moving to wake her with a kiss. His stomach growled.

He pulled back as if burned.

Bean's eyes opened in a flash. She jumped up—every muscles tense. "What? Did you hear something?" Her gaze darted around their impromptu campsite. "Where is he?" she whispered down to Stephen. "I knew we shouldn't have trusted him. Probably a scout. Leading a whole group to us."

"Talking about me?" asked Durham, coming around from behind a tree while zipping up his pants. "Sorry, didn't mean to cause you to freak out. I just had to water a tree and figured you'd prefer I do that elsewhere." His teeth gleamed. "That is, unless you're into that sort of thing?"

Bean's eyes flashed. "That's a no."

Durham shrugged. "You'd not believe how many times I've asked that question and gotten a different answer."

Bean glanced at Stephen. "We're leaving."

The grin disappeared from Durham's face. He held up a hand. "Listen, I'm sorry. I don't mean to sound like an asshole. Truly, I don't."

Bean arched an eyebrow. "I'd hate to be around when you're actually trying."

Durham snorted. "Seriously, though, I am sorry . . . I say things I don't mean—they just sort of come out. Like I don't have a filter. Especially since—actually, I have no idea how long I've been like this. One minute I'm heading into yet another death-by-PowerPoint presentation, and the next minute, I'm waking up in what used to be the basement of my office building but is now a pile of rubble."

Stephen and Bean shared a look. "Let me guess, you found yourself in a metal tube," said Stephen.

"Yeah. Oddest thing. I can't remember going into it." He scratched his hair. "What the hell happened, anyway?"

"That's where the end of the world started," said Stephen.

The remaining trace of humor fled Durham's expression. "So, it's all like this? Everywhere?" His shoulders slumped. "That's what Juliane suspected, but I was really hoping this was an isolated event. That someplace—"

"Not everywhere," said Bean.

Stephen frowned. Alan's warning sprang to his mind unbidden. How could he explain the full extent of why sending Durham to the Sorcerers' home turf was a bad idea without letting it slip that she might still be under Damien's control?

"Don't look at me like that," said Bean. "There's nothing we can do for him." She crossed her arms, shooting him a look that dared him to argue. "And he's like a baby out here. At least the tower has running water."

They're monsters. You said so yourself, back at the Watchtower, he projected at her.

Bean shrugged. *Yeah, well what do you call us?*

Stephen's wanted nothing more to pull her back into his arms, but the ever-present ache in his stomach reminded him of the potential risk. "I've told you before," he whispered to her. "You're not a monster." *But I am,* he finished the sentence in his head, making sure that no trace of the thought inadvertently made its way to the datastream.

"You say there is a place that still has showers?" Durham perked up. "Say no more. Point me in the right direction, and I'll be on my way just as soon as I catch up with Juliane."

"He's not going to be any safer there than he is out here," continued Stephen, loud enough for Durham to hear. "The beastmen are planning an attack. Hell, they could've already done it by now." Stephen trusted Alan to hold off the attack about as much as he trusted himself around other people.

Her back straightened. "Those guys are nothing more than a bunch of has-been football players who caught us by surprise. It won't happen again." She drew herself taller. "Especially if they think for a second, they can get past our defenses."

Us, thought Stephen. She'd rejoined the Sorcerers after Alan tricked him into going with the Watch. If he left her now, would she go back there again? His stomach tied itself in a knot. She might not view the beastmen as a threat, but Stephen knew differently. The image of her mangled body lying on the floor of the operating studio filled his thoughts. *If I hadn't gotten to her in time . . . if there hadn't been a storm to pull from . . .*

Bean glanced at Durham. "Why are you still out here looking for her, anyway?"

Durham scratched at his hair. "Like I said, we were separated and—"

"I mean, I assume you've at least *tried* simply sending her a message asking where she is. Haven't you?"

The smile returned to his face. "Of course I did. Like I said, nothing's going through. But it has been a while. Maybe I'll get lucky this time." His eyes took on the glazed expression of someone accessing the datastream.

"Well? Were you able to reach her?"

"No." Durham blinked as a smile broke across his face. "I still can't send anything, but it turns out she thinks about me after all. Sent me a message from a place called Woodspring."

"Where's that?" asked Stephen.

He shook his head. "Beats me, but she says it's just outside of New York."

"I know where it is," said Bean. Her eyes narrowed, and her voice took on a razor's edge. "And if she's there, she's in more trouble than she realizes. That's where these anti-tech nut jobs settled after they came to the conclusion technology had enslaved humanity." She closed her eyes and shook her head. "Morons. They're the ones that started bombing places in the beginning. Caused the whole chain reaction." She shot a pointed look at Stephen. "I get why he's clueless, but seriously, didn't you ever ask your parents about what triggered the initial rush out of the cities in the first place?"

"Oh, I don't know. Things like keeping the windmill turning and figuring out how we were going to have enough food to last the winter seemed a bit more important than wondering what was the motivation behind some wackos."

"Whatever." Bean turned her attention back to Durham. "The only problem was they neglected to plan out what would happen after humanity's so-called liberation." She shrugged. "Personally, for all the effort they put into it, I don't think they ever really believed their plan would actually work. At least, not everywhere." She gestured at the field surrounding them. "We think most of them left the movement after their crazy leader, Louis Evans left the scene. Those of us who stuck around in the city have kept an eye on them ever since, in case someone else ever tried to pick up where Louis left off."

"You heard Ahman," said Stephen. "Juliane and Louis had an argument right before he . . . you know . . . went poof." He made an exploding gesture with his hands. "We have no idea what they argued about or if she caused the bomb to go off early. He said the people holding Gena acted like the first explosion was a surprise. They might not care about Louis or their original mission anymore, but if they do, and if they come to the conclusion Juliane's somehow responsible for messing up their plans, then . . ."

"So, I guess we're going to Woodspring," said Bean.

"Er . . ." started Stephen. Bean knew a lot more about the world and the history of the panic than he did. More than might be expected of someone who'd spent most of her childhood as a lab rat. Doubt wormed into his thoughts where it multiplied and mutated like cancer. Was Damien feeding her information? What if Bean hadn't stayed with him after the battle entirely by choice? She cared about him. Stephen wasn't questioning that. He knew it to his bones, but it didn't mean Damien hadn't influenced her decision to stay with him.

Stephen had already proven capable of locating lost things. Damien might have encouraged Bean to stay so he'd have a way to sabotage their mission if needed? If Bean found Juliane on her own, and Damien *was* pulling the strings . . .

An image of Alan's knowing smirk sprang to mind. Stephen's mouth soured. *Damn it, Alan. Why do you have to ruin everything?*

"I'm going with you," said Durham.

Stephen clenched his fists. Woodspring was close to the city, which meant Alan had to be near there, too, if he planned to attack in just a week. He opened up his map application and ran the numbers. If they changed course now, they'd reach Woodspring before the week ran out, but that wouldn't leave Juliane much time to brush up on her coding skills and develop a cure.

That also assumes we can convince her to help us in the first place. Stephen turned to Durham. If Juliane trusted him, Durham might be the key to convincing her to help them in spite of whatever plan Damien had in store. "Guess that means you'd better saddle up, then," he said.

His stomach growled. *And if Juliane doesn't agree . . .* He shook his head. *Don't even think it.* He might still be forced to leave Bean and seek out Alan. Because one thing was sure, no matter how he looked at it, he was running out of time. Alan's words played over and over in his mind, *I encourage you to hurry. For both your sakes.*

chapter thirteen

JULIANE

Clouds grew in the sky as Juliane walked back to Rebecca's room, still fuming. If only she hadn't spent the last several years locked away under that pile of rock. She could have stopped events from reaching this point. She didn't know how, exactly, but she was certain, given enough time, she would have found an answer. She smiled to herself imagining Dr. Thomas being led away in handcuffs to serve a long and difficult sentence behind bars once society was functioning again as it should.

Inside, she looked around for an additional source of light. An oil lamp sat on a shelf. However, light switches and electrical sockets had been removed. Juliane traced the spot on the wall where the hole had been filled in. It seemed like an unnecessarily permanent step. An antique spinning wheel stood in the corner. Juliane had never seen one of those before, outside of the fairy tale stories her mother forced her to listen to.

"Lyall found you," said Rebecca in a quiet voice. She lay in the bed, still snuggling with her child.

Juliane banished thoughts about the past so they wouldn't affect her bedside manner. Rebecca hadn't asked for the doctor. She'd asked for her. She plastered on a smile. It occurred to her she didn't need to join forces with those living in the city. She forced her hands to stay by her side rather than touch the sore spot at her neck again.

The people there allowed the doctor to continue running around practicing medicine, knowing he was unstable. Clearly, Manhattan was not the remaining beacon of civilization she'd hoped it would be. She sat down on the edge of Rebecca's bed. She'd convinced herself that in order to make a difference in this world, she needed to be a part of something bigger, but did she really need anyone else? She'd already made a difference with two lives.

"How are you feeling today?" Juliane asked.

"Like I might go crazy if I am forced to stay in this bed for the next two weeks. My husband, Rob, says I've lost too much blood and need to stay off my feet. I thought you might be able to tell him otherwise."

"He's not wrong," said Juliane with a half-smile, touching the woman's forehead. "You did lose quite a lot and do need to rest. But the human body is surprisingly resilient. I suspect you will be able to move around after a day or two." Juliane hadn't ever had much time for streaming programs, nor had she ever really gotten sick, but she channeled what she'd seen of actors in commercials for medical dramas. "However, even then, you will need to be very careful not to outdo yourself."

Rebecca pursed her lips and then looked at her baby. "Do you hear that, my love? We're stuck here." She turned her face back toward Juliane. "I'm sorry. I shouldn't have said anything to Lyall about wanting a second opinion when he poked his head in. And I definitely didn't intend for him to run out and wake you up about it. You probably *want* to be in bed right now."

Juliane chuckled. "It's all right. I'm afraid I'm not quite ready to close my eyes just yet." She pointed at the spinning wheel. "You don't actually use that thing, do you?"

"I don't." Rebecca smiled and shook her head. "At least, not with much success. I keep trying, but I suppose I just don't have the patience for it." The baby gurgled. "Will you be staying here for a while?" The question was asked in a light tone, but a tightness to Rebecca's eyes as she gazed at her baby indicated that there was more to it than casual interest.

"I suppose I'm too tired to travel very far today," said Juliane with a yawn that wasn't faked. "I'll talk to my friend about staying one more day."

Naked relief flooded Rebecca's eyes. However, it had become harder to see the rest of her face as the light in the room dimmed further. A glance out of the window showed ominous clouds. If the effort of staying up the entire night wasn't threatening to knock Juliane down now, the pending storm was another excuse to delay leaving a little while longer. When she turned back, both baby and mother's eyes were closed. Juliane backed out of the room, careful not to disturb either's slumber.

Instead of going back to Lyall's room, she found herself lingering in the yard where the party had been held the night before.

"I was hoping I might see you one more time," said a man's voice. Sam crossed the yard from the direction of the chicken coop holding a basket of eggs. He had salt-and-pepper streaked hair and a thick but well-maintained beard. "Juliane, right?"

"And if I recall, you're Sam," said Juliane.

He grinned. "That's right." He glanced down at the basket. "You've got to be starving after what you did for Rebecca last night. Let me make you something to eat."

"Have you seen the woman I was traveling with? There's something I need to talk to her about."

"Morgan? Yeah, I saw Lyall running after her through the gate the way he always does." He lowered his voice. "You're better off waiting for them to return on their own time." He leaned toward her and whispered with a wink, "If you get what I mean." Sam straightened. "Don't worry. He'll bring her back before too long." He looked up at the clouds. "Or the weather will."

Her stomach rumbled. "I suppose there's no need to rush. I only need to find her to tell her that I've decided to stay another day."

Sam beamed. "Outstanding. Lyall will be thrilled if you can convince Morgan to stay, too, even if some of the others . . . ah well, that doesn't matter. Come on in." He gestured for Juliane to follow him as he made his way back inside the cottage. A wave of heat struck her as they turned left and entered a small kitchen. Metallic sheets and silver tubes hung along the wall, reflecting the natural light streaming in from the window. Though the panes were open, a lingering scent of cooked grease and ash hung in the air.

"What's with all the mylar?" asked Juliane, touching one of the silver tubes in passing. "You're not trying to protect your brains from alien invaders, are you?"

"Oh, those?" said Sam. He snorted. "Solar cookers." He nodded toward the window and the dimming light. "Works great most days, but not so well on a day like today."

Curiosity satisfied, Juliane shifted her attention to the rest of the room. An antique cast iron stove stood positioned in the corner. "That must come in handy, then," she said.

"Yeah, but it isn't the easiest to clean," said Sam. "And honestly, I hate to use it. I was a fire fighter back before. Seen what happens first-hand when people don't properly use one of these things. Cooking on it is now my job for the same reason." He placed the basket of eggs down on the kitchen counter, grabbed a piece of split wood, and tossed it through the stove's metal grate.

Sam walked over to Juliane until they were separated by mere inches. She stiffened. After her near-kidnapping, she wasn't inclined to let anyone get that close. Even if he wasn't the worst on the eyes. He leaned in. He had a musk about him—a mix of sweat and long hours in the sun. It wasn't entirely unpleasant. She shifted backward. *Damnit. Why did he make me think of Durham?* Sam smiled and grabbed a large skillet from behind Juliane's head. She bit her lip, realizing a second later she could be sending him the wrong message.

Sam lowered his arm holding the pan but did not immediately turn to go back to the stove. "I have to ask. Do you ever get the feeling that you've met a person before?"

Juliane cringed. *Ugh. He's recognizing me from the tabloids.* Her cheeks heated. She ducked under his arm, putting more space between them. *I should have introduced myself with a fake name.* "I've been told I have one of those faces."

Sam's brows quirked up. "By whom?" He shook his head. "A blind person? You were gorgeous enough in the moonlight, but now . . . A person could lose hours memorizing your every expression."

Juliane closed her eyes and shook her head. "That sounds suspiciously like a line you've used before."

"Doesn't make it any less true," said Sam with a twinkle in his eye.

Juliane caught her hand before it rose to smooth her hair. *It's reactions like that, that give people like him and Durham the impression those sorts of lines work.* Her nails curled into the meat of her palm. Durham wasn't going to be using cheesy pick-up lines on anyone ever again. Durham wasn't going to be doing anything. Her throat tightened. She itched to send him another message in apology. *An apology for what?* She bit her lip a second time and instructed her nervous system to release another dose of mood stabilizer.

It was taking more and more of the concoction to calm her mind and control her impulses. Feeling the task silly, but necessary all the same, she placed a block on Durham's contact record. It wouldn't keep him from popping up in her thoughts, but at least it would prevent her from sending messages that would never be answered. Perhaps then she would finally accept that he was in the ground.

"Did I say something wrong?" asked Sam.

"Not wrong," said Juliane. He must have seen something in her expression. "You just reminded me of a . . . a friend for a moment. That's all." She centered her thoughts around a happier place—her lab—and forced a smile. "You mentioned breakfast."

"That I did." He returned to the stove, placing the pan on its surface. He then picked up a pair of eggs and dunked them in a nearby bucket of water. Juliane hoped it wasn't the same one from the night before. Then he cracked them over the pan's heated surface. Minutes later, Sam handed Juliane the steaming eggs on an earthenware plate.

Juliane's mouth watered at the sight of food. Sam gestured for her to get started while he cooked up another batch for himself.

The first forkful burnt her tongue, but even so, tasted like ambrosia. Juliane's plate was empty much too soon. Without being asked, Sam picked up her plate and tossed it in the sink. He frowned at the contents of the water bucket. "Good thing we've had so much rain recently." A roll of thunder boomed in the distance.

His brow wrinkled. "Hmm, I wanted to give Romeo some time with his Juliet away from the others, but it may be time for them to return to the compound."

"You said something along those lines earlier. Do the others not approve of their relationship?"

He wrinkled his nose. "She's from the city. Lyall's family founded this place." He sighed. "It's ... well ... it's complicated."

"So? Why doesn't he ask her to move here, then?"

"He has. A least a dozen times. She always turns him down. Says her people wouldn't like that. And between you and me, I can't say that most of his would be thrilled by the idea, either." He scratched his beard. "I meant it when I compared them to Romeo and Juliet."

Juliane scowled. "I don't understand why anyone other than the couple involved feel that they should have a say in a relationship."

"Families," Sam said with a shrug. Something large hit the glass pane of the window, followed by something else.

Juliane jumped. Visions of birds flying into the glass at the top of the Apex building flashed across her mind. Ice flowed through her veins. She hadn't realized she'd issued the command for another dose of artificial calm. She pulled at the hem of her suit. That was troubling. She'd need to put a block on that particular command as well, if for no other reason than for the sake of her memory. The chemical mixture was known to cause recall issues when used in excess.

Sam went to the window and glanced down. "Hail," he said. "It's going to be a bad one." He gazed out at the horizon. "And I don't see either of them."

"There's a make-shift shelter at the ramp to the highway," said Juliane. "It's no four-star hotel." She thought of the stain on the mattress and cringed. "And it definitely wouldn't be my choice for some alone time, but I guess it gives them privacy. Lyall met us there, so he obviously knows about it. I'm guessing that's where they are."

"Oh," said Sam. "And where would be *your* choice for some alone time?"

"Not out there."

Sam chuckled. "You know, it wouldn't have to be the same for you," said Sam. "I mean, if you stayed here." Sam searched her face. "I'm not asking for myself. Though I'd be happy enough if you wanted to give it a try." He waved the comment away. "But before you say anything, I'm asking on Rebecca and the baby's behalf. You and I both know she would've died last night if it hadn't been for you. They both would have." He rubbed his face. "Frankly, we need a doctor."

"Hmm . . . about that," began Juliane. "There's something I should tell you—"

"You're not a real doctor and that you just got lucky last night."

Juliane blinked. "No, I *am* a doctor, but that's not . . . well—"

He crossed his arms. "Whatever you're about to say—it doesn't matter. The point is you have options."

The rain outside intensified, making it more difficult to hear Sam's voice above its growing rage. "I'm willing to consider it," said Juliane. The sound of rain outside coupled with warm food in her belly also made it impossible to hold her exhaustion at bay any longer. "But for now, all I want is a place to lie down."

Sam nodded. "I'll take you back to Lyall's."

"That won't be necessary," said Juliane.

"I know it isn't," said Sam. "I just want to." He followed her out of the kitchen and back into the hall. Jogging ahead, he grabbed an umbrella from a can near the door and gestured outside. "After you."

This place might not be bursting with technology, but at least its people still have manners. Sam struggled with opening the umbrella outside, making it obvious the device hadn't been used in some time and was being brought out just for her. His offer came back to her.

I have much to think on, indeed, she realized.

chapter fourteen

STEPHEN

S tephen sought a break in the clouds; anything that might hint that the storm would hold off until they reached the next town and possible shelter. All he received for his effort was rain in his eye. The wind pushed against him, making each step forward a struggle, while Durham and Bean shared the saddle.

Remind me why you aren't the one up here? said Bean's voice in his head.

I told you—the horse can only carry two, and you weigh less than I do.

I'll rephrase. Why is he up here with me instead of you?

Stephen pretended not to see the same hurt and confusion on her face that came through in her projected thoughts. *Because we need him, and he can't keep up. We've been through this already.*

She'd challenged the idea they needed Durham to gain Juliane's trust more than once. Explaining the real reason why he'd accepted Durham's offer to come along would only end in an argument. That much he knew. She'd accuse him of not trusting her, and she'd have a point. However, the truth was he did trust her. He just didn't trust Damien.

He also couldn't explain why he couldn't risk touching her. *She's not affected by the drain like you are*, Alan's observation came back. Stephen's lips twisted. Knowing Bean, if he said anything about either Damien or Alan and his warnings, she'd feel compelled to prove him wrong. He couldn't risk that. *Say goodbye now, while you still can.* Stephen couldn't tell if the words were his or Alan's. *If you still can.*

He turned his thoughts to the events of last night. *That happened, didn't it? No dream is that good.* Doubt began to creep in as they put more distance between them and the creek. He hadn't brought it up because if he did, she might remember their promise to talk afterward, but some hint about last night would have been nice. *We can talk about it after we find Juliane,* the voice in the back of his mind offered. More drops fell from the sky. *Who's the liar now,* whispered the voice, sounding suspiciously like Alan.

He focused on the road ahead and the excuse he'd made as more water fell from the sky. When he'd first suggested he walk instead of ride, Bean accused him of being possessed by a misguided sense of chivalry. The second time she'd brought it up, she reminded him that if it had been up to her, they'd have taken the horse and ridden away—Durham was in no condition to stop them if they did, even without their extra abilities.

The third time she'd brought it up, Stephen had simply said he'd made his decision, after which Bean grumbled about him being an idiot again.

Oblivious to his role in their silent argument, Durham passed the time by attempting to send messages to Juliane. So far, he'd let her know they were on the way. He'd also sent a warning to her about the Serpentine. However, he claimed that both messages were returned as "undelivered." This seemed odd to Stephen, considering she'd supposedly sent a message claiming to care about him, but he hadn't pressed.

It'd only serve to convince Bean further that Juliane was no longer interested in reconnecting with their tagalong.

"We should find shelter," Durham shouted.

While the horse helped, their progress had remained slow. Too slow and each pained glance Bean sent him chipped away at his hope that they'd reach their goal in time. "We're miles away," Stephen shouted back.

"It won't do Juliane any good if we're struck by lightning out here," said Durham.

Speak for yourself. Stephen continued walking. He looked back up at the sky. He'd absorbed the power of a lightning bolt's strike the same way he'd consumed Nadia's life-force. It had given him the power to bring Bean back from death's door during the attack on the Watchtower. His gaze darted to Bean before looking back toward the sky. He grinned as large drops of water pelted his face. Another strike like that would keep Bean safe from him for hours, if not days.

He sent his consciousness out, looking for anything that might give him an idea where the next bolt might strike. Thunder crashed around them. The horse reared, apparently agreeing with Durham on the need for shelter. Stephen abandoned his efforts to locate sensor clusters as Durham clutched the reins, and Bean yelled.

Bean grabbed Durham around the waist, but the effort wasn't enough to keep either of them in the saddle, and both tumbled to the ground in a pile. The horse, no longer burdened, galloped down the road without them, taking its saddlebags and their remaining supplies with it.

"Well, that's just great," muttered Bean.

Stephen watching the horse grow smaller and smaller by the second. He extended his hand to Bean. "Are you okay?" he asked.

"More bruised ego than anything else," she said, taking his hand. "Would have helped if someone had held onto the reins a second longer."

"I've never had to travel cross-country by horse before," said Durham. "Unless you count that time with Vanessa . . ." He frowned and rubbed his head. "Sorry, what I mean to say is I was caught by surprise and panicked."

Bean snorted. "Yeah, that's pretty obvious."

"Will you two stop it!" snapped Stephen. Thunder punctuated his words. Something struck him on the head. Then struck again. Rain transitioned to hail. He covered his head with his arm, while the others did the same and broke into a run after the closest tree line. Larger chunks of ice struck the open road as the wind picked up in strength.

Durham's face went blank as he accessed the datastream. "Nor'easter," he said.

"You think?" Bean scowled as chunks of ice the size of coins piled up around them. One managed to cut through the protection of the branches, coming to rest by her foot.

"Right," said Stephen. "We can't stay here." He opened his virtual map. "Looks like there's a service station a mile up the road. We can wait the storm out there."

"The only problem is we'd have to go back out in that," said Bean, kicking the hailstone by her foot.

"I don't know that we have a choice," said Durham.

Stephen and Bean shared a look. "You always have a choice," said Stephen.

Durham pressed his lips together. "Yeah, well, personally I prefer to live to see the consequences of my decisions." A nearby tree groaned, then a limb snapped. "We need to go, before it gets worse out here."

Stephen nodded. Taking a breath, he ran back out onto the road and into the storm. The hair on his arms rose. He smiled. Maybe lightning would still find him after all. He slowed his pace. Both Bean and Durham had launched into a run at the same time as he did, but when Bean noticed, she hung back until he caught up with her.

"Why'd you slow down?" he asked.

"Why did you? I'm not going to have to carry you, am I?" An icy pebble landed next to her feet.

"Har, har," said Stephen between strained breaths.

"Seriously, are you okay?" She searched his face.

"I'm fine," said Stephen through clenched teeth. Alan's smirking face popped into his head. "Just double-checking the map. Rain makes it too easy to go the wrong way. Don't worry. I'll be right behind you. See if you can find the station."

Bean nodded, breaking into full speed. Stephen watched as she grew smaller, much as the horse had done. He found himself slowing as more ice struck him on the arms. Unfortunately, it would seem this storm would not be producing the electricity he needed. Another chunk struck him on the temple. Hot blood, a stark contrast from the icy precipitation, ran down the side of his face. *Let her go*, the voice in his head said. *You want to trust her. Prove it. Turn around and let her go.*

A broad shoulder wedged itself under his armpit, causing Stephen to lurch forward. He'd been so focused on Bean, he hadn't paid attention to where Durham was. The man's lips had taken on a shade of blue, making the bruise around his head wound all the more distinct. Even so, Stephen couldn't help but notice how the man's warmth radiated off him. The craving rose up within him. "I don't need your help," shouted Stephen, pushing the man away.

"Yeah? Unfortunately, I need yours," said Durham. He gestured at the bruise above his face. "I can't run in a straight line to save my life. Zigzagging all over the place. Happened to me enough on the field to recognize what that means. Figured if we teamed up, we both might have a better shot of actually reaching this shelter of yours before another rock falls from the sky and gives me a more permanent injury." He pointed forward.

Stephen followed the direction of Durham's finger. Bean was turning off the main road. The mixture of wind, water, and ice had reduced visibility up ahead, but she must have found the service station. Before Stephen had a chance to respond, Durham once again thrust his shoulder under Stephen's. Together they ran forward, and Stephen found that as long as he put all his concentration into the act of putting one foot in front of the other, he could hold the hunger at bay. A patch of icy road caused Stephen to slip.

"I got you," said Durham between heavy breaths. "Almost there."

They turned where they'd last spotted Bean. Stephen glanced around, but he'd lost sight of her figure in the storm.

"Over here," she shouted from his right. He spotted her underneath a canopy thick with ivy, which had completely covered what was left of the man-made structure. Stephen and Durham ran toward her, each supported by the other's weight.

Bean's eyebrow shot up in question as they reached her side. "He needed help," said Stephen as he tried to catch his breath.

Her lips twisted. She turned toward the abandoned structure. The glass protecting the entrance was broken. Bean kicked it with her shoe until the opening was large enough for them to step through without causing further injury. She gestured at the door. "After you," she said.

The insides of the former service station were as Stephen expected, based on the condition of the exterior. The air smelt thick with mold and dirt. However, the roof over their heads provided welcome protection from the other elements. Though the light was dim, there was enough to show Durham's breath as he rubbed his hands together. "We're going to need to start a fire." His gaze darted around the shop. "See if you can spot anything flammable."

"Too risky," said Bean through chattering teeth.

"You'd rather risk freezing to death?" replied Durham. "Besides, who else is going to be as stupid as we were to be caught outside in this and see it?"

Stephen's head ached as much as the rest of his body. Dread coiled inside him as he put space between himself and the other two.

"Bingo," said Durham. He dipped under the remains of a desk and emerged with a box labeled Air Fresheners. Placing the box on top of the desk, he opened the flaps, exposing a plastic bag filled with thick paper cutouts shaped like evergreen trees. Durham grinned, pulling one out of the pile.

"Gotta love the classics." Durham brought it to his nose. His grin turned into a grimace followed by a sneeze as he returned the cutout to the pile. "Well, they might still work as kindling. That chair over there looks like it is made of wood. We can use it to dry out some of the fallen limbs from outside. Now, all we need to do is find a match."

Bean swooped the box up in her arms. "I'll take care of it." *You're sure you're fine?* Her voice whispered in Stephen's head.

He nodded and turned away as if to continue searching for anything they might burn. Instead, he found the door to a back-room office. He supposed it would be too much to hope there'd be a cot inside.

The corners of Stephen's lips twitched at the memory of the night he'd met Bean for the first time back at Jim's tavern. They'd hidden together in a back-room office just like this one until an inferno and the Watch's pursuit forced them out. She'd been rude. Bossy. An absolute nightmare. He couldn't wait to get away from her then. He couldn't bear the idea of leaving her now.

Something moved in the darkness as he stepped into the room. Stephen's fingers curled around the body of a snake before he registered what he was doing. The creature's hibernation must have been disturbed by the opening door. The snake hissed, then its body fell limp in his hands. Its life energy didn't provide the same rush as the old man's had, but Stephen was relieved to note his head no longer ached. He reached out with his consciousness in search of the building's nanobots or sensors that might divulge the location of similar beasts.

An occupancy sensor confirmed he wasn't alone. Another query returned the image of not one but a den of at least twenty or more. Stephen shuddered. "Do what you have to do," he muttered. He stepped further into the room and shut the door.

Minutes later, Stephen's hands were full of dead serpents. His nose twitched at the scent of smoke in the air with a hint of evergreen. He emerged from the back room to find the other two huddled next to a small blaze underneath a broken window. Bean must have gotten the fire going while he'd been occupied with the snakes.

Bean looked his way as he approached. *Where were you?*

"I found us something to eat," said Stephen, raising his hands. Dark bodies hung from his fingers like ribbons of death. Durham drew back in disgust as he continued his approach. "Found a whole den back there," said Stephen, nodding in the direction he'd come from. "We just have to figure out how to cook them."

"Cook them? As in, for dinner?" asked Durham. He glanced at their meager fire.

"Might as well," said Bean with a shrug, coming to Stephen's side. "Here, give them to me," she said, extending her hand. "I noticed a metal rack we can probably use as a grill over by the desk."

His hand brushed against hers as they made the exchange. A warmth that had nothing to do with the fire rushed through his body. He pulled back. He'd hoped the snakes' lives would have been enough to satisfy the dangerous craving. It would seem they'd acted more as an appetizer. He moved to the other side of the fire, making a point to rub his hands together as if still forcing out the chill from the weather outside.

Bean remained where he'd left her a moment longer. Could she sense what had almost happened? His gaze fell to his hands as he ran through how close he'd come to doing the unimaginable. *You're out of time.* There was no more point in lying to himself about it.

His shoulders slumped. Maybe Bean would go on to find Juliane. Maybe she wouldn't. It no longer mattered to Stephen whether she went to Woodspring or back to the city. Wherever she went, she would be safer as long as it was without him. *Time to say goodbye.* His throat tightened. Thunder crashed outside. *I'll go,* he promised himself—and this time he meant it. *As soon as the storm breaks.* He would just have to keep his distance until then.

Bean returned with the makeshift grill covered in pale slick bodies. While he'd been lost in thought, she not only found the means to cook their dinner, she'd dressed the meat as well.

"It's a bit disturbing how fast you did that," said Durham, looking at Bean's handiwork. "Hot . . . but disturbing."

Her eyes narrowed. "Still not interested."

He held up his hands. "I told you. No filter. Stuff like that keeps slipping out the wrong way, but I meant it as a compliment. Nothing else. Besides, even if it wasn't obvious you two are together, if I'm being completely honest, my heart is set on another."

"Your *heart* isn't the part of you that bothers me," muttered Bean.

Durham chuckled and then sighed. "Yeah, I find it hard to believe, too." He gazed into the fire. "It certainly came as a surprise to me, but I guess when you meet the right person, it . . . it . . . changes your whole perspective—about everything—even about the things you thought were all you needed. It's like my final year with the Dragons—we played the Lionesses."

Durham's babbling made it difficult for Stephen to think of how to break the news to Bean.

"It was supposed to be one of those novelty match-ups— a publicity stunt, more or less. We'd joked around. Said things like for them not to worry, as no one wanted to send anyone to the hospital."

Bean snorted and flipped the snake meat with the knife she'd used to skin them. "Let me guess, they surprised everyone by winning."

"Hell no, they didn't win," said Durham. His teeth, exposed by his smile, shone in the firelight.

How would the conversation even start?

"As I said, I was with the *Dragons*." Durham followed the words with a roar. His smile turned into a pout as it became clear that the name meant nothing to either Stephen or Bean.

I love you, but I want to kill you. No, that wouldn't work. She'd laugh it off. Probably say she wanted to kill him, too. Worse, it sounded suspiciously close to a line from one of the old novels Nadia read when the chores were done.

"The way the game ended doesn't matter. What mattered—to me, at least—was how they played while the clock was running. This energy all around them. It filled the stands. We had a few matches after that, against good teams—"

Bean stabbed at the meat.

Look, Bean, I've found someone who can cure me—in the datasphere. Er . . . yeah, you definitely don't know him. Stephen shook his head. Weren't they already going to someone who supposedly had a cure? Wasn't it the whole point of their journey? Bean would roll her eyes, but considering how willing she'd been to go first to Worcester and then to Woodspring, she'd probably just shrug and follow him to their new destination, too.

"But it was never the same. Those other teams . . . I started to realize they were only good on paper. Sure, they could run play."

Listening to Durham's story was worse than walking into a cloud of gnats at dusk.

"And there was a close game or two now and then, but no fire. Speaking of which . . ." He stood up abruptly and grabbed a sign hanging from the ceiling advertising some long-abandoned product. "Here," he said to Bean. "Whenever you think the meat is done, feel free to use this as a plate. We can toss it in afterward."

Stephen looked at Durham as something he said registered through the noise. *I found someone.*

Durham held up a flask. "I also found a little something extra to help wash it down. Guess somebody here liked to drink on the job." He settled back into his spot on the floor and placed the flask in front of him. "When I saw my teammates pose for pictures following the championship that year, I realized it was just another trophy for us. Sure, for the rookies it was worth celebrating, but for the rest of us, it was just another ornament for the case."

Bean picked up the flask. Sending Stephen a look that spoke volumes, she took a long drink. Liquid dripped down her chin. She grimaced and wiped her lips before she passed it to Stephen. Stephen followed suit. Its contents burnt his throat, but then a pleasant warmth filled his insides.

"That's when I realized that the game had lost its thrill for me," continued Durham, taking the flask from Stephen. "I talked to my coach about leaving the next day. Said something about wanting to go while we were on top, but deep down, I think he knew the real reason." He took a swig. Then another. "Now it seems the same can be said about pursuing other women."

Durham looked over at Stephen. "If you're smart, you won't let this one slip through your fingers." He nodded at Bean meaningfully. "You might not get another chance."

Stephen's heart sank.

Durham reached over and picked up a piece of the charred meat Bean had placed on the make-shift plate while he'd been talking and immediately dropped it. He blew on his fingers. "Wow. Glad I don't mind mine well done."

Stephen risked picking up a sliver of meat as Bean and Durham each drank from the flask. Though Bean's sip could just as easily been classified as a chug. Stephen pretended he was holding a hot dog in his hands rather than a slithering creature. Not that Stephen remembered eating a hot dog recently. The meat itself lacked flavor other than char, but Stephen wasn't going to complain as chewing gave him something to focus on other than the life energy pulsing on either side of him.

There has to be another way. His eyes widened. *If only he truly had met someone else who could figure out a cure.* What was he doing? Alan said it was a virus, but it just so happened he had met another computer genius in the datastream. The fire in front of him dimmed and was replaced by the rolling shadowless landscape he'd come to associate with the virtual world. "Yo, Wes? You listening?"

His friend appeared as a series of pixels. "And when am I not? What's up?"

"I need—" Stephen cut himself off. Wes had been a victim of the virus. How do you tell a person that their death could have been avoided? "Er . . . when we were on the train . . . why didn't you do something?"

"Do something?" Wes's cocked his head. "About what?"

"About the drain," said Stephen. It occurred to him that if Alan could lurk in this place without Stephen suspecting anything, Damien could, too. Even so, he found himself asking, "Did you ever try . . . ugh, this is going to sound terrible . . ." *You're wasting what little time you have left with Bean,* Stephen berated himself. *He brought a freaking antenna with him, didn't he? He had to have known what caused the drain and hadn't been able to stop it. All he was about to do was remind Wes he'd failed.*

"Never mind. Forget I said anything."

"No, seriously. Tell me what's going on."

"It's nothing," said Stephen. His shoulders slumped. If Wes couldn't defeat the virus while he was living, what chance did his ghost have? Stephen summoned a map. "So, we've made it this far." A blue dot appeared over the top of the former service station. "But the weather's going to be a problem." Another dot appeared over a neighborhood just outside of what used to be New York City. "Durham says Juliane is currently here, which is where we've been going."

"Durham?"

"This guy we met along the way. Knows her." A ring of red appeared, expanding several miles out from the city's center. "If the beastmen are going to attack the tower in a matter of days, that would mean they've got to be camped somewhere in this radius."

"So, you want me to figure out where they are so you can avoid them?" Wes stretched his fingers.

"No." Stephen took a breath and glanced around. There was no sign of Damien anywhere. "Actually, I'm hoping you can help me figure out where they are so I can . . ." *This is it. Decision time. No turning back.* "So I can join them."

"Er . . . what about Juliane? If she's where you say she is, you don't have much further to go. Don't you want to find her?"

"Yeah, I do, but, well, there's been a development." He looked at his feet. "Can't go into the details, but Bean's going to have to find Juliane on her own. Assuming she still wants to."

Wes lowered his face to meet Stephen's eyes. "And Bean agreed to this?"

Stephen shrugged, then straightened. "Well, technically she hasn't yet, but she'll come around."

Wes's brow furrowed. "For some strange reason, I doubt that very much."

"Yeah, well, she's going to have to have to." *Because I'm an energy-sucking vampire, and if I am going to kill everyone around me, it might as well be the beastmen.* "It's the only way to stop the war."

"You?" Wes laughed. "You've been out in the wilderness too long. You've lost your mind. You. Stop a war."

"Please."

"Fine," said Wes, grinning. "That's right folks, my best friend. Savior of the world," he muttered with a grin. "Let me see . . ." His grin slipped as a large cluster of dots appeared on the map. "Are you sure these people are planning an attack? On the Sorcerers? On him?"

"It's fair to say I have that on authority."

"Well . . . something isn't right about this. I found them *way* too easily. It's like they want to be found."

"They're probably trying to send Finn a message," said Stephen. "Like, look how many of us there are. Oh, and by the way Finn's real name is Damien."

Wes' lips twisted. "Maybe . . . but that would only work if they were sure they had the Sorcerers outnumbered." He nodded toward the map. "Which even *I* don't know, and I've been living there most of my life."

Stephen looked at the map. The man who'd raised him was out there, somewhere—Chad, his real dad. He'd seen Stephen for what he was. After Nadia, Chad made it clear that he wanted to put as much distance between them as possible.

Stephen's gaze dropped to his hands. If only he could walk away from Bean as easily.

He sighed. Wes was right about Bean, though. It was going to take something truly spectacular to convince her not to follow him into the beastmen's lair. It was kind of funny that in order to show he trusted her, he had to lie to her, and to protect her, he was going to have to hurt her like he had Chad—make her never want to see him again.

Something touched him. He blinked and in an instant, the landscape in front of him transformed back into a campfire that had grown smaller while he'd been in the digital world. Bean's hand rested on his shoulder. "You looked like you were ready to sleep sitting up, like Mr. Romantic over there." She pointed. Durham had repositioned himself while Stephen had been accessing the datastream so that his back was to the wall. His head hung low. "Lightweight," she said. "Anyway, you took care of all the snakes in the back, didn't you? As in, they're all gone."

Stephen nodded. "Yeah, about that—"

"So, if we were to go back there to, ah, let's say lie down, we shouldn't have any unexpected company, right?"

Stephen sighed. This was going to be more difficult than the battle at the Watchtower. "We need to talk."

"You sure about that?" Her voice deepened. "Because I can think about a few things I'd like to do right now other than talk." She smiled suggestively.

The blood rushed from Stephen's brain. Before he knew what he was doing, he'd let her help him stand upright. Warning bells rang in his mind as she wove her fingers in his hair, pulling his head closer to hers. Then her lips were on his with a heat that burned more than any fire and was more intoxicating than any liquor. His arms encircled her waist, drawing her closer. Her body relaxed.

He broke away from their kiss, alarmed, and released her. The voice in his mind screamed at him to stop what he was doing now, before he did something worse.

The corner of her lip turned up in a sly grin. Her eyes were dark pools. If the sun were up, they'd be the color of jade he now associated with strong emotion. She stepped back toward the back-room office. He couldn't look away. He might as well fight gravity. She took his hand. "Aren't you coming?"

Her husky tone made it painful to remain standing in one place. It would be so easy to give in. *And so easy to lose control*, the panicked small voice whispered in his brain. "Bean . . ." he started.

"Stephen . . ." she mimicked. She pointed at him. "Don't you want to get out of those wet clothes?" She drew her hands down her sides and pulled at the hem of her shirt. "Because, I know I do."

She makes a good point. His groin agreed. He bit his lip and looked anywhere but at Bean. "You're drunk," said Stephen.

"So?"

"So . . ." Stephen searched for an excuse, but his brain was no longer being cooperative. "So, it wouldn't be right."

"It's not my first time, if that's what you are worried about," she said with a laugh. Her voice changed. She released her shirt. "Oh . . ." she covered her mouth with a hand. "I'm sorry," she said. "It's yours . . . Isn't it?" She dropped her hand. "It will be okay," She smiled. Her eyes sparkled like gems in the firelight. "You have nothing to worry about," she said, reaching toward him. "I promise." She took a step closer to him.

"It's not," he said, taking a step back. The time in the virtual world counted, right? It had seemed real enough to him. "Er . . . I mean it's not about that."

"So." She took another step closer, trapping him between her and the fire. She traced a finger down his chest. "What is it, then?" She looked around his shoulder at their companion. "Are you worried about him?"

Durham was still slumped over. The flask lay on the ground beside him, completely drained.

"Because I'm not," she said placing her hand on his cheek and bringing his attention back on her. Durham snored behind them, emphasizing Bean's point.

Her eyes were like magnets, pulling him in. His resolve started to chip away. He wanted nothing more than to taste her lips, her skin, her very essence. *I found someone who can help.* He shut his eyes. *I found someone.* "It's not working out," he said between clenched teeth.

"Liar," she purred.

"No, I'm serious," he said, opening his eyes and stepping to the side. "We need to take a break."

Bean's mouth fell agape. Her features twisted. "A break," said Bean. Her eyes flashed in the firelight. "You. You want to take a break? Now?" She snorted. "As in, right this moment." Her eyes narrowed. "That's not funny, even for you."

"I didn't mean it to be," said Stephen.

"A break," she repeated. "After what we've been through?" She gestured wildly. Her expression softened. "Look, if this is about us going too fast—if you're not ready—it's okay. I mean, I thought . . . what I mean is, I can wait."

"I already told you, it's not that," said Stephen, forcing himself to look her in the eye.

"Then what is it?"

"I can't—" He steeled himself. *I can't control myself around you—and not in the fun way.* "Look, last night was a mistake."

She tilted her head to the side.

"And I haven't been entirely honest with you."

"I know." She held up a hand. "Whatever it is, I don't care." She waved his words away.

"What?" Stephen blinked. "But I haven't even told you what it is."

"It. Doesn't. Matter," she said.

He wet his lips. *But it does. It matters quite a lot.* The conversation wasn't going the way it had to, and if he wasn't careful, he'd confess everything, and she might start thinking there was still a chance she could save him. *What if there is?* the voice whispered in the back of his mind. *She might not be connected with Damien after all. It could be just another of Alan's lies. Tell her what's going on—what's really going on.*

No. He forced the thought down. If Alan was telling the truth, Damien could kill her right in front of him.

"It actually does," he said, hating himself for what he was going to have to say and do next. "I . . . er . . . There's someone else."

Bean's brow furrowed. "Someone else," she repeated. She crossed her arms over her chest. "And who exactly would that be? The only people we've seen since the Watchtower are Ahman, that creepy old man by the trailer," she tapped a finger on her arm she spoke, "and that guy." She glanced down at Durham. "You're not telling me you and the Rugby-Wonder-Guy shared a moment on the road. Did you discover some deep personal connection limping here together? What, are you soulmates now?" She snorted. "Well, I hate to be the one to ruin your happily ever after, but I'm pretty sure when he was talking about being in love with someone else, he didn't mean you."

"Wes wasn't the only person I've met online. I've been . . . er . . . I've been meeting her at night while you were sleeping. In the digital world. And we . . ."

"You what?" Her eyes shimmered with danger in the firelight.

"Like last night." He grimaced at what he had to say next. "Only not with you."

"What'd you think . . . ?" Her mouth twisted. "No. Better question, why are you thinking about a computer game when there is a woman, a real woman, standing right in front of you, practically begging for it?"

"Because you need to know. And because I didn't want to keep living like this."

Bean's eyes narrowed. "And there it is." She pursed her lips. "You think I didn't know you weren't sleeping at night?" She shook her head. "Don't tell me a story about a relationship with some datastream woman who you've never actually met. I know what you're really saying. You'd rather not live at all. That's what you mean." She clenched her fist.

"It's not that." *Not exactly.* "You don't understand." Stephen turned away. Bile built up in his stomach. "I can have everything there." He watched as his words struck into her like a blade.

"You can have *me* here."

Stephen looked down at his feet. "It's not that simple," he muttered.

Bean reached out and grabbed his chin and forced him to look at her again. "So, you have issues. Who doesn't? It doesn't mean we stop trying." She tilted her head to the side and batted her eyelashes. "You seemed to like trying before."

He pulled her hand away. He couldn't risk her changing his mind. "No, *you* liked me trying. I, on the other hand, didn't get nearly as much satisfaction out of the process."

"But you do when you're in *there.*" Water began to well in her eyes. "With this imaginary girl who's probably nothing more than a sexbot. Or," she glared through the wall of tears, "some guy like you who has nothing better to do than pretend to be someone he's not."

Stephen's cheeks heated in a way that couldn't be attributed to their makeshift fire, but once again, he refused to look away. "I do." He swallowed. His embarrassment was only temporary, he told himself. Soon, he'd never have to worry about having a conversation like this again.

"She's not even real."

"She is to me." *Time to twist the knife.* "Listening to Durham go on tonight. I guess it made me realize it was time to tell you the truth."

"Truth." Bean grabbed his hand and placed it on her breast. "Do you feel that? That's the truth. When you are with her, can you feel her heart beat like mine does?" She pulled him closer. "Is she warm to the touch?" She looked up at his face. "Can she ever really know you like I know you?"

Stephen twisted out of her embrace. "Don't you get it? That's exactly why I want to be with her and not you."

Bean's lip quivered for a moment, then twisted into a snarl. She closed the distance between them and pushed him. "Fine. Go then. Make digital babies with Ms. Perfect. Drain yourself dry."

"Don't be like that."

"Oh," her eyes flashed in the darkness, "what, now you care?"

"Bean, it's not that I stopped caring for you, it's just—"

"I was right to call you an idiot that first day I met you."

"Bean . . . Look, this is for the best. You. Me. It was never going to work out between us. I mean, I wanted it, too, but . . . we're kids. The Watch. Going on the run. Nearly dying. Of course, we were going to think we were in love. But deep down, we must have both known—"

"The only thing I know is wrong is the garbage coming out of your mouth right now. Do you even hear what you are saying? You love me. I love you. It's that simple."

"No, you don't. That's what I am saying. You only *think* you do."

She crossed her arms over her belly. "Have you developed new powers, then," she said with a snort. "Oh, so now you can read my heart as well as what is in my mind?"

"I don't want . . ." He turned away. "I never wanted to hurt you."

"Well, guess what, you failed. Just like you failed to save your mom."

He staggered back. She couldn't have picked a more lethal barb.

Bean straightened. "What a loser you've turned out to be. And to think here I thought I would follow you to the end of the earth. Guess I should thank you for showing me the kind of person you really are before I made that mistake." She pointed to the service station entranceway. "You want to take a break? Well, fine. I suggest you start by going out that door."

chapter fifteen

JULIANE

Juliane made her way to Lyall's room with Sam close behind. However, upon opening the door, it was clear sleep would have to wait a while longer. An older woman sat on the bed, her hair plaited in a thick white braid hanging down to her waist.

"I'm Mags," said the older woman, making no effort to move from her spot while her breasts rose and fell arrhythmically. Her skin might have grown paper-thin with age, but that softness hadn't reached her eyes.

"I would say it is nice to meet you, but I'm afraid I've been up all night." Juliane shot a pointed look at the bed and tried to hold in a yawn. It was disconcerting how many people let themselves in another person's bedroom. Perhaps this wasn't the place to make her fresh start after all. She glanced around the room. If she was ever going to get any real sleep, she was going to need to find something to use to block the door.

"You don't belong here," said Mags.

Juliane crossed her arms over her chest. "Funny, because I just was asked to stay."

Mags's attention locked on Juliane as if Sam wasn't there. "Sam was in no position to ask you that."

"Why not? He's a grown man." Juliane was beginning to understand why Morgan and Lyall preferred to conduct their relationship in the car lot.

"He's grown soft. He's forgotten why we first started this place."

Juliane sensed Sam stiffen behind her. "Does this have anything to do with the fact that I've undergone the Gene Assist procedure?"

The woman's lips twisted like they'd tasted sour. "It's unnatural what you've done."

"No, it's evolution."

Mags snorted. "Evolution happens on its own. It doesn't require needles."

"So, you're saying you'd be fine with what I can do if I'd gained these same abilities through natural selection."

"I would," said Mags. "Because it would have been part of the Plan. But that would have never happened. Never been allowed. Humans were only ever meant to be caretakers of this place. Not gods."

Great, a zealot. Losing her temper with this woman would do nothing but draw out the conversation further.

"Mags, she's not from the city. You saw Rebecca," said Sam. "You know what she did."

Mags glared at Sam. "Yes, I saw Rebecca. And the baby." She turned back to Juliane. "However, I know who you are." Her knuckles cracked. "And I know you haven't been completely honest with us. I'll admit, your skills may have proved . . . helpful." Mags looked like she'd eaten a slug at the admission. "It's the only reason I didn't come here sooner, but we're perfectly able to take it from here." Mags nodded to herself. "I expect you gone tomorrow."

Mags grabbed her braid, threw it behind her back, and rose from the bed. Her legs wobbled. Sam rushed forward to catch her arm and helped her rise the rest of the way. Mags shot a look at Juliane of such smug satisfaction, Juliane wondered if perhaps the other woman wasn't as frail as she let on.

Juliane bit her tongue, watching the older woman hobble out of the room with Sam. Each of her steps took an age. Juliane glared at the door when it finally shut. She wasn't about to take orders from some old woman who wouldn't allow herself to see the larger picture.

Whether she decided to stick it out here, go on to New York, or travel to places unknown in search of other survivors, Juliane would decide for herself what her next steps were. However, she couldn't deny sleep was first in order. With one decision made, Juliane slipped between the sheets and fell asleep to the sound of pelting rain.

Juliane awoke to darkness. She pinged the datastream. She'd slept until four forty in the morning. The sun wouldn't rise for several hours yet. However, Juliane found she could sleep no longer.

The bed groaned as she sat up, and floorboards creaked as she padded her way to the door and down the hall. The courtyard outside was a mess of debris, littered from the storm that must have raged while she slept the remainder of the day away. A layer of snow and ice coated the roof of the chicken coop as well as the surrounding buildings.

Juliane's breath crystallized in a plume as she blew on her fingertips and rubbed her hands together. Once again, she was glad to have had a place to shelter under the storm, even though some of the residents hadn't rolled out the welcome mat. A breeze teased her hair, causing a shiver to dance down her spine. She wondered if Morgan and Lyall were still huddled together in the back of the cruiser with no source of warmth other than the proximity of each other's bodies.

She turned to go back inside. She likely had until the sun came up before Mags decided to pay her another visit. She might as well make the most of that time. However, a motion at the side of the yard caught her attention.

Lyall sat huddled next to the gate in a tight ball. His body shook. Juliane went to his side. "Have you been out here long?" She rubbed her arms at the sight of him. "You should have woken me up," she said. "I would have given you your room back. I didn't mean to sleep that long in the first place." She scanned the perimeter of the yard. "Where's Morgan?"

He broke into a sob. "She's gone."

"She's already gone to the city?" Juliane's brow wrinkled. "Without me? Did she talk to Sam?" Juliane's questions were punctuated by misty breath. She tugged at her sleeves. "He better not have said anything. I hadn't made my decision yet. She was supposed to wait for me."

"She's gone," repeated Lyall. His sobs grew louder. A light flared in the house where Rebecca and her baby rested. It disappeared, only to reappeared at the entranceway. Hinges squealed as the door opened and closed. A man-shaped shadow emerged holding a lantern. Though it was difficult to see his face in the pre-dawn light, Juliane recognized the pair of shoulders.

"Lyall?" asked Sam, joining them. "I heard voices. What are you doing out here? Why didn't you come inside?"

"I was sleeping in his room. He must not have wanted to disturb me." Juliane touched the icy ground and shivered. "Go inside. You'll freeze out here."

"She's gone," repeated Lyall, as if the phrase was all that was left to him.

Sam looked at Juliane. "You need to get back inside, too," he said. "Before—" The door squealed again. "Never mind. Too late," muttered Sam under his breath.

"What's going on out here?" asked another man, coming outside. "Do you have any idea what time it is?"

"It's Lyall, Rob," said Sam.

"I see." Rob crouched in front of Lyall. "I told you nothing good could come from chasing after that girl."

Lyall's eyes shone in the early morning light as he straightened his back. "You won't have to worry about that anymore."

Rob searched Lyall's face, then shot a questioning look at Sam, who slowly nodded. Rob reached out and put an arm on Lyall's shoulder. "Did she . . . ?"

Lyall stared ahead. "I caught up with her. At the ramp— our spot. That's when I saw him."

"Him?" asked Rob.

"The other doctor—the one from the city. He was lying on the ground." Lyall's words were clipped and spilled out behind chattering teeth. "Unnatural. Then she saw me and smiled—I've never seen her smile like that before. It was like she was another person. She . . . She . . ."

"Let's talk about this inside and where it's private," said Sam, nodding his head at Juliane.

"Your new friend isn't the one in danger here," said Rob, glaring at the other man. Sam's mouth tightened. "I hope you now remember why." Rob stood and turned to Juliane. "My wife's condition gave them the perfect opening to exploit. I was blind. I see that now. I should have known something was wrong when I heard she'd asked to see you before me."

He tightened his jaw. "Mags told me she found a needle in your room. Tell me, is that even still my wife up there?" Rob gestured back at the house. "Or have you already corrupted her?"

Juliane straightened her back. "Your wife asked to see me because you give bad advice."

Rob clenched his hands into fists.

"Rob, you stood in the doorway the whole time," said Sam. "Did you see her inject Rebecca with anything?"

"She could have done it afterward. There was plenty of opportunity."

"Except she was with me. She didn't go back to the room until I took her there."

"I'm not surprised that Lyall fell under one of *their* spells, but you, Sam?" He shook his head. "I couldn't believe it when Mags told me."

Sam moved in a blink, inserting himself between Juliane and Rob. "She's not like them," he said.

"They're all like them," said Rob, shaking his head again. "You know this."

"I know her."

"You just met her."

"No, I didn't," said Sam. He glanced back at Juliane in apology. "Mags isn't the only one who recognizes you. We actually met years ago."

Juliane's eyes widened. She took a step back, covering her mouth. "You were a fireman." A memory of being trapped in a dark room flashed through her mind as an ax hacked into the doorway. A pair of men waited for her on the other side, only every instinct told her that they hadn't been sent there for her rescue.

Sam's brow knit. "I was," he said, sounding as confused now as she'd been a moment before.

Juliane remembered those fear-fueled minutes like she was living them for the first time all over again. It was when she'd learned the upgrade allowed them to do more than access information. She'd disguised her features like an octopus might camouflage its body. When the ax finally had broken through the door, she'd appeared to the outside world as a diminutive blonde. She'd escaped by simply walking past Sam and another man.

He doesn't recognize me from that day. He couldn't, which means he met me somewhere else. The pre-dawn sky had continued to lighten while they stood in the cold and it outlined his body in silhouette. "It was you," she gasped. "In the lobby." It wasn't a question. Missing memories came at her with the power and warning of a tsunami.

He'd been there the day Juliane's world went insane. Juliane's breath caught in her chest. Sam had been the one to block her exit and part of the group that had bombed factories, labs, and technology shops in the name of liberation. What had the news called them? The Serpentine, for the rapidness of their strikes and the signature red cloth they'd wave in the air like a tongue following an attack. Louis had joined the group, or likely created them, in the days following his wife's death.

In her mind's eye, Juliane saw Louis's face before he'd gone into the elevator—it was the face of a broken man— and a million years apart from the man who'd once held her heart in the palm of his hand only to toss it away with a laugh. She'd hated him for what he'd done, but a part of her still loved him, too, even at the end—especially at the end. She'd thought she could save him. He'd rejected her again in the most unmistakable way possible. Then the door shut, and her world both figuratively and literally came tumbling down.

Her legs trembled. She refused to allow them to give way. *Grieve later. He was never yours to lose.* Mentally, she kicked and swam against the flood of memories until her head resurfaced in the present. Her body ached for another dose of instant calm, but now that the wall protecting her from her memory had fallen, she was reluctant to risk putting it up again.

His head dropped. "I was," he said. However, this time his words were soft and drawled out.

"Sam," said Rob. "Where did Lyall go?"

Both men looked to the fence where the younger man had sat. Nothing but mud and grass remained. Juliane took advantage of their momentary distraction and ran for the open gate. She'd thought of Mags as a zealot, but it was worse than that. She was a terrorist. They all were, and she'd spent the night with them.

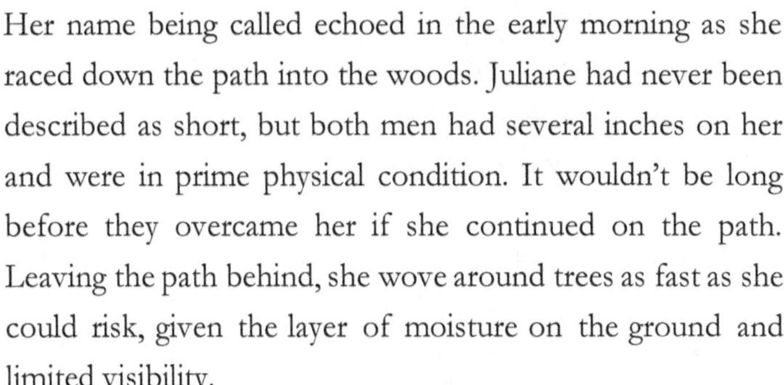

Her name being called echoed in the early morning as she raced down the path into the woods. Juliane had never been described as short, but both men had several inches on her and were in prime physical condition. It wouldn't be long before they overcame her if she continued on the path. Leaving the path behind, she wove around trees as fast as she could risk, given the layer of moisture on the ground and limited visibility.

The tree line broke, and Juliane found herself in a clearing. Her heart raced as her ears strained to detect the sounds of continued pursuit. At least one of the men was close behind.

Taking advantage of what little time she had, Juliane issued the same cellular command as had protected her in the past. Within seconds, patches of dark bloomed across her skin, providing camouflage. Unfortunately, her clothing offered none of the same protection.

Her gaze darted around the clearing, looking for someplace to crouch behind. *Ditch the outfit.* Her skin prickled in anticipation of the cold. *It will only be for a few minutes.* The adrenaline in her system made it hard to think rationally. She pulled at the hem.

Twigs snapped. She spun around. A figure emerged from the woods. "Juliane, stop," said Sam. "What are you doing? Let me explain."

"Explain what?" asked Juliane, taking a step back. The dark patches on her skin swirled liked clouds as her cells attempted to adjust to her nearby surroundings. "Why you bombed an office tower? I hardly care." Fear transformed into rage.

Sam grimaced. "It wasn't supposed to be like this," he said after a moment, gesturing at their surroundings.

"No?" Juliane scowled. "You never considered what would happen after you ruined the world's economy?" Her fists curled. Headlines and missed alerts describing the collapse of the economy and the rise of a mysterious plague scrolled across the bottom of her vision at her command. The dates on the alerts abruptly ended less than six months after the attack on the Apex building and Louis's suicide.

"I thought we were just breaking up corporations. Giving the little guys a chance. I had no idea . . . Never expected . . . Then people started dying . . ."

"People were already dying," said Juliane. She now understood the facility she'd run and its workers had been among the first casualties. "Innocent people." Her nails dug into her flesh as she tightened her fists further. "The so-called little guys. Your bombs killed them."

"I've never bombed anyone," said Sam, stretching out his arms. "All my life, all I've ever wanted to do is protect people."

"You might not have pushed the button, but don't for a second tell yourself you weren't just as responsible as the people who did."

Sam hung his head. "I know . . ." He looked up, "But I'm trying to make up for it now."

"Let me go, then," said Juliane, terminating the camouflaging program.

"I'm not stopping you," said Sam. "But I hope you will stay anyway."

"Why on earth," she snapped, "would I want to have anything more to do with you?"

"Because . . . because . . . I need help making things right." He held his hands open. "This place—Woodspring— it was always intended to be something greater than any one person. A place where people can live and truly start over." He reached out to her. "Not like that place." He nodded at the city's skyline. "With you here, with your skills and that beautiful brilliant mind to lead us, it can still be that place." He nodded back toward the compound. "Mags and Rob— they've got good intentions, but they don't understand. Not like you do."

"Understand what?" asked Juliane, making a point to look at his open arms. "There hasn't been a single thing that's made sense. You brought a building down on my head."

He grimaced. "That everyone deserves a second chance. That we're all victims." He lowered his arms back to his sides.

"Maybe not in the same way, but we were all manipulated into doing things. Terrible things." His shoulders slumped. "Every last one of us." He pressed his lips together and took a deep breath through his nose. "The plague—the riots—the panic. People like to think those things were a perfect storm of unfortunate events. Nothing more than a chain reaction." Sam shook his head. "But I know it was planned. By them. Or more specifically, by *him*. He set everything in motion. He's behind it all." He met her gaze with his own. "And you know it, too."

His words cut through her anger, making sense in a way that nothing else did since she'd woken from the tube. The final missing piece of her memory fell into place—the name that went with the voice that haunted the edge of her thoughts. She remembered his dark confession as clearly as if he was still whispering it into her ear as the needles in the cryogenic cylinder came ever closer Juliane's eyes narrowed. "Damien."

chapter sixteen

STEPHEN

The view over Stephen's shoulder hadn't changed in the minute since the last time he looked back, or the minute before that. His shelter from the evening before was nothing more than a speck in the distance, and there was definitely positively not a figure standing in front of it watching him go. "You did what you had to do," Stephen told himself, kicking a rock. "She wouldn't have stayed away for any other reason." Still, the knowledge hadn't made turning his back on Bean and walking out the door any easier.

He'd made his decision, told his lie, and now he was going to have to learn to live with the consequences. He forced himself to look forward and toward the horizon. His stomach rumbled, and he grimaced. Unless he found another nest of animals or a similar energy source, it wouldn't be long before he succumbed to the drain, just like Wes had. *At least I won't take Bean with me.*

His vision became fuzzy and unable to focus on anything in particular, like it did whenever he was about to access the online world. Stephen slapped himself. He couldn't afford to lose himself in the datasphere. Not unless he wanted to give up before he'd even started. "If Bean *were* here, she'd tell you you're being an idiot and to pull yourself together." The thought of Bean's expression she used when she was in one of her moods popped into his mind. He shook his head. How could he have ever wished her away before?

"Right, so time to start acting like a man," he said straightening his back. A bead of sweat dripped down his spine. The cold front that rolled in ahead of the storm had given way to heat today. It would seem that summer wasn't quite done with them. "Good thing I don't need the map anymore." He hadn't noticed at first—likely because he didn't want to—but with each step closer to New York, he'd grown more and more certain he could find Alan blindfolded. He couldn't help thinking it must be how a moth feels, attracted to a flame.

"Acting like a man would probably be easier if you would stop talking to yourself." He tightened his jaw and pressed his lips together as if he might be able to stop the words from spilling off his tongue with a little extra muscle control and picked up his pace.

The storm from the day before had left a large swath of destruction in its wake. Tree limbs and broken branches lay across the roadway, and more than one tree had fallen altogether. The road he walked on would be impassable for anyone who wasn't on foot.

The urge to access the digital world returned as Stephen maneuvered around a particularly large wooden casualty. The former king of the forest lay on its side—more hill than tree. By the size of it, it must have stood for at least a hundred years. Unfortunately, the ground, saturated from the recent string of storms, must have been too soft to hold it when the winds picked up. The tree's extensive network of roots hadn't stretched far enough to keep it secure. Stephen allowed himself a slight smile. If something as mighty as that tree could fall, then maybe regular people stood a chance against those like Alan and Damien, too.

Newly-sprung mushrooms dotted the roadway ahead of him like snow as Stephen rounded the other side of the massive trunk. Luckily, he didn't need the datasphere to recognize them as the edible variety.

He plucked one from the ground, brushed off the dirt from its base, and bit in. His nose wrinkled. They tasted much better the way Nadia used to prepare them; however, he kept chewing all the same. Calories were calories, and he was in no position to be choosy.

He ventured off the roadway to collect more that might sustain him through the balance of the journey while also looking for water. He grinned. The storms had provided for him in that regard as well.

Plastic litter, more than a decade old, held rainwater. He knelt down and lapped it up like an animal rather than risk spilling the precious contents by picking up the trash. He stood back upright. He would still need more, much, much more, but perhaps he might just survive this trip after all.

Leaves crunched behind him. Stephen spun as a man, large enough to be mistaken for a bear, stepped out from behind a tree. Given his size, Stephen wasn't sure how he'd missed him.

Bloody stomach. "Hello, there," said Stephen out loud. His fingers twitched. If the man tried anything, he'd find out the hard way that his size wouldn't protect him. The corner of Stephen's lip curled up. A few weeks ago, he might have gone running, hoping that speed or agility might be the skill that saved him. He took a step forward, making eye contact. Stephen realized he *wanted* the man to try something. The thought stopped him in his tracks and chilled his blood. The stranger hadn't done more than surprise him, and here Stephen was, not only ready to kill him, he was eager to do it. His stomach turned.

"You're Stephen." The stranger's words weren't a question.

Stephen cocked his head. "I am." He blinked. "How—?"

"I was told you might need a guide."

"Oh." Alan must have known he was coming and sent him.

The man gestured for Stephen to follow. "Come on. I'd rather not miss lunch," he said. Together they left the countryside behind and trudged down empty streets until the open road became lined on either side by abandoned shops and former homes. After what felt like an age, they came to a stop in front of a multi-level brick building that had seen better days.

Cracks rose from its foundation. Many of its windows were just as blackened or broken as the even taller buildings located in nearby boroughs of New York City proper. He turned to ask his guide why they'd picked such a beaten-down location as their headquarters, but the man had disappeared as silently as he had arrived.

"Guess this is home," said Stephen to himself.

"For now," said Alan, opening the door and stepping outside. He looked over Stephen toward the skyscrapers. "I see you managed to leave the girl behind. Good. I wasn't sure you would be able to honor that particular condition of our bargain."

Stephen's lips twisted in disgust at the sight of the man. Did he have nothing better to do than come up with new and crueler ways to ruin his life? It had been one thing knowing the man would be there to greet him. It was quite another thing to actually live through it. Even worse was the sense of wholeness he felt standing so close to Alan. It was a feeling that he should have only shared with Bean. "And if I hadn't?"

Alan scratched at his chin. "Isn't it nice we didn't have to learn the answer to that question?"

Stephen clenched his jaw. "So, what now?" he asked after he trusted himself to speak.

"Now?" Alan had altered his appearance at the cellular level using a technique similar to the one Bean employed to blend into their surroundings. He wore the leader of the beastmen's face and spoke with Jeremy's voice, however, it did not entirely disguise his eyes, which sparkled as if Stephen's question were some part of a private joke. "Now, let's get you inside and fed before a breeze knocks you over."

From the inside, the building contained a central lobby leading to former individual office suites. Its marble floor had been swept clean; however, large gouges intersected the stone's natural veins where something large had been dragged across its surface. A sculpture stood in the middle of the room. Stains on its side made it obvious it had once been a water feature back when water ran for no other reason than to provide enjoyment for the viewer.

"It's not Buckingham Palace," said Alan, gesturing with a sweeping motion of his hands. "But it will do until we find something more . . . permanent." He looked at Stephen sideways. When Stephen didn't respond, Alan added, "Isn't this the part where you try to convince me not to attack?"

"Would it make a difference?"

"No," he laughed. The smile slipped, and he took a longer look at Stephen's face. "You're different than that boy I met before. What happened?"

Stephen shrugged. "I guess I was forced to grow up. Now, you mentioned something about feeding me."

"Ah. Yes." His mouth twitched, then he cupped his hands to his mouth and shouted, "Everyone, we have a guest today. I want you all to be on your best behavior. So, don't kill him."

Stephen raised his eyebrow. "Did you think they would?"

Alan mimicked Stephen's shrug from a moment before. "That's another one of those things I find best not to find out the hard way. Wouldn't you agree?"

He gestured for Stephen to follow him, clearly not expecting an answer. They made their way across the lobby and down a flight of stairs. A moderate-sized diner had been repurposed into a mess hall.

Beastmen, some with more obvious alterations than others, lounged in booths and at tables. A handful hustled in and out of the kitchen.

Stephen's nose twitched, detecting fire. "Should they be cooking inside?" he asked. The farmhouse he'd grown up in had been equipped with a wood-burning stove, but it had an exhaust pipe sending fumes safely outside. They'd also had a solar one, which Nadia, in particular, preferred Chad use, but Stephen didn't see a similar setup here.

"Probably," said Alan. "But this is one of the few areas where I am not in charge." He walked over to the counter where a pair of stools were unoccupied. "What's the special today?" he asked a scale-covered man rummaging through drawers on the other side.

"That joke hasn't gotten any funnier since yesterday," said the lizard-man.

Alan turned to Stephen. "See, what did I tell you? No one respects me when it comes to dining."

"That's because Jeremy here wouldn't know how to make a sandwich if a person handed him a jar of peanut butter and a loaf of bread."

"No respect," said Alan again.

Lizard-man grunted, then disappeared into the kitchen area through a pair of swinging doors. "Between you and me, in my former life, I was actually quite the accomplished cook, but I found it's helped morale to allow them to keep their preconceptions."

Meaning about the guy he's pretending to be. When the beastman reemerged, he carried a pair of gray plates covered by something that appeared to be a roasted chicken with field greens. Stephen's mouth watered at the sight.

"See, there are worse things that can happen than to allow my people to be in charge." Stephen grabbed the chicken with his fingers and bit into the meat. It was every bit as delicious as it appeared.

Alan did so, too, though with the speed of someone confident that their next meal is a few short hours away, rather than days. To Stephen's surprise, Alan allowed him to enjoy his meal in peace. Only when there was nothing but a bit of bone left on the plate did Alan resume their conversation. "You may be wondering how I knew where to find you."

"Nah," said Stephen, licking the last bit of chicken juice from his fingers.

Alan pressed his lips together. "You and I are still connected," he said.

"Yeah, I got that," said Stephen. "Before. Back when you hijacked my dream." He waved to the beastman who'd brought them their meal. "You don't have anything more to drink back there, do you?"

Lizard-man handed both Stephen and Alan narrow plastic glasses filled with a bitter brown liquid. One sip informed Stephen that it was home-brewed ale.

"One cup limit," said the beastman. He looked at Alan. "Boss's orders."

Alan nodded, and the beastman turned back to his work. Alan leaned over and said, "He says that as if I don't know full well that the kitchen crew imbibes a few extra after the meal hours." He shook his head. "The things I allow . . . I can't turn the blind eye though, for the rest—they have to stay sharp. It wouldn't do for the others in the city to get the jump on us."

"You mean the Sorcerers."

"The who?" His mouth opened. "Oh, I'd completely forgotten that was what they were calling themselves." He made a tutting noise before patting Stephen on the back. "I'm glad you saw the wisdom in not going back to them." He stood. "Now, how about we see what we can do about that virus you're carrying around inside that head of yours."

Stephen looked around the room. "What? Here? Now?"

"I'll admit that the circumstances are less than ideal, however," he pointed at Stephen's forehead, "I can't have you walking around with that ticking time bomb in your head, either." He gestured at the other beastmen in the room. "You see, they're my children now. Just as much as you."

Lucky them, thought Stephen. "Fine," he said, sliding off the stool. *Might as well get it over with.*

Alan's eyes narrowed. "You agreed to that rather quickly."

Stephen shrugged. "I didn't realize I was supposed to argue."

Alan's forehead wrinkled. "I've found that when most people are asked to stop talking and actually put a theory to the test, they usually do. Especially when there's potential death involved."

"Let's just say I've come to terms with either outcome."

Alan blinked. "Perhaps I didn't make the risks clear?" He cocked his head. "Oh, now I see. This is about the girl, is it?" His lips pressed together. "Feeling guilty, are you?" Alan sighed and placed a hand on Stephen's shoulder. "Look, whether you intended to do it or not, I've found breaking a girl's heart is an inevitable part of growing up. But I've also found the female heart is remarkably resilient." He patted Stephen, emphasizing his point. "She'll get over you." He released Stephen. "And you, her."

Stephen's fist clenched reactively. He leaned over and took one last sip of ale. "Now who's talking too much. I said I'm ready."

Alan frowned and glanced around. "Hmm, on second thought, you were right about this not being the right place. Much too public." He gestured for Stephen to come with him. "We'll use my room."

"Whatever."

Alan led him back up the stairs to an office suite located on the third floor. The suite contained several smaller rooms. Faded posters with things like "Teamwork" and "Success" printed on them in big block letters hung on display. They stopped in front of a thin wooden door. Alan pulled at the knob. "It sticks from time to time. Just a sec." Then he twisted it. The room on the other side was pitch black.

"You didn't demand a room with a view?"

Alan closed the door behind them. A ball of light appeared in the palm of his hand, casting his features in sharp relief. He walked over to the desk where a pair of lanterns sat and turned them on. "The lack of windows is why I didn't immediately suggest we come here." The light disappeared from his hand.

"Why don't you just tell the bots to come back on?" asked Stephen, snapping his fingers. "Like you did on the road."

Alan smiled. "Because Jeremy doesn't know how to do that."

Stephen snorted. "Ah, I get it. Just like he doesn't know how to debug a computer virus or cook a meal."

"Precisely," Alan clapped his hands. "Now you understand why I changed my mind about staying in the cafeteria."

"And here I thought you were trying to be considerate."

"Considerate? How is bringing you back to a windowless room being considerate?"

"Beats spending my final minutes as the dinner show for dozens of strangers." Stephen placed his hand on his throat and pantomimed gagging.

Alan rolled his eyes. "You're being unnecessarily dramatic."

A cot stretched out in the corner of the room. "Should I lay down?"

Alan's eyebrow arched. "Why ever for?"

"So that I'm easier to carry out when this goes wrong."

"You trust me that little?"

"Absolutely."

Alan frowned, reached into his pocket, and pulled out a small box.

"What's in there, a pill? I thought you'd just send me a file or something," he said tapping his forehead. "Like Damien did."

"You think I have the resources to manufacture a pill? Did you not notice that this place hasn't seen running water or reliable electricity in over a decade? No, I'm not giving you a pill." He opened the box and pulled out a narrow pendant suspended from a thin chain.

"A necklace?" Stephen's forehead wrinkled. "Your grand solution is jewelry?"

Alan held the chain up. The pendant shone in the glow of the lantern as it slowly rotated on its chain. He admired it for a moment before handing it to Stephen. "Put it on."

"Jewelry," Stephen muttered, more to himself than to the other man.

"Jewelry, yes, but it's more than that. I'm giving you a *chance*," said Alan. "Put it on and make sure you tuck it under your shirt."

The second the pendant slipped under his collar, Stephen felt different, like a fog rolled in and took up residence in his brain. However, what he didn't sense, or more importantly who he didn't sense was Alan. He touched the mound on his shirt that shielded the pendant from view. "It's like being at the Reef," he said, recalling the name of the stadium where the beastman had lived in Worchester.

Alan's smile returned. "I managed to access one of the devices limiting players' access to the datastream while they were out on the field and repurposed it. It isn't a perfect solution, by any stretch. For one, the range isn't very good, but as long as you wear it next to your skin, it will prevent the virus from doing more damage."

"Can you make another one?" asked Stephen, forgetting for a moment his distrust. He'd send a message to Bean, apologize to her, and explain everything. Then the two of them could live happily ever after as normal human beings.

The smile slipped from Alan's lips as he shook his head. "I was only able to produce this one as the components were relatively easy to access. However, the rest is buried somewhere underground—who knows how deep. Even then, if I was able to dig another one up—there would be no guarantee that I could get it to work again. Unfortunately, I have to admit circuits are one of the few skills that elude me."

"I could do it," said Stephen, hope building in his chest. "I've rebuilt plenty of machines."

"I'm sure you have. However, have you ever done so without accessing the datastream for instruction?"

"Considering the whole datastream thing was news to me a month ago, plenty."

Alan shook his head. "I wouldn't be so sure if I were you. You were accessing the datastream without thinking about it as a toddler. You wouldn't have known you were doing it. How can you be sure you have a natural talent?"

"So, I take it off while I work," said Stephen, picking at the chain.

Alan's hand snapped out, placing his palm on Stephen's chest over the top of the pendant. "Don't do that. All this pendant has done is cut off your access to the datastream. However, the virus is very much still active and will continue to replicate its code—including whatever causes the drain on your body."

Alan paced around the room as much as the space would allow. "I told you there were risks involved." He stopped and turned, facing Stephen. "Pretend your body is made up of a series of pipes. The virus is like a leak—a constant drip. That," he pointed to the chain under Stephen's shirt, "in this example, is the equivalent of covering the hole with a bit of tape. It works for now, but if you were to remove it, there's a good chance it wouldn't work again. At least, not as well. The pressure will continue to build up on the other side, even while you wear it."

Alan placed his hands on Stephen's shoulders. "I've run the calculations. Unless Damien built in a way to switch the virus off, the pressure is going to cause your pipes to burst. When that happens, you'll be dead in seconds. This is why it was so important you joined me when you did."

Stephen glanced at Alan's hands with a scowl before meeting the other man's eyes. He smirked. "Funny, the way you say that, it almost sounds as if you care."

"What will it take to get it through your head that I'm not the bad guy? I never have been. Well . . . not really." Alan dropped his hands and rolled his eyes. "You aren't still fixated on that whole abandonment thing, are you? I thought, based on the fact you came here *alone,* you now understood how sometimes removing yourself from an equation is the only way to protect the people you care about."

Stephen snorted.

"Fine. I'll answer your question with one of my own, then. Why are you so convinced I don't?" Alan held up a finger. "I sent someone out to meet you on the road so you wouldn't lose your way before you could find nourishment." He held up another. "Even before then, I called off the fight at the hospital, sparing your girlfriend. And though you're determined not to believe me, it was also *my* decision to allow Chad and Nadia to raise you in my absence." He shook his head as he lowered his hand. "I knew the risk of what we were doing. They, of course, didn't have a clue, but I made sure you would be taken care of in any eventuality."

Alan had made a similar statement about the people Stephen considered his parents before. He wanted Stephen to ask him to explain how he managed that particular feat when he'd been in cryosleep. Stephen clenched his fists. He wouldn't give him the satisfaction.

Alan shook his head and made a tutting sound. "Such a shame about Nadia. She wasn't my type, mind you, but I admired her spirit. Now, that was a woman who wasn't afraid to tell you exactly what she wanted." He waved the comment away. "We've spent far too long cooped up in this dark room." He chuckled to himself. "The others are bound to start wondering what we are up to."

He gestured to the door. "I'll make sure the team fully understands you are no longer a threat. All I'll ask you to do is to remember to call me Jeremy and try to act as if you haven't spent the last fifteen years hating my guts."

Stephen scowled. "That's a big ask."

"I only said try, and you only have to keep it up until after we've defeated my old friend, and you're cured permanently. Then, if you still hate me, you will be free to leave me behind and never look back."

"So we're clear, that's exactly what I will do."

Alan held the door open. "Fine. Now that that's settled, let's get you reintroduced to the team."

They returned to the lobby and exited the building. The parking lot was now filled with people engaged in various activities, though at the sound of Alan's shout, they all halted what they were doing and gave him their full attention.

"Some of you may remember meeting this young man before." A couple of the beastmen barred their teeth in toothy grins that were anything but friendly. "A few of you might even still hold a grudge." A man whose hair and beard made him appear to have a lion's mane spat on the ground.

"I'm asking you today to let it go." Alan patted Stephen on the back hard enough to cause Stephen to take a step forward. "This man is no longer a threat to any of us. In fact, this man is no longer a threat to anyone, as it seems his abilities were burnt out in the storm." Alan patted him on the back again. "Isn't that right?" he said, lowering his voice. Stephen made a face, but nodded.

Alan smiled. He raised his voice and said, "He understands now that he was on the wrong team and has humbly asked to join our side." Stephen glared at Alan through the side of his eye and bit his tongue.

"I have accepted," said Alan. The man with the mane of hair scowled and made a move as if to protest. Alan raised his hand, then closed his palm so that a single finger remained extended. "On one condition."

Stephen closed his eyes. Whatever the other man was about to say next, he was pretty sure he wasn't going to like it.

"For the past several days, we have been working on various game plans designed to go through the barricade and gain access to the Sorcerers' stronghold with minimal bloodshed. I have found us a solution. Gentlemen, I would like to introduce you to our bait."

chapter seventeen

JULIANE

"**D**amien? Who's Damien?" asked Sam. "No, the guy in charge over there goes by Finn." Juliane's eyes tightened. *Who's Damien? Wasn't that the question?* His name might have been the signature of her initial paychecks after she'd left the ACI, but he'd been more than that. He'd invested in her research, given her free rein on her resulting business, and treated her like a daughter. Was it any wonder then that her brain had attempted to shield her by creating a firewall around the memories of his madness and betrayal?

"You said one person is responsible for this." She waved her arms at everything and nothing in particular. "All of this." Her memory fully restored, she could hear his voice as he whispered his confession. "He's the one." Her heart raced. A vision of the cylinder's metal door sliding over her face came to mind. The sound of birds in the trees became the rising crescendo of the whine of whirling motors. Branches became needles coming ever closer to her skin.

"Whoa, whoa," said Sam, closing the distance between them and pulling her to him. Juliane, paralyzed by the memory of being forced into cryosleep, had no choice but to let him fold his arms around her. "I've got you," he murmured. Then, without further warning, he leaned forward and crushed her lips with his.

Juliane shoved his chest. "What are you . . .? No," she said. He pulled back, but did not completely let her go.

"Sorry," he said with a sigh, though his eyes said something else entirely. "But if the end of the world has taught me anything, it is to live each day with no regrets. It could all be over tomorrow—I had to try." He sighed. "I thought we had a . . . I don't know what I thought. I guess I thought it would help snap you out of whatever that was. Looks like I was right—at least about that last part."

She touched her lips. She couldn't deny being wanted felt good, especially with the reminder of both Damien's betrayal and Louis's final rejection so raw in her mind. However, it didn't change the fact that the man holding her now had once been part of the group responsible for destroying her legacy, even if he did regret it now. "If we did, it is only because you reminded me of someone else, but that was only for a second. And I can't stay here with you," she said, infusing her voice with a confidence she hadn't felt since the morning of the presentation. She stepped out of his arms.

His eyes lost some of their sparkle. "Is it because of Mags and Rob? The others will come around," he said. "After I explain who you really are. Mags only knows you from the tabloids. She's never considered . . . she doesn't appreciate . . . Look, I'll make them understand how and why you're different from the rest."

"It's not that," said Juliane. "I've spent a lifetime not caring about what other people think about me, and I'm not starting now. I simply can't stay here. Especially now." In her mind's eye, she saw Durham in Apex's conference room. The building shook as birds struck its sides from all directions. Most people had run outside, but not Durham. He'd come back for her, tried to help her get away, only to be reduced to a near-vegetative state for his trouble by Alan. He had cared about her *before* the attack, not just in the days since they woken from cryosleep. She had been blind not to see it.

When Durham had been struck down, she'd thought Alan had lost his mind. She hadn't understood the half of it. Alan wasn't alone in his insanity either. *I gave the order*, Damien had whispered in her ear, explaining that Alan was working at his direction. He'd made it sound as if Alan had gone along with the plan willingly, but ultimately Damien was the one pulling the strings. He'd confessed to that and more, secure in the knowledge that Juliane couldn't do anything about any of it. He'd made a mistake. She set her jaw. "I made a promise, and I intend to keep it."

Sam released his hold on her, defeated. "It won't be easy," he said in a resigned voice. "Taking him down directly, I mean. Believe me, we've tried." He ran a hand through his hair. "Lyall's mother, Irene, was captured on a mission once. She claimed they'd let her go with a warning. Only they did something else." His eyes remained fixed on the horizon.

"Irene killed five people that night, just by touching them. Even worse, she had no remorse about doing it. Afterward, we found her lying next to one of them—Lyall's dad. Laughing about power. Stroking the body like she was on ecstasy or something."

A cloud passed over his expression. "At first, we didn't realize what had happened. It was Mags who figured it out. Irene had been 'upgraded' while in the city."

Juliane stopped paying attention to Sam as she lost herself in her restored memories. Damien had orchestrated the murder of thousands of factory workers. He'd made it look like their deaths were nothing more than a tragic accident caused by unsafe working conditions, greed, and corporate callous. *Loose ends had to be eliminated.* The event had given Louis the idea to bomb technology centers.

"We didn't kill her, if that's what you're wondering," Sam continued. "We don't—won't—do that anymore. But she died all the same. They'd wanted to use her to send us a message." He grimaced. "And we got it." He paused as if reliving the event. "Once delivered, she just dropped."

Betty had suspected there was a flaw with the Gene Assist program—that it had been altered and was being passed on through other means than the clinical procedure they'd developed. She'd tried to convince Juliane that it was the source of her son, Stephen's wasting sickness. She'd given her an encrypted flash drive too. Juliane had dismissed Betty's theory, but Damien had confessed to being behind that too. *The plague.* Stephen's illness hadn't been isolated. However, misinformation about its cause had spread throughout the press, adding to the mystery, and fueling panic.

Sam looked into her eyes. "The group gave up after that. Now we don't go there except to trade, and that's only when we absolutely have to. However, if you cross that bridge—all alone—looking the way you look now . . . It doesn't have to be this way. With you here . . . can't you see? You're needed here."

If only she'd listened to Betty that day—truly listened. She'd convinced herself Betty was being paranoid. She'd told herself the medical community was better equipped to diagnose and treat Stephen's illness than she was. She'd made the biggest mistake of all. She'd doubted her abilities.

"Think of Rebecca, if not yourself." His gestures grew more animated. "Imagine what you can do for them. Each and every life you save. Each and every person you keep from crossing that same bridge—it'd be spitting in his eyes. You'd be treated like a queen here."

Juliane gazed back up at him. His eyes shimmered in the early morning light, begging her to change her mind. Starting over with him would be easy. However, starting over would be to ignore her role in what had happened since Project Gene Assist's first experiment.

Durham's face flashed in her mind and Louis's, too. For all her education, she'd been so naïve back then. If she hadn't lowered her guard and allowed herself to be manipulated by Damien's machinations, they both might be alive today, along with millions of others. She shook her head. "I've never wanted to rule the world—only save it."

Sam's shoulders slumped like the air had been let out of a balloon. "Unfortunately, I expected that would be your decision." He turned away. "If I can't convince you to stay, at least let me take you as far as I can."

Towers that once rose into the sky as symbols of humanity's success were now reduced to nothing but hollowed-out pillars of shattered glass and empty concrete. Each footfall echoed as they made their way across a bridge that had inspired songs and more than a few dreams of grandeur in days past.

"It's strange," said Juliane, taking the sight in, "not seeing other people here. I'm still not used to it."

Sam nodded. "If we're lucky, we won't see anyone until we get on the other side of the gate."

"Gate?" Juliane asked, looking around. "What gate?"

"It's a checkpoint." Sam paused pointing into the distance. "You'll see."

The streets became more difficult to navigate as they penetrated deeper into the remains of the city. Rusted cars that had been abandoned to the elements blocked much of the way. Sam began weaving them around one car and then another.

"Is there a particular reason you are directing us like a drunk person?" Juliane asked.

"Several reasons, actually," said Sam. "And many of them have the ability to blow us up. We called this section of road 'the maze,' back when we were still trying to do more than the occasional scavenge from this place."

The space between the cars became narrower and narrower. "We're almost there," offered Sam as he took a sharp right turn. He walked three more steps and stopped short. Then he turned away.

"Is there a problem?" asked Juliane.

"We'll have to go a different way."

Juliane looked up at the sky. They were losing daylight. "Do you think that is wise?"

"Doesn't matter. That way is blocked."

Juliane craned her head and saw that the car closest to where Sam stood had a large dent in its roof. She looked up again. "Did something fall?"

"Not *something*. Someone."

Juliane's eyes widened. She went over to Sam's side. A body lay on the payment next to the crushed vehicle. A dark red stain spread out from limbs twisted and bent at unnatural angles. Juliane tilted her head as she realized what the blood on the ground and the lack of decomposition meant. "This happened recently."

Sam pressed his lips together. "I recognize her. Tabitha. Passed through Woodspring a couple of years ago." He sighed. "Couldn't convince her to stay either."

The corner of Juliane's lip pulled down. "I hate to ask, but is there any chance it was an accident?"

Sam turned away. The gesture was all the answer Juliane needed. Together, they left the corpse and continued through the maze. Though as they walked past more empty buildings, Juliane couldn't help but wonder who would take care of burying the body.

Gusts of wind blew down the avenue, bringing with them the chill of imminent evening when Sam and Juliane passed under a long series of metal pipes and scaffolding. The structure had once protected pedestrians from the dangers of building construction, but likely now protected them from being squished by a fallen billboard instead. A man appeared out of the shadows as they emerged from the other side, coming at them in a run. His eyes grew wide at the sight of them, and he stopped short.

"This is going to be awkward," Sam muttered under his breath. "Paul," he said louder, with a slight nod of his head in greeting.

"Oh," the man said. "It's you." He stretched his body to look over Juliane's shoulder. "You wouldn't happen to have seen anyone else on your way in, would you? I've been looking everywhere for . . ."

Sam walked over to the man, putting his hand on the other man's shoulder. "I'm sorry, Paul."

The man's body seemed to collapse under the weight of Sam's hand. "Where?" he managed to ask after what felt like a century.

"By the plaza," said Sam holding him steady.

Paul straightened. The corner of his lip twitched. "She always did like that place."

Sam patted the man's shoulder once more, then let his hand fall to his side. "This is Juliane," he said pointing back at her. "I found her on the road. Thought she might be more comfortable living with you guys, if you get what I'm saying."

Paul's features stilled as if he'd covered his face with a mask. He nodded.

"After I take her to the gate, I . . . er . . . I could come back and help you. With Tabitha, I mean."

Paul pressed his lips together into a fine line before answering. "I'd appreciate that," and with that, he passed Juliane without sparing her a glance and disappeared through the tunnel archway.

"Tabitha is . . . *was* his wife," offered Sam as he gestured for Juliane to follow. "We've cleared out the rest of the booby traps on this side, so we will be able to take the more direct route from here. Next stop, the wall."

They walked the rest of the way in silence and came to a stop in front of a massive wall made up of twisted metal and large blocks of steel and reinforced concrete. Juliane detected a change in the datastream signal. In the time before she went into the cylinder, there had been so many active users, she hadn't noticed any one particular person's use, nor the resulting electrical signal, but now, with so few people around, the other users might as well have an arrow pointing over their head. "We're not alone," Juliane said. "There's someone up there. On the ledge."

Sam shot her a sideways glance. "Let me do the talking. Morgan told Lyall once that Finn . . . er . . . Damien likes to play favorites." He chewed on his upper lip. "Be aware, not everyone is here against their will. Some of his followers . . ." Sam's jaw tightened. "You can't let them see you as a threat to their position. Don't mention your previous association if you can help it, and if you can't . . . don't give them any reason to think you remember anything that happened that day."

"I wasn't planning to," said Juliane, keeping her gaze focused on the figure above.

"Just making sure." He cupped his hands around his mouth and shouted, "I've brought you a new recruit." A portion of the wall blurred as a man deactivated the same sort of invisibility cloak Morgan had used when they first met.

"Sam," the man answered with a laugh. "Is that you? How long's it been since any of you've come this way? We'd figured you had to be dead by now."

"Been busy getting the last of the harvest ready." He shrugged.

"That storm yesterday was something."

"Yeah, good thing the snow didn't stick this time."

The man jumped from ledge to ledge as gracefully as a cat. He looked over at Juliane and eyeballed her from head to toe. Juliane noticed his gazed stayed on her breasts and hips longer than was strictly necessary. "A new recruit, huh?"

Sam scowled. He'd seen where the man's eyes had lingered, too. "Should I have said it slower?"

The twinkle returned to the man's eyes. "It's just a surprise. That's all." The man's tone changed. "Though I do have to wonder why a person of your . . . hmm, how do I put this . . . history . . . would take it upon themselves to escort anyone here." He leered at Juliane. "Then again, I can see why you wanted to spend a little extra time with her." Sam's fist clenched and unclenched.

"Hoped I could convince her to turn around, but she's a stubborn one," said Sam after a heartbeat. The men exchanged a look. "Juliane, this is Colemin. Served on the force back when." He looked at her like he wanted to tell her more, but then thought better of it.

Juliane tilted her head at the introduction, but then turned her attention back to Sam. "I assume this is where we say goodbye?"

"No need to go so soon, Sam. There's a place here for you, too," said Colemin with a smirk. "Even if you once were on the wrong team. No hard feelings."

"I'll think about it." He leaned over as if to kiss her cheek and whispered in her ear. "Whatever happens, remember who you are."

A mask of cold professionalism took over Colemin's face as he gestured for Juliane to follow him into an opening in the mass of debris.

The path was narrow, forcing Juliane to walk several paces behind the former officer. Much of the metal was rusted as well and puckered outward with jagged edges that scraped her arms or caught on the fabric of her clothing. Though the view of the sky above was blocked for the most part as they traveled, every now and then, a pocket of light would shine down. At first, it seemed as if the skylights were random, but Juliane's mind picked up a pattern as they walked which made her think their placement was much more strategic than they appeared at first glance.

Colemin had been standing watch much higher. Anyone passing through the barricade's pathway would be at the mercy of anyone stationed high above. Part of her marveled at how much effort must have gone into creating the medieval-style defense. The other part of her shuddered that anyone thought it necessary. She was beginning to see why Sam's group had given up.

The path came to an abrupt stop in front of a door. A scuffed bronze plaque named the place, The Pinnacle. He held up her hand to a pad next to the sign. A light flashed along with the clicking sound of a bolt moving from within. She pushed the door open, revealing a wide-open lobby.

Juliane looked about the space. The furniture was well worn, but in decent condition. She walked over to a nearby lounge chair. An electronic reader screen lay on an end table. She picked up the device and turned it over in her hands. "I haven't had this model in years," said Juliane.

"It doesn't work anymore," said Colemin. "I think the only reason it's still there is for spare parts, but no one's taken the time to break it down to see what's in there." Colemin froze in place. His expression took on the dulled appearance of someone accessing the datastream. Juliane's skin tingled. He blinked. "Finn says I'm to send you straight up right away." His head tilted. "Seems he's taken a special interest in you." His eyes narrowed. "Which makes me wonder, who are you, really?"

She bit her lip. *Time to deflect.* "Do you always jump when he commands?" She shook her head.

Colemin nodded with a solemn expression. "People usually do. Unless they want to be forced to fend for themselves on the outside."

Act intimidated. Juliane ran her fingers through the side of her hair and glanced down, as if taking in the status of her attire. She needed to appear eager, but not *that* eager, to meet the man in charge. It wasn't that hard to pretend.

In the clearing, her goal seemed so straight-forward. She'd confront Damien, stop him from continuing to pervert her creation, then go about righting past wrongs. However, the sheer size of the wall and what it had taken to put it in place reminded her that he'd had years to establish defenses. Defenses that weren't necessarily limited to the physical world. She would need time to familiarize herself with the person he'd become since she'd gone into the tank. "Well, tell Finn that I'll be happy to join him for dinner tonight, but I would like the opportunity to clean myself up first."

Colemin paled. "He's waiting to meet you."

This isn't going well. You know what you have to do. Juliane batted her eyelashes and stroked her collar bone as bile formed in the pit of her stomach. Colemin's gaze locked on the motion. "Please?" She asked, hating how pathetic she sounded. "You only get one chance to make a first impression." She was going to need more than a quick shower to feel clean again after this encounter.

His forehead wrinkled.

He's not buying it, thought Juliane. *What else will I have to do?* She wet her lips as she tried to come up with another way to gain his trust. Preferably one that wouldn't involve debasing herself further.

Then his expression blanked again. When his eyes refocused on her, they were filled with surprise. "He must be in a good mood today. Said he'll set a place for two at seven, and I'm to show you to apartment 1401. You'll find everything you need up there." He started to move, but then paused. "I don't recommend getting in a habit of asking Finn for many favors, though, if I were you." His leer returned, "but feel free to ask *me* as many as you want."

Juliane nodded her head. "I'll keep that in mind." She hoped the man standing in front of her assumed her voice was breathless because she was still attempting to sound sultry, when in reality, it was all she could do to keep herself from gagging.

Colemin never broke stride as he passed the elevator doors and opened another, exposing the emergency stairway. Juliane allowed herself a brief pause at the threshold, but matched the man's pace as they climbed flight after flight. Eventually, he came to a stop at a landing marked with a sign that said fourteen. He hesitated at the door. "To be honest, I've never been up this high," he said in between heavy breaths. "Even Finn prefers to stay on one of the lower floors."

"And why is that?" asked Juliane. "He's not afraid of heights, is he?"

"Definitely not heights," said Colemin.

Juliane raised an eyebrow but did not question her escort further.

Colemin pushed open the stairway door and pointed into the hallway. "The doors are numbered."

Juliane glanced back at her companion. "Not staying to see that I am able to get inside?" There had to be cameras watching their movements if Damien wasn't concerned about giving a stranger free access to an entire floor of his tower.

"Should be unlocked." He turned on his heel and disappeared down the stairs.

Only then did Juliane realize the man had neglected to tell her where she might meet up with Damien, or Finn as he was now calling himself, later. She traced her hand on the wall as she made her way down the corridor. A pair of large vases filled with silk plants broke up the space. The plants themselves were gray from a layer of dust. An enormous frame lay on the floor between either planter. Juliane pulled the frame back as she passed and discovered there was a mirror on the frame's other side. She left it where it was, propped up against the wall.

The door to apartment 1401 opened with ease, revealing a room with bare walls and a single chair facing the external window. "Whoever used to live here wasn't much of an interior decorator, were they?" Juliane said to herself. Her voice echoed in the space. The room opened up to a small kitchen featuring stainless steel appliances and bare granite countertops. A simple stool fit under the lip of the countertop. Juliane pulled it out. Its leather surface, riddled with cracks, flaked with her brief touch. Leaving it, Juliane made her way into a short hall where she found a bathroom.

She turned the handle in the shower, and after a brief sputter, was relieved to see the flow of running water. The muscles in her shoulders loosened as she stripped out of her garments and stepped under the spray of the showerhead. The water was cooler than she would have enjoyed previously, but Juliane gloried in it all the same. Streaks of red, brown, and black swirled around her feet as dirt and dried blood made their way down the drain.

She stood under the shower's onslaught until the water soaking her toes ran clear. Turning the faucet off with some reluctance, she stepped out onto the tile floor. Her clothing lay where she'd discarded it. Juliane wrinkled her nose, hating the idea of pulling them back over her newly cleaned flesh. *Maybe the previous resident left something behind,* she thought, opening the door to the adjacent bedroom.

Her steps left a wet trail of footprints on the hardwood floor as she made her way to the dresser on the other side of the room. The first drawer proved to be empty. Juliane sighed. A pounding at the apartment's front door interrupted her search.

Not seeing any other option, she threw her soiled clothes over the top of her naked body before returning to the main room.

She'd barely touched the door to the apartment's handle when it opened. A slight woman with nut-brown hair cut in a severe style let herself in. Eyeing Juliane from head to toe, the corners of the woman's lips turned up, though the expression was anything but kind.

"I suppose you are here to escort me to Finn," said Juliane, taking care to use her former mentor's fake name.

The woman nodded and turned away, leaving nothing else for Juliane to do other than follow behind. She turned a corner then was gone. Juliane scanned down the hall, looking for a doorway she might have disappeared into. She scowled. How was she supposed to confront Damien if no one bothered to hang around long enough to provide a decent set of directions?

She tried the first door. It was locked, as was the second and the third. The hall ended with a small table beneath a window that had been painted over. She frowned. *I must have missed something.* She retraced her steps, banging a fist on each door as she passed.

"Hello?" she shouted. "Hello?" Her voice echoed. "Well, that's just great," she said.

She started back toward the apartment where she'd showered, thinking that the woman would return there as soon as she realized Juliane no longer followed. However, when she turned the corner, the hallway on the other side no longer looked anything like it had before. Where the walls were once dull and gray, a pattern of black and gold vines twisted their way down the sides of the hallway. She glanced up at the nearest door to her right. The plaque above the knocker declared it to be apartment 1417.

So, I'm still on the same floor, she told herself. She placed her hand on the wallpaper and pulled back as the vines moved. *That's not creepy at all*, she thought, as she wondered about the mental state of the person who'd come up with the design and the effect in the first place. *It was probably the same designer who came up with the idea of cloaking the entrance to an entire building in stealth material*, thought Juliane, recalling her old laboratory space.

She touched the wall again. Silhouettes of flowers bloomed into existence. A memory of Louis, the day they'd first met, popped into her mind. Though the entire campus had been his to command following his ascent into the company's presidency, he'd been forced to wait by the flowerbeds for someone to show him the way inside. That someone had been her. Her eyes tightened. Events might have played out very differently if that particular doorway had been easier to find.

An idea struck her. *I wonder . . .* Accessing the datastream, she issued a couple of commands. Within seconds, she'd isolated the code for the digital wallpaper. The vines disappeared, and the walls were once again a dull gray. She returned to the corner where she'd last seen the brown-haired woman. However, this time she noticed an extra door where she hadn't noticed one before. She cocked her head. *Clever.* She pushed it open, revealing a staircase.

Colemin said Damien doesn't go up this high, so I should go down, thought Juliane as she stepped inside. The door behind her closed with a slam, causing her to jump. A strip of wall on either side of her glowed with warm light as she made her way down. The brown-haired woman met her two flights down. "Took you long enough," she said.

"You didn't exactly make it easy," said Juliane.

The woman sneered. "That's the point." She turned and pushed open the stairway exit. "We like to test newcomers. See what they can do. Now, go on. He's expecting you."

"Which apartment is his?"

The woman shrugged. "Any door will do. They all go to the same place." She gestured at the door once again, encouraging Juliane to enter the hallway, though she remained where she stood on the stairway side of the entrance. Juliane crossed the threshold. The door closed behind her with a soft click. Juliane found herself in a hallway much like the one she had left upstairs, with the same pattern-changing wallpaper dancing up and down the walls, although the pattern was different. This time, it was more like a scenic landscape than geometric lines. Clouds seemed to float along the length of the hallway. A river navigated across its length. She paused at the first door on her right, which featured a small square pad mounted on the wall. It was a simple security device, designed to alert occupants inside when someone lingered outside.

The door opened. Taking it as an invitation, she stepped into the apartment on the other side, where she found a table set for two. Classical music played over built-in speakers. A pair of candles flickered on the table. The room itself smelled like a glorious mix of properly cooked meat and freshly cleaned linen.

Juliane's mouth watered at the scent of food cooked in a civilized kitchen; however, her host was still missing. She glanced back over her shoulder at the door. A mechanical arm fastened to its top must have allowed the door to open without the need of a human hand.

"Finn?" she called out, hoping the name didn't sound as much like a lie to his ears as it did to hers. "I was told you were expecting me. Is anyone home?"

"My apologies," a voice called out. "I'm just pouring us something to drink."

Juliane tensed. The urge to fight or flee threatened to take over at the sound of his voice. Phantom pain, stemming from the memory of more than a dozen needles piercing her flesh, overcame her senses. She fought to control her breath as she recalled how her body had seemed to fade until she was nothing more than a speck floating in an endless sea of nothing.

She'd accessed the datastream and managed to issue a series of commands the cryogenic sleep took over. She didn't have enough familiarity with the cryogenic tank's controls to stop its operation, nor did she have the time to figure it out through trial and error. Instead, all she could do was attempt to safeguard her mind while enacting a small revenge on Damien.

She'd told herself at the moment that larger payback would come later. However, it troubled her that it had taken her days to recall anything specifically about Damien or his involvement. She supposed the mental block could have been a result of post-traumatic stress, or a side effect from over-dosing on artificial calm, but standing in his apartment, knowing what she knew now, she found herself questioning if her last-second protections had been enough.

"I've been waiting for an excuse to open this bottle," said the voice that had haunted her nightmares for the past several days. "It's a '72."

Anger pushed doubt to the side. How dare he talk to her like she wasn't a threat or was pleased to see him. He might have kept her from remembering for a time, but the memories *had* returned. Therefore, at least some of her protections must have done their job. *But Damien doesn't know that. He thinks he altered my mind. That could play to my advantage.*

If Damien thought she was nothing more than another one of his pawns, it would give her the time to better formulate a plan for vengeance. *Unless* . . . A chill went down her spine. *This is about finishing what he started as much for him as it is me* . . . Her body shook with another spike of adrenaline.

Right now, he might only suspect something. But if he sees you panicking, he'll know for sure. She started the process which would force her system to produce an artificial calm, but stopped before her cells and glands could react. She transformed her expression into one of steel. *You are Juliane Faris,* she told herself. *You don't do dependency. Remember who you are. You have no reason to be afraid. If anything, he should be afraid of you.*

The man rounded the corner, holding a pair of glasses filled with dark red wine. "Are you alright?" He asked. "I thought I heard you gasp."

He looked different. His hair was lighter, more a mix of chocolate and honey resulting from exposure to the sun than the pure ebony it was the last time they'd shared a room, but there was no mistaking his eyes, which narrowed at her inspection. She realized she'd gone too long without speaking. She forced her breath to calm while she relaxed her features. She unclenched a fist to smooth her hair.

"I thought I saw something. A bug perhaps, that's all."

Damien laughed, and Juliane fought the urge to cringe at the sound. He gestured at the table. "Please have a seat. I assume you're famished. Most of our new arrivals typically are."

"It does smell wonderful," said Juliane, walking toward the dinner table as calmly as she would a board table. "I can't say that I've eaten very well the last few days." She looked down as she patted her stomach, hopeful that by doing so, Damien would interpret her as cowed.

"Food and drink are some of the best parts about living as we do. We were fortunate enough to find a stockpile of ready-meals which helped us in the early months following the panic. It gave us the freedom to wait for our crops and livestock to be cultivated to their full potential so they might be harvested responsibly, rather than cut too early like so many others were prone to do. Once you try some of this steak, you'll understand why so many people who come here can't imagine living anywhere else."

She plastered a smile on her face as he placed the glasses on the table and pulled the chair out for her. "The fact that you have running water here was enough of a sales pitch for me."

His lips curled in a predatory grin. "I'm glad you were able to make yourself at home."

Juliane didn't like the glint of his eyes one bit. How had she never seen it in his face before? *I didn't want to.* She'd been blind in so many ways. Damien had promised her a freedom she'd never had with the ACI and the opportunity to show Louis exactly why he shouldn't have been so quick to let her go. *That's why.*

Damien tilted his head to the side. "Are you sure you are alright? You look pale."

Juliane picked up the glass nearest her and held it up as if admiring its contents in the light. "I'm just tired from the walk, that's all. I've been on the road for days." She swirled the glass and took a sniff. It smelled of oak, with a darkness that reminded her of those first confusing moments when the cylinder opened. She tipped the glass back and took a sip, but did not swallow right away. Instead, she sent out a ping to the datastream. If the beverage was spiked with nanobots, the simple command should detect them.

Damien nodded his head. "Delicious, isn't it." He pointed at his glass where he'd placed it on the table. "I'd been saving it for a special occasion."

Juliane raised the glass back to her lips, though instead of taking another sip, she let the wine from her tongue trickle down and join the rest. "Oh," she said. "And what occasion would that be?"

"Your arrival, of course. I've been looking forward to this day for some time."

This could be a test, thought Juliane. *He's probing to see how much you remember.* "Hmm," she said as a way of buying herself more time to figure out how best to respond without giving more away than she should. She let her gaze slide across the room.

A buzzer sounded in the adjacent kitchen. Damien held a finger up. "That story will have to wait for just a moment while I get our dinner ready."

Damien disappeared around the corner, and when he returned, he carried with him a large platter containing sliced steak. A pair of plates piled high with salad greens balanced on his arms. Her mouth watered. Thoughts of strategy vanished in the face of the bounty in front of her. She reached for a fork. The cool touch of metal in her hand, so much like the interior of the tank, reminded her of the danger she faced by assuming things were as they appeared.

Damien returned to the other end of the table where he sat down. "This is nice," he said, picking up his own fork and knife and cutting into the steak. Juices streamed from the newly revealed pink center. "Wouldn't you say?"

As much as Juliane wanted to do the same, she decided to try her luck with salad first. She picked up a forkful and said, "You've grown this yourself? How industrious of you."

"I can't claim all the credit. No, we've been quite fortunate to have recruited some of the best and brightest in all aspects, including horticulture. You're not going to find anything like this anywhere else in the entire world."

"No, I suspect I wouldn't." *Because you destroyed everything else.* "Which makes me wonder, how have you been able to maintain this level of civilization?" She tilted her head at her full plate. "As far as I can tell, the rest of the world is going to hell."

"Sacrifices had to be made, just like anywhere else. I like to think we've made the right ones."

Juliane held the leafy greens up to her lips. The dressing glistened in the candlelight. Her taste buds begged her to abandon caution and devour everything in front of her. "I would think you have plenty of mouths to feed here. Can you really accept another one?"

"There's always room for someone with talents like yourself. It's my understanding you were escorted here by a man from one of the nearby towns. Sam, yes?" Damien smiled. "It was good to see his face again. Between you and me, I'd almost forgotten he was still alive."

Not knowing what else to do, Juliane nodded. "The other man. Colemin, I believe he said his name was, mentioned something like that."

"But you also met Morgan, before that."

Juliane returned the fork to her plate with the lettuce still impaled on its end. *How would he have that information?* She recalled the bit of conversation she'd thought she'd imagined between Morgan and Dr. Thomas and how Morgan's voice had changed. What if that change hadn't been the result of drug-induced hallucination? Lyall's mother had been turned into a killer. He'd turned Morgan into one too. Damien had the ability to do far worse than alter a person's memories.

She stared at the lettuce. A bead of salad dressing dripped onto her plate. It was now clear to her that Damien had been the one to stop her kidnapping, not Morgan. He'd spoken to Dr. Thomas through the other woman's mouth. Which meant the man sitting across from her could have just as easily been watching her through Morgan's eyes as they made the trip south or listening to their conversations. Damien's perversion of her technology made Louis's sex games seem like child's play.

Her stomach turned. If her memories had returned right away . . . if she'd given them voice, or indicated what she intended to do next, he could have killed her while she slept. "I did . . ."

"Sad news. About Morgan. When she didn't report in . . ." Damien leaned back in his chair. "Unfortunate, but not entirely unexpected. Morgan always did like being in the wild. More than anyone thought was truly wise. We could never keep her here for very long. It was only a matter of time until some accident or wild animal found her."

Wild animal. Juliane thought of Lyall and the look on his face when she'd found him sitting by the fence. *Act like the fool he thinks you are,* thought Juliane. She folded her hands on her lap and forced her features into what she hoped was a confused expression. "What happened that day? Back at the office. I have a fleeting memory of some birds and going into a big meeting—I was supposed to present something that day, if I recall." She pouted, then tapped her finger on her chin.

Damien beamed. "You do recognize me, then. I didn't want to presume." He held up a hand before she could say anything, "I wouldn't have blamed you if you hadn't." He ran his fingers through his hair and shook his head. "Quite a number of things have changed since you were last in New York, haven't they?"

"It's been a lot to process."

"I expect it has. And you say you are having difficulties remembering why you went into cryogenic sleep?"

"I assume that's one of the side effects, but yes." She rubbed her forehead where the needle had bored into her skull. She then dropped her hand and changed the subject before the rage she felt inside could show on her face. "Although, now that you bring it up, they said I was meeting with a person named Finn. Why the name change?"

He laughed, "I'm sorry if it caused you any additional confusion. I started using it shortly after the whole unpleasantness, mostly for my own safety. After all, I was meeting with a number of strangers. I thought it wise to protect my identity. The name, I guess, rather stuck."

Damien looked down at her plate, which remained as full as it had when she'd first sat down. "And here my chatting away is keeping you from enjoying your dinner. How rude of me." He gestured at the uneaten food. "Please, eat while it is still hot. I promise you'll hear nothing more from me until you have cleaned your plate."

Juliane picked up the fork with the bit of dressed greens. Seeing no other choice, she bit through the crisp lettuce while initiating another scan of the interior of her mouth. The flavor of the dressing made her traitorous taste buds sing in approval while she waited. Digital text overlaid across her vision flashed the words "No signal found." Relieved she no longer had to fear its flavor, she returned the fork to the salad plate for another bite.

Damien raised his wine glass as in toast, though kept his promise and did not speak. Instead, he tilted his head back and drank deeply.

Juliane intended to claim the salad alone had filled her up, but her body, it would seem, had other ideas following the long trek to the city. She swallowed a small piece of meat before she'd realized what she'd done. For a second, she contemplated letting it go. After all, the rest of the meal had been innocent enough, but then she looked at Damien's face and didn't like what she saw.

She issued a command to her body to stop the meat's descent down her throat. She coughed and pushed herself from the table. She coughed again, more forcefully than the last time, then again.

Damien stood. "You're turning blue," he said, coming to her side.

She tapped the base of her throat frantically as she continued to cough.

"You're choking," he said, stating the obvious.

She nodded. Panic began to take over her brain. If he didn't do something soon, she would be forced to allow the piece of steak to pass and hope that if it did contain any nanobots, she would be able to detect them and disable them before they could do too much damage.

The stunned expression on Damien's face returned yet again to one of confidence as he wrapped his arms around her from behind and struck her abdomen. She could feel the lodged meat move in an upward direction as he struck her again. She coughed, and the bit of steak flew from her mouth, landing on the floor next to her chair.

Damien, however, continued to hold her close. Her body betrayed her by sagging in his arms as her lungs filled with oxygen.

"You gave me quite the scare. Feeling better now?"

She straightened, and his arms fell away. Turning, she wiped the tears from her eyes and nodded. "I'm afraid I've lost my appetite. I need to call it a night. I'll show myself back to my room."

His body stiffened. *He doesn't like that idea.* She looked up. *Is he now attempting to exert his control?* She touched his cheek. Satisfaction flashed across his face. She shifted her gaze to the table. "It was a lovely dinner, though. So, if you don't mind, I'll like to take it with me. Perhaps I will be able to finish it later, once I've had a chance to recover somewhat."

His lips pressed together in a fine line for a moment, as if he intended to argue, but then his expression softened. "But of course," he said, picking up her plate from the table. "If you would give me just a moment, I'll wrap it up for you so it is easier to carry back upstairs."

Before Juliane could protest, he'd taken the plate back into the kitchen area. Juliane heard the sound of drawers opening and closing and things being rummaged around. Every fiber of her being urged her to exit the apartment while she still had a chance; however, if he wasn't already suspicious of her, that would finish the job.

A moment later, he returned from around the corner, holding her dinner plate wrapped in plastic. "There you go, my dear," he said. "Oh, and don't worry about returning the plate. I have more than enough in here."

"Thank you, again," she said with a slight nod of her head. "I'm sure we will have plenty of opportunities to catch up another time. Based on what I've seen since I arrived, I have no plans on leaving any time soon."

He grinned at her final comment. "Then until next time." His eyes twinkled. "Good night, Juliane."

"Until next time," said Juliane. *And next time, don't expect me to be so polite.*

chapter eighteen

STEPHEN

Alan abandoned Stephen the moment the speech ended and led a pair of beastmen away. Not entirely trusting his father's people to behave, speech or no speech, Stephen maintained a distance from the others. When the dinner meal came, he grabbed a plate from the make-shift mess hall and took it outside to eat under the setting sun. His skin itched like he'd lost a limb, and he found himself more than once rubbing the pendant from the outside of his shirt. Stomach full for the first time in days, if not weeks, his thoughts cycled around Bean, and sleep, and sleeping with Bean.

Frustrated, he took a walk around the complex-turned-beastman headquarters. The main building, housing the mess and Alan's room, was rather non-descript and could easily be lost among the remains of the New Jersey suburban skyline. It would be even harder to spot from nearby Manhattan. However, it wasn't the only building now occupied by two-legged fangs and fur. Stephen noted that a few of the other beastmen disappeared into the other neighboring buildings and was surprised when moments later, at least a dozen regular-looking people appeared in their place and filed into the main building. It would appear that he wasn't the only new recruit to the cause.

Although the knowledge there were other people at the camp who didn't resemble the stuff of nightmares should have caused comfort, Stephen chose to keep his distance from them as well. He rubbed the pendant again.

The moon replaced the setting sun in the sky. Although Stephen stood alone in the empty parking lot, he assumed there were one or two look-outs hidden somewhere close by standing watch. He covered a yawn with his hand. *I guess it's time I found someplace to call it a night*, he thought, looking around.

The office suite containing Alan's quarters had been modified to hold other sleeping quarters, but he had no interest in spending the night under the same roof with that man. He also had no desire to risk exploring any of the other buildings at night, especially without a light source. *Guess it's another night for me under the stars.* A blast of cold air ruffled his hair, sending a shiver down his spine.

He frowned. There weren't enough trees in this place. It meant there would be nothing to block the wind nor leaves to cover and soften the broken asphalt. More importantly, there would be nothing to insulate him from the changing weather. He rubbed his arms. Though the day had been comfortable, the weather this time of year could be unpredictable, with dangerous results for those caught outside. The night before was proof of that.

He snorted to himself. *Wouldn't that just be great? You manage to fight off whole teams of genetically modified beastmen along with psychos bent on controlling the world, and you get taken out by a case of frost.*

He could imagine only too well what Bean would say about the situation he found himself in. For the millionth time, he wished he could contact her, explain, and beg for her forgiveness. He fingered the pendant again. *It's only been on for a few hours,* he thought, *it couldn't possibly be that dangerous to remove it yet.*

He reached under his collar and pulled at the device.

"There you are," said Alan.

Stephen dropped the chain. "Yeah, here I am. You found me." He gave Alan a little wave. "Good job."

Alan frowned at Stephen's words. "You promised to try, remember?" He made a small gesture with his thumb back at the headquarters building.

"This is me trying," said Stephen.

"Well, try harder."

Stephen's mouth twisted, biting off a callous retort. "So, where should I sleep?"

"That's the reason I came looking for you. I forgot I had to deliver additional instructions in person. It's been a while since I've needed to do that." He chuckled. Stephen didn't join in his mirth. He sighed. "After consulting with my captains, we decided it would be better for you to sleep with the other regulars rather than in the main building with me."

"Yeah, I'd prefer that, too."

The corner of Alan's mouth twitched. "I didn't think you'd take much convincing." He started walking toward a squat brick building to their right. He stopped at the top of the stairs and waited. The door opened and out came a man Stephen hadn't noticed before, holding a lantern. "Stephen, this young man is Lyall," said Alan. "He's another stray we picked up wandering aimlessly not far from here a short time before you. He'll be your partner in your upcoming mission. You may find you also have a few other things in common." Introduction made, Alan wasted no time turning and disappearing back into the growing darkness.

Lyall wasn't wrinkled or marked by other signs of age, like the bulk of people Stephen had met since leaving the farm not associated with the Sorcerers were. He also lacked the beastmen's physical enhancements. This meant he had to be only a few years older than Stephen—in his mid-twenties if Stephen had to guess; however, the light from the lantern made Lyall's face look like a twisted skeleton. "I know why I volunteered for this mission. What's your reason?"

Stephen shrugged. "I didn't have anything else important going on. So, I figured, why not?" He realized only after the words were out of his mouth how they might sound, but he hadn't been able to help himself. Lyall's youthful appearance reminded him of Wes, and the joke was the sort of thing they'd shared before launching a mission in their game. Wes would have chuckled and made a witty comment in kind. Lyall's mouth didn't so much as twitch.

"Follow me," he said instead.

The lantern cast just enough light to help Stephen avoid walking into a wall or stubbing his toe on a piece of ill-placed furniture, but not enough to give him a feel for what used to be housed under its roof. Stephen supposed it didn't matter, but wondering about the building's original purpose gave him at least something to think about as they made their way through the narrow hallways.

"You'll sleep here tonight," said Lyall, coming to a stop in front of an unmarked door. A narrow cot lay stretched out in the middle of the small room, and nothing else. "We'll head out first thing in the morning so that we can get to the gate before the majority of people wake up. I've crossed the bridge before but never made it as far as the tower itself, so your job is to make sure we don't accidentally trip any booby traps before we reach the barricade."

"Problem. While I've been on the inside," said Stephen, "I don't know how great a guide I am going to be. I was there only for a day, and if there are traps, I didn't see them." He explained how he'd arrived at night and by boat. It had been too dark to see much of anything, and if there had been hazards along the way, Wes hadn't bothered to point them out.

Stephen had been given a digital map from Finn, but he wouldn't be able to access it anymore. At least, not while wearing the pendant. His fingers itched to scratch at it again, but he kept them at his side.

Lyall looked away and started to leave the room. "Well, I guess that means I'll go first."

If Lyall was right about there being traps, they could well be going on a suicide mission tomorrow unless Stephen could remember the route they'd taken. Stephen's brow wrinkled. "Not that I am complaining, but why?"

Lyall looked back over his shoulder. "Why not? How did you put it before? I don't have anything else important going on," he said, echoing Stephen's words from before with a smile that looked anything but joyous.

Stephen understood then why Alan said they had things in common. The expression on Lyall's face was of one who'd lost it all and just wanted a way out. He'd seen a similar look on Chad's face, too, the night of the battle. Words of comfort and understanding, the sort of things Nadia would say while he was growing up whenever he was feeling down, bubbled up on his tongue. He crushed the lies before he could give a single one of them voice. "So, tomorrow at dawn, huh?"

Lyall shook his head. "No. Even earlier."

"Guess I should get some sleep, then."

"Guess so." The door closed behind Lyall, leaving Stephen in the dark in more ways than one.

chapter nineteen

JULIANE

Sleep eluded Juliane after dinner. Though tired to the bone, she'd tossed on the bed. Damien or one of his people might intrude upon the apartment at any time. They'd have no difficulty gaining entry to the place, considering the entrance featured an electronic lock. She padded her way over to the door and attempted to twist the handle. The handle refused to budge. As she'd feared, she was locked in.

Scowling, she moved to the apartment window. She pushed the set of dusty curtains back. The glass on the other side was blackened. Damien may have treated her like a guest downstairs, but it would appear he was more inclined to treat her like a prisoner up here. *Now, all I have to do is figure out a way to stop him before anyone else falls for his scheming.*

She tapped her chin. If Durham were still alive, he probably would have enjoyed finding a way to break out of here. Before she knew what she was doing, she'd removed the block on his contact record. She shook her head in disgust with herself.

Her mental cursor hovered over the record. She was just about to toggle the block back on, when a text flashed across her vision. "Message received. Read." She covered her mouth with her hand. *Durham.* The time stamp on the automatic read receipt showed he'd opened her email long after they'd been separated. *Which means . . . which means . . .*

She blinked tears away. *He's alive.* She leaned on the wall for support. She caught her reflection in the darkened glass and straightened. The news was wonderful, to be sure, but she was caught off guard by how much a simple message had affected her. *Of course he's alive,* she told herself. Why had she ever allowed herself to believe otherwise? The man didn't have enough sense to die.

She began drafting a message in reply, but stopped mid-word. Morgan could have simply found the bloody shirt and jumped to a conclusion, but that would have required Durham to have taken the time to remove it in the first place. *Unlikely.*

Morgan had also said she'd seen the body, which meant she'd lied. *Why?* Juliane supposed Damien could have been controlling Morgan at the time and made her say things that weren't true. Juliane tried to recall if Morgan's voice had sounded unusual, but couldn't be sure. She hadn't known the other woman long enough to recognize the difference. But even if the lie was Damien's and not Morgan's, what would be the point?

Because he wanted Juliane to believe Durham was dead? *No,* Juliane realized, he didn't just want her to *believe* Durham was dead—he wanted him dead in reality but had failed.

There had been several times Morgan acted like she'd wanted to say more but had held back—had she let Durham get away? The lie, then, could have been intended for Damien just as much as it was for her, which also meant Damien's control over his followers wasn't absolute as Sam made it seem to be.

Juliane tapped her lip. Then again, Morgan had been helpless when forced to turn against Lyall, who was clearly dearer to her than some random stranger. Did Damien's control have something to do with distance? Pieces of the puzzle fell together, though the full picture remained irritatingly unclear.

Then again, her theory didn't explain why Damien bothered putting Durham into cryogenic sleep in the first place, or then waking him if he ultimately wanted him dead. The problem gnawed at her. She was now certain Damien had sent Morgan to collect them. The timing of her arrival was just too coincidental to believe anything otherwise. Damien, therefore, had to have been monitoring the cryo-tanks from afar. He'd have known more than one tank was powered down. He'd likely been the one to key in the reanimation sequence.

Had Durham's reanimation been an accident? Juliane shook her head. A person who'd gone to such pains to bring about the end of the world wouldn't have been sloppy enough to make a mistake like that.

If the death of billions hadn't been enough, Morgan's death made it clear Damien didn't care about sparing lives once a person had outlived his uses. He must have thought he still needed Durham. So, what had Durham said or done to change his mind? She rubbed her temple. What was she missing? She paced the room, trying to recall their last conversation, but no matter how many times she crossed the room, a logical explanation eluded her.

She needed to ask the source. Juliane returned to the window and pulled up Durham's contact record again. Another message could alert Damien that Durham remained a loose end. Then again, if her online activities were being monitored that closely, the damage was already done. Durham, then, would need as much advance warning to stay alert and as far away from here as she could give him.

She pressed her lips together. Indecision didn't sit well. She fired off a quick message with a link instructing him where to meet her in the datasphere and waited.

The darkened glass in front of her dissolved as her consciousness entered the digital world, and in its place was the interior of a luxury jet with a chessboard set up in front of her.

Her avatar picked up a knight. Her brain registered its touch as cool marble. The corner of her lips turned up as she gazed around at her creation. At least some part of the world she'd known before being forced into that tank had survived.

A figure materialized a short distance away.

Juliane placed the knight back on the table. After believing for so long that she'd never see him again, she had a difficult time focusing on anything else. Suddenly, she felt very small. She should never have agreed to go with Morgan. Not without seeing his body for herself—no matter what condition it was in. "You were dead." Her voice quivered with unshed tears more than she would have liked.

"Aw, and here I didn't think you cared." His tone made it sound like a joke, but there was no humor in his eyes.

"Why would you . . . of course I . . ." Did he think she'd left him because she wanted to? What kind of person would that make her? She turned away. "I mean . . ." she said, straightening. "You should have called."

"I tried. So many times. You might have been right about the concussion. I don't think I would be able to talk to you now if you hadn't sent the link."

It was all she could do not to confess exactly how much she'd missed him and how deep she was willing to admit her feelings for him ran. If Damien was monitoring her activity . . . *she couldn't give Damien a weakness to exploit.* "You need to stay away."

His shoulders slumped. "Why?"

Contacting Durham had been a terrible idea. There was no way to warn him of the danger he was in without the risk of alerting Damien she remembered more than she let on. She needed to watch what she said. "It's better if I don't tell you." She bit her lip. "It's not that I don't want you here—"

He held up his hand. "You don't have to explain."

"But I want to . . ." She pursed her lips. "I just can't right now. It's complicated," she said, holding up her hands.

"I already know you're in danger."

Juliane blinked. "You do?"

"Yeah. These people I'm with—they told me all about Woodspring. I'll agree to stay away from there as long as the next thing you tell me is that you're getting yourself far away from there, too."

"Woodspring? Oh, you mean—" She flicked her wrist. "I'm not there anymore." She swallowed a curse. The words had come out before she could stop them.

His brow creased. "Then why?"

She clenched her hands. She needed to reclaim control of the conversation. *If he knows about Woodspring, he might know something else that you can use now.* "Have you remembered anything more about the day we went into the tanks?"

Durham's mouth narrowed in a fine line, and as the pause continued, Juliane wasn't sure if he was going to answer, but then he said, "Bits and pieces. You were making a presentation. The whole group was supposed to be there. I'd gotten there early, gone to review some paperwork for Damien. He asked me if I wanted to get a sneak peek at the setup in the basement before the rest of you guys showed up. I think we shared a drink or something 'cause the next thing I know, the meeting's started, and Camille's pissed off her Wand thingy is already obsolete. Then nothing until you helped pull me out of that hole."

Juliane frowned. "What sort of papers?" she asked. Had Durham inadvertently seen something he shouldn't have? She shook her head. That couldn't be it, or he'd still be sleeping the years away with the rest of their colleagues.

Durham shrugged. "Pretty standard stuff. A lease agreement for an apartment in New York called the Pinnacle." He looked at her with fire in his eyes. "You're in New York. Aren't you? You found Damien."

Juliane looked away.

"I'm on my way," he said.

"That's exactly what I just finished telling you not to do." The man had an infuriatingly stubborn streak. How he'd managed to work his way into her affections in the first place was a puzzle she might never solve, but she could no longer deny that was exactly what he'd done.

"Juliane . . ." he said.

Her heart betrayed her mind's resolve at her name being spoken from his lips. There was a longing in his voice that demanded to be answered. She couldn't trust herself to stay with him any longer in a place where a touch could feel real. If he kissed her now . . . if they did more than kiss . . . and

Damien found him before she could stop him. She couldn't bear it. "I'll contact you again. When it is safe. Until then, stay where you are."

Then, before he could protest further, she exited the datasphere. She blinked, and her view transformed back into the abandoned apartment and the blackened window. She returned to the bedroom, though paused in the doorway, looking at the large empty bed. Would Durham listen? She doubted it, which meant she had even less time to figure out a way to defeat Damien. She slipped under the sheets, twisting the fabric in thought until exhaustion took her.

chapter twenty

STEPHEN

The door creaked open, and Stephen rose from the cot. The faces of those he'd hurt haunted him in the darkness as he followed Lyall. Neither of them said a word. Outside, a murky gray light of pre-dawn illuminated a layer of frost on the ground, making Stephen glad he'd found a place to pass the night protected from the elements.

So now what? Alan hadn't shared his plan with Stephen beyond the fact that Stephen and Lyall were supposed to somehow gain access to the barricade and convince the Sorcerers they weren't a threat long enough for the beastmen to pass through.

The corner of his mouth twitched. For a guy that was supposed to be some sort of innovative genius, his biological father hadn't exactly come up with the world's most original plan. It was pretty much the exact same thing the Watch had concocted, with him serving as bait in both. The fledgling smile slipped from his face.

Their footfalls echoed as they made their way down the empty streets. Then the buildings on either side of them were replaced by a line of trees, broken only by a cabled bridge stretching out across the water. "You ready?" Lyall asked. It was the first words he'd spoken all morning and effectively broke through Stephen's thoughts.

"Sure," he said. "I was born for this."

Lyall's lips twisted, but he continued on.

Wes would have laughed, thought Stephen as he followed behind. *Bean would have, too.* He traced the outline of the pendant. If anyone had bothered to ask him, he would have told them the whole mission was pointless, but no one had. It was just as well. If they had, they might have expected him to offer another suggestion, which would put Bean in danger.

Without him forcing her to stop every half hour to forage for food, she should have reached the tower by now. If she had, the Sorcerers would know they were coming. Warned, they'd see right through distraction. They were likely already preparing some nasty surprises. After the way he'd broken it off, he couldn't expect Bean to hold back either.

And if she hadn't reached the Sorcerers' home base . . . He scraped at the frost with his toe. She made it there, he told himself. Likely took a hot shower and slept in her old bed. He touched the pendant again. He was probably going to die today anyway. He might as well take the darn thing off if only to send Bean one last message. He reached under his collar.

Lyall's hand shot out, grabbing him by the shoulder. He pulled him over to a portion of the bridge's roadway blocked by a rusted school bus. "What's wrong?" asked Stephen in a whisper.

"Movement. Up ahead," whispered Lyall back.

"And that's bad how?" asked Stephen, straightening. "I thought the whole point of this was to get them to see us."

"Not yet, it isn't," replied Lyall. "The plan—"

"You might as well come out," shouted a voice from the other end of the bridge. "We know you're there."

"Guess we're going to have to improvise, then," Stephen said to Lyall in a low voice before walking out from behind the bus. "Thank goodness you found us," he shouted. "I was afraid we were lost out here."

"I recognize you," the man shouted. "You're that kid. Supposed to find the Wand for us. Heard you died."

"Yeah," Stephen shrugged. "That's kind of a long story."

The man came closer. "You don't have it now, do you?" He glanced down at his hand. "I wouldn't mind shaving a few years off."

An idea occurred to him. The plan to infiltrate the Pinnacle and the Sorcerer's home might be a bust, but maybe they didn't need to get inside. Maybe all they needed to do was get Damien out instead. Stephen held up his hands. "Nah, but I know who does." He lowered his voice conspiratorially. "And where to find him. Tell Finn I'm here."

The man's eyes narrowed suspiciously. "Why can't you tell him yourself." He tapped his temple.

"Like I said. It's a long story."

The man's lips tightened into a narrow line, and his gaze slid to the bus. "I take it your friend doesn't know what you're offering."

Lyall had remained hidden behind the bus and shouldn't have been visible to the naked eye, but it was clear to Stephen the man in front of him wasn't relying on sight alone. Distracted or not, if Alan thought his beastmen would be able to sneak up on the Sorcerers, he had another thing coming. Once again, the thought made Stephen wonder if that truly had been the real plan or if there was a larger game being played out.

"Lyall," shouted Stephen. "Come out. I need to introduce you to . . ." He nodded his head at the other man. A rustle to his side told him Lyall was making his way out into the open.

"Name's Henry," the man answered. His eye's narrowed as he took in Lyall's appearance. "Your friend looks familiar."

"He's got one of those faces," said Stephen. "Don't you?" Stephen assumed Lyall's answering nod was enough, because Henry didn't press further. "Right," said Stephen. "As I was saying—"

"How did you stay alive out there so long, anyway?" Henry looked off into the horizon. "Personally, you couldn't pay me to spend another night out there. The stories I've been hearing ... beasts that move like people ..." He shuddered. His gaze returned to Stephen.

Stephen heard a rustling behind him, which had to be Lyall emerging from his hiding place. "Yeah, well it was touch and go a couple of times. This is Lyall."

Lyall came to a stop next to Stephen. "He wants to join us."

Henry's gaze swept Lyall from head to toe. "Don't take this the wrong way, kid," he said to Stephen, "but he doesn't look to me like the joining type."

Lyall's body relaxed, and a smile broke out across his face. "I'm sorry," he said, extending his arm. "I've been on my own for so long, I guess I just forgot how I am supposed to act around other people."

"That's close enough," said Henry. The easy-going greeting had the opposite of its intended effect, making Henry grow tenser.

Lyall picked up the change in mood in an instant. His face became less jovial, and his movements more cautious. Stephen made a mental note not to trust anything his companion said based on how easily he'd slipped into whatever character he was intending to play. Lyall held up a hand. "Sure. You're the boss."

The phrase worked on Henry like magic. He stood taller and puffed out his chest. "Wait here," he said. "I'm going to call this in."

"Is that really necessary?" asked Lyall. "I've heard that the people who live here now have all sorts of powers. Like, I've heard it said you can shoot laser beams out of your eyes and are strong enough to lift trucks as if they were toy cars. I know for a fact, a person like me doesn't have a chance against a single person with those abilities."

"Whoever you have been talking to has been reading too many comic books," said Henry.

"The rumors aren't true, then?"

Stephen opened his mouth to speak.

Henry answered before he could get the words in. "I'm not saying anything other than follow me."

Stephen scratched at his neck where the chain rubbed the skin under his collar, missing the ability to communicate telepathically. It was now clear he and Lyall were each working a plan B that neither of the other was party to.

The sun continued its ascent in the morning sky. Stephen realized as they wove their way through the city streets that his stomach hadn't complained all morning, though their breakfast had been nothing more than a piece of dried meat and a leftover biscuit from the dinner before. *At least that's something*, he thought. After traveling inward for several blocks, Henry raised his hand. "Wait there," he said, pointing toward a recessed former display window. His gaze took on the blank expression of a person accessing the datastream.

The pair sat down on the narrow slab of concrete while they waited. "How far is the barricade from here?" Lyall whispered, though Stephen was pretty sure they could speak at a normal volume and not break Henry's concentration.

"I don't know," whispered Stephen back. "I didn't come this way before."

Lyall frowned.

"I told you I was going to be a terrible guide," he whispered.

"They should have sent me alone. Would have been better for everyone," said Lyall.

"Maybe," said Stephen. "But they didn't. So, here we are."

Henry blinked and came over to them, silencing further conversation. "You're in luck," he said to Lyall. "Seems the boss is more interested in what you know than concerned about the real reason you are here. I'm to take you to him."

Stephen started to stand. Henry turned toward him. "Not you," he said.

Stephen's brow knit for a moment. "Oh, I get it. He wants to question us one on one," he said, wishing he and Lyall had spent the time at the window sill formulating a plan together rather than arguing. "No problem. I'll stay here."

Henry shook his head. "That's not it," he said. "I told him how you've been cut off. You're of no use to Finn. Not anymore." He lowered his voice. "You seem like a good kid. Head back wherever you came from. Before Finn gets here."

Alan wasn't going to be pleased by this turn of events, thought Stephen. *No, not one little bit.*

chapter twenty-one

JULIANE

Juliane woke with a start. While the windows blocked much of the light from outside, her body told her morning had come. She padded to the door and peered out through the keyhole. She jiggled the door handle, but the apartment remained as locked as it had been the evening before.

Juliane let go of the door. She could likely figure out how to bypass the lock, but she wasn't ready yet to show her hand. Instead, she moved into the kitchenette. A cup of coffee would go a long way.

She reached into a cabinet and pulled out a glass. The water from the tap ran crystal clear, tasting as good as it had the day before. However, outside of a handful of plates, the rest of the cabinets were bare. The only foodstuff in the apartment was the leftovers from her dinner the night before, which remained wrapped on the counter, exactly as she'd left them.

Juliane frowned. She was going to have to do something about them. He'd only agreed to let her cut their meal short when she'd offered to take them. Clearly, Damien wanted her to eat the food he'd provided, which meant she absolutely, positively did not want to do that. At the same time, the leftovers' presence would be another giveaway that she was still in control of her own brain.

She decided to break the problem into smaller, more manageable chunks. She peered into the sink. The kitchenette appeared to have a disposal unit, but that device would be connected to the grid powering the tower, and though the electrical surge would be small, it might be noted, depending on how closely the apartment was being monitored. Throwing it in the garbage would also be too obvious.

She carried the plate to the bathroom then tossed a small portion of the food into the toilet and performed a test flush. The food swirled around in the bowl, and for a second, Juliane wasn't sure it would go down, but eventually the bowl cleared.

Juliane took another handful of food off the plate and mashed it in her hands, attempting to soften it so it might go down the drain with less of a fight as she waited for the tank to refill. Her ears strained over the sound of the running water for any hint that someone may be coming to check on her. *This is taking too long,* she thought to herself, flushing the contents a second time.

She removed the lid from the tank as if she could will it to fill itself faster. She wrinkled her nose and dumped the rest of the dinner into its opening. It was a less than ideal solution and would likely cause plumbing issues she would have to deal with if she wasn't able to figure a way out of her current imprisonment, but it would have to do.

She'd just finished dropping the now-empty plate into the sink and washing her hands when the door to the apartment opened. "Is that housekeeping?" she asked, turning toward the door, infusing her voice with as much of a calm demeanor she could muster. "I'm afraid you'll need to come back later."

"Good, you're awake," said Damien letting himself inside. "I hope you are feeling better this morning."

"Much," she said drying her hands on a nearby dishtowel. "Thank you."

"I apologize if you tried to leave the apartment earlier," he said. "I'd locked the door."

"Locked?" Juliane raised an eyebrow, attempting to look like it hadn't even occurred to her to test the door.

"Yes, well some of the people who live here can be somewhat . . . eccentric. I thought it best if you didn't go wandering around last night. Just a temporary measure, I assure you."

"But I'm free to go where I please today, yes?"

He glanced at the sink, noting the empty plate. "I see you were able to finish your meal after all. Excellent."

She patted her stomach. "Nothing like steak for breakfast. Even cold. Thank you, it was delicious." She clenched her abdominal muscles. It wouldn't do for her stomach to growl at this moment.

"Ah, good, I'm glad you liked it. It took me ages to get the recipe right."

"So, other than experimenting with steak recipes, what *is* there to do around here during the day?"

Damien smiled and held out his hand.

Juliane drew back, realizing too late that she might have given herself away, but his gaze had gone blank. She moved toward the open and unlocked door without thinking. Her hand touched the knob. Damien's head swiveled towards her. He blinked, and his vision was clear once more.

Juliane smiled, fighting the disgust that threatened to come up like vomit. "Are you not taking me on a tour of your kingdom?" she asked. She'd run through a multitude of options during the night as to how to stop him, but thus far, the only solution she'd come up with was to kill him.

Unfortunately, he'd likely planned for the possibility of his death. After all, he'd brought about the end of civilization. He would have made sure his madness lived on through one of his pawns.

No, in order to take him down, she had to first sever his control over the rest. To do that, she needed to find a weakness, which meant spending more time with him.

Damien's expression relaxed. "Unfortunately, the tour will need to wait as it would seem my people need me, but don't you worry. I won't be gone long."

Juliane released the handle. She gazed into the apartment. Her nose wrinkled at the sight of the blackened window. "I'd like to go with you," she said. "I might even be able to help. You know I can't stand to let a problem go unsolved."

Damien chuckled. "True, but unfortunately, this isn't the sort of problem you have experience with."

She drew herself up. "That's never stopped me before," she said. She gestured at nothing in particular. "Please," she said, hating to sound like she begged. "Everything has been turned upside down since I woke up. This could give me something I can sink my teeth into."

Damien's smile slipped. "I don't . . ." he began. His vision dulled for a moment. "Well, that's an interesting development," he muttered to himself. He turned toward her. "Perhaps it *would* be better for you to come with me after all."

Juliane's eyes took a moment to become accustomed to the natural daylight after having gotten used to the inside of the tower. Shards of broken glass and twisted metal made the light seem even brighter from where she and Damien stood. The view would have looked less out of place in a landfill than in the former major thoroughfare.

A handful of people materialized out of the heap's nooks and crannies at Damien's appearance. A few cocked their heads as if being instructed by words Juliane couldn't hear before disappearing back into the city streets.

No, she thought, *that's exactly what was going on.* Juliane pressed her lips together. She'd hoped he could command only a single person at a time, but the scene before her suggested otherwise.

Two figures came into view. Juliane wrinkled her face trying to make out more detail. *Was that Lyall? Why was he here?*

"Is something the matter?" asked Damien.

"No," she said, shaking her head. "Nothing the matter. It's just I recognize the one on the right. I met him on the way here." Juliane curled her lip in disdain. "Dreadfully boring place," she added. "I can see why no one wants to stay there."

"Oh?" said Damien. His gaze went blank. The man escorting Lyall gestured for him to continue to follow him. Damien blinked. "In that case, why don't you come down and help me welcome him to the community. I am sure he's understandably nervous and would appreciate hearing from a friendly face."

"Well," said Juliane. "I don't know how much of a difference that will make. We only met in passing. He probably won't even recognize me."

Damien smiled. "You don't give yourself enough credit, Juliane. You're not the type of person who people forget easily."

His words brought up memories of being chased by the tabloids long after her relationship with Louis ended. However, if she'd been hard to forget back then, it wasn't because of what she'd done, but whom. "That's kind, but I disagree."

"Disagree all you want, but I am right," said Damien. "In fact, I'm rather counting on it."

"What do you mean?" she asked, but Damien had already started down a path cut into the wall of debris. Not seeing any alternative for escape that wouldn't put herself and Lyall into danger, she hurried after him.

"It's Lyall, correct?" said Damien reaching the bottom. "How nice to meet you. People here call me Finn." He extended his hand.

Lyall's mouth twitched. "Oh, I know who you are." Before anyone could react, Lyall pulled out a knife. "This is for Morgan." He plunged a knife into Damien's chest. He pulled the blade out and stabbed Damien again. "And this is for my mother. My father." He took a step back.

Damien looked down at the stain of red spreading across his shirt. He grasped the bloodied handle and clucked his tongue. "Well, that's a shame," he said, looking down. "This was my favorite shirt." He eased the weapon out of his flesh. It left large gashes in the fabric, making it easy to see Damien's skin knit together. Juliane expected Damien would be hard to stop, but she hadn't anticipated an ability like that.

Lyall sank to his knees. "Go ahead and kill me, then," he said. "I'm ready."

"Oh, I don't think you are," said Damien with a predatory grin. "Most find they aren't, when the time actually comes." His gaze slid toward Juliane. "However, consider yourself lucky. That time isn't now." Addressing Juliane, he said, "You said you met this boy on the road? Where was that, exactly?"

Juliane cocked her head and wrinkled her brow as if what she'd just witnessed was normal. "I'm not entirely sure," she said after a pause. If she could have shaken Lyall, she would have. Sam, Rebecca, the baby girl—they were all at risk if Damien believed their truce was over. "The suburbs all look the same to me. All I know is it was on the other side of the river." She shrugged. "I suppose I could have asked, but then the storm hit and, well, I had other problems to worry about."

"No? Well, that's unfortunate." He directed his attention to the young man on the ground. "Luckily, I'm fairly certain I know where this boy comes from. As well as how many people live there. A place called Woodspring," Damien grinned. "Am I right?"

"They had nothing to do with this," Lyall spat on the ground. "This was my idea, and my idea alone."

"Now that's a lie, and we both know it." Damien crouched down next to Lyall. "That said, I have every reason to believe my old friends haven't regrown their spines since the last time I had to teach them a lesson. More like worms now than Serpentine. No, if I were a betting man, and I am, I'd say Alan put the idea behind this little tantrum in your head."

Juliane wasn't surprised Alan had been released from the sleeping death. The ruin around her was just as much his fault as Damien's. The day she'd gone into the tank, they were allies. However, it would seem that even more had changed while she slept. Thankful once again for the upgrade that allowed her to command her features, she adjusted her expression until her face was in her usual resting position and devoid of emotion.

Lyall's forehead wrinkled. "I don't know who or what you are talking about."

"That may well be true, but unfortunately, I don't have any reason to believe you. At least not yet. But I will." Damien stood and nodded at the man who had escorted Lyall to the wall. The man nodded back before reaching down and grabbing Lyall by the arm. He hauled Lyall back upright. The boy twisted for a moment but then went limp. A brown-haired woman Juliane hadn't noticed before joined the first man, and together, they carried Lyall away.

"What are they going to do to him?" asked Juliane as the trio departed.

"Nothing for you to worry about, my dear. They're simply giving him a shower."

"A shower?"

"Yes, a shower. You must have gone nose blind after spending so much time on the road, but trust me, he stunk." He laughed. "The people who come to visit us. They go through so much effort to try to hide from us, but none of them ever bother to wash up before they arrive. We don't have to see them. We can smell them from miles away."

"And then?"

"You'd be surprised at how much more agreeable people are after experiencing hot running water."

Steam, Juliane realized. *That's how he's managed to take control.* A shower's mist and jets of water could hide nanobots, and be the perfect way to get a person to unknowingly inhale them. She recalled the muddy puddle next to her clothes. No wonder Damien hadn't pushed back on her request to clean up before their dinner appointment. She hadn't needed to worry about laced food. She'd already played right into his hands.

She immediately issued a command for her body to run an internal scan. If he had done the same to her, it hadn't taken effect—at least, she didn't think it had, but that wasn't to say there wasn't a time delay. She had to erect a firewall of some kind *now*.

Damien's mouth twitched. "Feeling okay?"

Beads of sweat formed on her forehead. "I'm fine," she lied. "It's just very hot up here."

"We'll go inside soon enough. Now, come with me," he said. "I've been told there is someone else here who you'd be interested in meeting."

"I think I would rather go back inside." She would be better off solving this problem in the virtual world, but that would leave her real physical body defenseless while she worked. She could be injected with any number of substances while she was distracted or worse.

"It will only take a moment," he said. "Then I'll leave you to whatever it is you feel you need to do."

One of Damien's other minions came closer. The threat of what they might do if she didn't obey couldn't be clearer.

"Fine," she said, infusing her voice with control, though she was anything but in charge at the moment.

He led her down a path cut through the barricade which she might never have found on her own and down a ladder. The streets, now empty, echoed with their footsteps as they made their way around the corner.

chapter twenty-two

STEPHEN

Stephen glanced up at the sound of approaching footsteps. Henry looked at him with regret. "You should've run when you had the chance."

Stephen's stomach turned. That didn't sound good. Lyall must have done something stupid. He touched the pendant. The virus running inside of him couldn't have replicated itself that many times during the night. He had to have at least a couple of minutes before the drain took over. Worst case, he could take Damien down with him.

Stephen's lips tightened. That was probably Alan's real plan after all. *I'm not bait.* He'd sent Stephen to take out his enemy and didn't care that he'd die in the process. *I'm a bomb.*

Damien rounded the corner. Unlike the other tower dwellers, he didn't hide his appearance. Nor did he make any effort to cover his chest where the fabric of his shirt was torn and bright red. A woman walked with him.

Stephen did a double-take. The woman walking toward him hadn't been at the tower the last time he'd been here. He would have remembered. His gaze returned to Damien. The raven-haired woman heading toward him might be gorgeous, but she was also no Bean.

"I don't believe I thanked you properly for locating the Wand," said Damien, coming to a stop in front of him. "Especially after how it was hidden from me." He glanced at his companion. "You might better know it as Camille's science project."

The woman's face creased in puzzlement. "What? Her anti-aging device?"

"Please, Juliane. This game you're playing—it was fun for a time—part of me wanted to see exactly how long you'd drag it out, but I've had enough. We both know you know exactly what I am talking about, as you were the one to keep it from me."

Juliane. Stephen took another look at the woman by Damien's side. The recording he'd seen in the datasphere hadn't done her justice. If anything, she looked younger now than she did in the recording—more alive.

Juliane's face paled, though she kept her chin up. "Then, that would make this boy—"

Damien grinned. "Alan and Betty's son, Stephen. Yes. See, I told you, you'd want to meet him." Damien glanced at Harry. A scowl replaced the grin. "I see what you mean," he said. He tilted his head. "Actually, it's not about what I see, but what I don't.

Damien turned to Juliane. "People who can access the datastream have a glow about them. An aura, as it were. It's how I can detect the gifted from the," he made a point of searching for a word, "not. I believe you were one of the first people to notice it."

"Some gift," muttered Stephen.

Juliane's eyes narrowed. "I didn't tell anyone about that."

Damien's teeth shone. "Maybe not in so many words, but I assure you, you did," he said. "You give away more than you think you do. For example, you were the one to give me a reason to visit your little factory. You also were the one who gave me the backdoor key into the power grid."

Juliane took another step back. "Those people hadn't done anything wrong."

"Except miss their production quota on a regular basis, I seem to recall you saying."

"You murdered them."

"No," he said. "I *had* them murdered. Completely different."

Henry moved as if to stop her. Damien raised a hand. "That won't be necessary," he said. "Dr. Faris here won't be going anywhere. I remembered how much she enjoyed analyzing patterns. I thought she'd enjoy piecing together how I gained control of the entire city on her own. But now that she has, she understands she has nowhere else to go." He turned his back on Stephen. "So, Doctor. Tell me, in your professional opinion, is the patient curable?"

"I'm not helping you hurt anyone else," she said.

"And I'm not suggesting you have a choice," said Damien. "Oh, don't be like that, Juliane. It's not like I enjoy taking away a person's will. I've found that a person loses a bit of spark whenever I do. Makes it harder and harder for them to come up with ideas on their own, but sometimes the greater good calls for a nudge."

Damien looked at Henry, whose face had taken on a look of puzzlement throughout the exchange. Henry's features went slack, and he turned and ran into the nearest wall without slowing. His head connected with a sick thud. Henry then stood and repeated the process. It reminded Stephen of a bird he'd once seen at the farmhouse who'd attacked the kitchen window over and over again after Nadia had left some seeds out on the counter.

Stephen wondered if he would be experiencing the same if either of the pair figured out how easy it would be to get him online again. He fought the urge to pull at the pendant. If he took it off now, he couldn't be sure that Damien would be his only victim.

"The greater good. You're still telling yourself that's what this is all about?" said Juliane, watching Henry with white knuckles. Stephen expected her to charge at Damien or rush to stop the other man before he could damage himself further, but instead, she looked to the sky.

"What else could it be?" asked Damien. "I would have thought you of all people would understand that our greatest growth as a species has always come following chaos and tragedy. The Roman Empire rose from the Middle ages. The Thirty Years' War gave birth to the ideas of the Enlightenment."

"Spare me the history lesson," she said. "My area of interest has always been the future, not the past."

"And this is your future, if you don't watch your step," said Damien, pointing at Henry. "Which would be a shame, not to mention so boring. A beautiful brain like yours . . ." he said, shaking his head. "I'd hate to spoil it, especially over such a small thing."

"And as I mentioned, I prefer," said Juliane. "to look up. You should, too, sometime. You never know what you might see."

A wave of an odor that reeked of death and excrement assailed Stephen's senses as darkness covered the sunlight, followed by a thunderclap. The odor grew stronger as a bird, larger than anything Stephen had ever seen, plunged down from beyond the skyscraper heights. A scream cut through the city streets. He wasn't sure if it came from the bird or if it came from him as his body was picked up by cruel-looking talons.

Then the ground beneath him receded, growing farther and farther away by the second. Wind rushed his cheeks as he struggled. They ascended higher and higher, until only the highest floors of the occasional tower surrounded him.

The bird screamed again—its call echoed by another. However, Stephen couldn't spot the other bird. Not that he was looking too closely. More of his attention was on the ground far beyond and the thought of how little the talons clutching his arms hurt compared to what he'd feel if the bird were to let go.

He allowed his body to go limp as the streets and skyscrapers stopped at the edge of the glimmering river.

Then they were on the other side. The bird holding him called out again to its friend or mate. *There are more of the bloody things.*

The air clapped around him like thunder. The ground beneath rose back up at an alarming rate. *Here goes,* he thought. *I'm going to die.*

Stephen's stomach flip-flopped as they plunged back toward the earth. His ears popped at the change of pressure. At this speed, the landing wasn't going to be gentle.

Just as Stephen resigned himself to becoming a flattened mash of entrails, the bird opened its wings. His body lurched as their descent slowed. The bird changed its course, and they were again over the river. Then the pain around his shoulders where the bird clutched him disappeared, and Stephen found himself free-falling as the river rose up to meet him.

He spread his arms and legs as if he could somehow force his body to glide to safety. However, all it did was expose more of his belly to the icy cold water as he crashed through its surface.

Stephen sank like a rock. He'd learned how to swim in a nearby creek, but that body of water had rarely been deep enough for him not to be able to touch the bottom if needed. This was a completely different experience; one made even more difficult by the fact that Stephen could no longer tell which way was up in the darkness.

A shimmer of light caught his eye. He turned his body toward it. *Please be up*, he thought. Pressure built in his lungs as his body called out for air. His muscles seized as his body's heat bled into the icy water.

The flash caught his eye again. It wasn't light, he realized, it was simply something white. His arms slowed. His kicks grew less determined. Out of all the ways he thought he would die today, being considered take-out by a monster bird and drowning hadn't been one of them. As panic took over, he laughed, releasing the remaining bubble of air from his lungs. His vision dimmed as the flash of white drew closer. Stephen's last thought before he lost consciousness was that he hoped whatever it was, it wasn't hungry.

chapter twenty-three

JULIANE

Damien glared at Juliane as a feather the size of a dog landed on the ground where his latest prisoner had knelt captive a moment ago. "I hope you are proud of yourself," said Damien. "However, explain to me how what you did to that creature is any different from what you find so distasteful about what I do." He gestured toward the other man, who now lay in a crumpled heap next to a bloodied wall.

"The suggestion I placed in that bird's brain is temporary, for one—and I only did it to save a life. You're killing people."

"People die every day." He glowered at her. "At least my way gives their deaths purpose. Besides, you say that as if saving a life is always the better choice. Take the boy, for example. You and I both know he should have died years ago. Instead, his life cost Betty hers. She should never have redirected her energy. All that talent. All that potential— wasted—and for what? A life that's proven to contribute nothing further to this world than act as another distraction."

Juliane's eyes narrowed. She clenched her fists. "I think we've talked long enough."

"Don't worry, you won't remember this conversation much longer." His gaze went slack. Juliane's gaze darted around, looking for something either blunt or sharp to strike him with if only to break his connection to the datastream. *No time*, she thought. She'd have to take the fight to the virtual world.

Juliane accessed the datasphere. Damien's data signature was easy enough to locate—so confident in his control, he hadn't bothered to shield it. She'd use that to her advantage.

She countered his command with one of her own, turning the signal into nothing more than a nonsensical series of ones and zeros. She readied herself for retaliation. He hadn't expected her to fight back this time. He wouldn't make the same mistake again. The scene in front of her was replaced with rolling hills of an unnatural green. Light poured in from all directions. "I won't make it easy for you," she said, leaping into the air and hovering there.

"You never have." The few small shadows pulled together, becoming more like a puddle than the absence of light. A shape arose from their depths, twisting and building upon itself until it resembled the figure of a man. "I understand why Alan was so obsessed with you." The figure shifted; however, it remained as dark as a shadow.

"Speaking of which, I truly did hope things would work out between the two of you organically. You were always a condition of our previous dealings together. It would have made things better for you in the next day or so, when I give you to him in exchange for the return of the Wand." He laughed. "Of course, that's also the reason I had to eliminate your other friend after I was satisfied you were on your way here. I know you've wondered. I wasn't sure how much you'd remember upon waking and needed someone you trusted to convince you to leave Worcester. But you weren't supposed to develop feelings for that fool. I guess I shouldn't have been surprised; you've never shown yourself to have any taste."

Juliane extended her arms and legs downward and grew until her feet touched the rolling hills. "Is this the part where you explain all your evil plans?" she asked with a smirk. "Because I feel I should remind you, I'm the one who invented this place. You're in my world now."

The man-shadow raised a hand and broke apart into a murder of crows, which flew into the air and darted about until they produced the shape of a face. "You may be its original creator, but I've been in control here far, far longer. I know all the tricks you do."

Juliane held her head like a queen. She flicked her wrist, and her body was once again her normal size. The sky darkened and filled with clouds. A single bolt of lightning arched across the heavens and struck at the mass of birds.

The face made up of birds dissolved as the flock converged into a single column of black. The column fell, striking the earth. The horizon shook, though Juliane remained where she stood. A crack appeared and made its way up the side of the column. More fissures appeared. Pieces of the column fell away as the crack raced higher and higher up its surface.

"Was that supposed to impress me?" Juliane crossed her arms over her chest and tapped her arm with a finger. Large sections of the column fell away, disappearing as they crumbed onto the grassy knoll, until only a man-shaped outline remained.

The stone figure rushed toward her like a freight train. Juliane held one hand out, summoning a gale-force wind.

The wind should have been enough to send Damien flying away, but his avatar dug his heels into the ground as stone turned to wood and roots wormed their way into the earth around him.

Movement out of the corner of Juliane's eyes was her only warning before a large root the size of a bus emerged on her left. It wrapped itself around her legs, then her chest, and squeezed. Her lungs became more difficult to fill as it wrapped tighter and tighter.

"Now who's the one who is being overly confident in their abilities?" said Damien with a smile. While his feet remained anchored into the ground, the rest of his body stretched and moved closer to her.

"I just wanted you closer," said Juliane, though the words weren't easy to say with the constricted oxygen flow. Her body became a white-hot flame.

Damien screamed and pulled his wooden tentacles away, but not before several were reduced to ash.

"Guess all those years of extra experience didn't give you quite the advantage you expected. Did they?" asked Juliane, returning to her normal form. She looked down at her dress and dusted away the remaining ash where it marked the fabric.

Damien snarled and charged at her. A cage of silver wrapped in a wire mesh materialized out of thin air, halting him in his tracks. "Hurts, doesn't it," she said. She took a deep breath and looked around the virtual landscape she'd created before focusing her gaze on Damien again. "It's also far less than you deserve."

"All you've done is piss me off," said Damien. He grabbed at the bars only to jolt back to the center of the cage. He scowled and clenched his fists. "Damn it." His eyes narrowed. "What have you done?"

Juliane's brow wrinkled. She hadn't designed the cage to do that.

"You have no idea how long I have been waiting for this moment," said a new male voice. A figure faded into existence where no one stood before. He was a young man with dark-rimmed glasses.

"Wes," Damien shouted from within the cage. "But how . . . that can't really be you. You're dead." Damien looked at Juliane with fear in his eyes. "He's dead. Who are you?"

The boy shrugged, but didn't look at his captive. He turned his attention to Juliane. "I do apologize for being late to the party, but you are one difficult woman to track. I mean, I knew you were somewhere around here, of course, but dividing your signal like that?" He kissed his fingers. "Well done."

"This doesn't concern you," said Juliane. The new arrival had to be part of Damien's back-up plan. Avatars could be made to look like anyone and anything a person pleased. She didn't trust that the real person looked anything like the man before her. In fact, she didn't trust anything about him, especially how young his voice sounded. It had to be a trick. One designed to make her lower her guard. Juliane took a closer look at the bars surrounding Damien. It was only a matter of time before Damien found a flaw in their design.

"He can't escape, if that's what you are worried about," said Wes. "While you were talking, I took what you'd created and made it better." He laughed. "Think of it as a Faraday cage. He can try to send commands to the datastream all he wants. He's not going anywhere." This time, the boy did spare a glance for Damien. "Now, tell me, how do *you* like being a prisoner in your own mind?"

"Overconfidence puts us both at risk," said Juliane. "A virtual cage won't hold him forever. What happens when you need to rest? It's simply a matter of time until he finds a way to break free."

"Oh, I don't need rest," said the boy. "In fact, I don't need anything. Not anymore." He glared at Damien. "You heard him. I'm dead. However, you have a point."

Damien began cursing. At first, Juliane thought the cage was simply getting smaller, but then she realized that the entire structure was sinking into the ground. Damien's curses became more frantic as the space between him and the top of his prison grew smaller.

Juliane pressed her lips together as she considered what would happen now that Damien was trapped in the datasphere. If the cage held, and that was a big if, his body in the real world would remain in a vegetative state. However, that would only solve the immediate problem.

He'd already laid the groundwork for worldwide dominance. There were bound to be people serving under him who hadn't needed that extra nudge from a computer program to join his way of thinking. If Sam hadn't suggested as much, Alan was all the proof she needed.

She looked at the glowing world that she'd once believed would serve as her legacy. It might be tomorrow or years from now, but it was only a matter of time before someone else decided to follow in his footsteps. And then what? Would the rest of her life be spent fighting Damien's followers and ensuring they never left their virtual prison? "It's the only option," she muttered to herself and started issuing commands.

At first, few of her efforts were noticeable to the naked eye. The air stilled completely, and not a blade of artificially constructed grass moved. The parts of the sky dimmed and faded away, exposing nothing but narrow bands of black as her new code wormed its way through the computer program she'd used to give this place life.

Damien's screams suddenly turned into hysterical laughter. She spared him a glance from the corner of her eye as she continued with her work. His body was sunk into the ground to his waist, leaving only his arms free, which were now pointing at the sky.

"What are you doing, Juliane," growled Wes.

"What I have to," said Juliane. She turned her attention back to her work. She couldn't afford to be distracted. Her original code had been a masterpiece. If she was going to destroy it, it deserved her full attention.

"I can't let you do that," said Wes.

"You don't understand," she said.

"No, you don't understand," said Wes. His voice was robotic.

Juliane's eyes widened as the things he'd said finally clicked together in her brain. "You're . . . you're not just an avatar. Are you?"

"I was once. Now, it's time for you to go." He held up a hand. Juliane flew backward as if she'd been struck by a wrecking ball. She was once again surrounded by towering skyscrapers.

"No. Not until I finish what I started," she said. She didn't need to see Wes to know he could still hear her. She clenched her fists and resumed her commands. The skyscrapers pixelated and jittered.

"Stop," Wes's voice boomed from all directions.

"I can't," said Juliane. Blocks of skyscrapers disappeared, exposing empty streets. "Not until I know for sure that history will never repeat."

"Then I have no choice."

Juliane had prepared herself to be struck by another blast of air by surrounding herself in an invisible shield. Instead, the entire cityscape disappeared, and Juliane found herself in a bubble floating in a river of starlight. Her bubble picked up speed until the bits of stars were nothing more than streaks of light, and for the first time, she realized that though she had created the digital world, she may no longer be its master.

chapter twenty-four

STEPHEN

Stephen floated in darkness until his body came to rest on a grassy shore. He gingerly rose to his knees, coughing up water from his lungs. A forest surrounded him. He blinked as he stumbled over rocks before straightening the rest of the way. He knew these woods, but they were miles away. A thick rope swing hung from one of the branches. He knew that rope, too.

He'd found it attached to one of the trees when he was a kid—a remnant of the family who'd once called the farm home. Whoever they'd been, they'd never returned, but somehow, he had. He continued through the woods until the tree line broke. There, exactly where he thought it would be, stood the farmhouse. He looked back over his shoulder at the woods. The bird was fast, he gave it that, but how had he gotten all the way back here?

He picked his way up the grassy path. The windmill turned in a breeze just strong enough to be comforting. *That's not right*, he thought. The last time he'd seen it, it was broken. Stephen held his breath. Was he back in the digital world, or had he died?

He reached up to touch the pendant but found only his chest. The protection against the drain was gone. So, *I'm dead*, he decided.

He grinned. The idea of being dead didn't bother him nearly as much as he thought it would. He raced up the remainder of the path and threw open the front door.

Stephen expected to find Nadia there ready to welcome him home. Instead, the room on the other side was dark and lifeless.

She's probably out working in the garden. It would be just like Nadia to still feel the need to do chores even in the afterlife.

The door slammed against its frame behind him as he made his way back outside. He cupped his hands around his mouth and shouted her name but received no reply. He scanned the horizon for any sign of where she might have gone.

Stephen looked at the barn. If he'd learned anything growing up, there was no surer way of summoning his mother than trying to goof off when she thought there was work to be done.

He opened the barn door and made his way over to his regular hiding place. *That's strange*, he thought, pulling at a floorboard. The board usually took very little effort to move. *Had Chad finally got around to fixing it?* Stephen wrinkled his brow. *What am I thinking? This is heaven.* He focused his thoughts and pulled at the board again. This time, the plank came away freely in his hand, revealing the old computer terminal he'd rebuilt from scratch.

He picked up the computer and pressed the button with the circle on it. The screen flickered and flashed as the operating system went through its standard power-up routine. Stephen sat back while he waited. The sequence could take a while to complete and often required him to reboot the system more than once. However, this proved not to be one of those times, as the familiar welcome screen was quickly replaced by a series of icons.

He didn't hesitate to click on one of the icons near the top of the screen. The display changed once more, showing the title cards for his favorite game with two buttons underneath. Single-Player or Multi-Player.

Stephen grinned, and he toggled the second option. With any luck, Wes was here, too. He pressed the enter key. The display flickered. Then the world around him went black, including the screen in front of him. Even the yellow LED indicator denoting the computer had power had gone off.

Shit, he thought. *So much for things working in the great beyond.* He stood and made his way back to where the barn door should be, if only to open it so that some natural light might shine its way in.

He found himself back in the farmhouse kitchen; only this time, he wasn't alone. The person he'd sought for the last several days sat the table. Considering how long it had taken to find her, Stephen felt he should have been more excited to see her. Instead, his shoulders slumped. The giant birds must have taken her, too. Was her body now being ripped and torn to feed some monstrous hatchlings or resting at the bottom of the river like his was? Another possibility occurred to him. "I'm not in heaven after all, am I?"

Juliane's eyebrows twitched. "No. This most certainly isn't heaven."

Stephen turned toward the door. "Yeah, well . . . If I'm not dead, I will be soon enough." He reached for the door, but the door refused to budge. "Why won't this thing open?"

Juliane smiled. "Exactly the question I was wondering as well."

If this isn't heaven then— "Wes," shouted Stephen. "I need you." His eyes narrowed. The big red button Wes created for him materialized at Stephen's command. He pushed it repeatedly. "Work, damnit," he muttered.

Wes appeared, but he was a faded version of himself, more ghost than digital construct. He looked forward with dull eyes, focusing on nothing in particular. "I'm sorry," he said. "I know I said that all you had to do if you ever needed to talk was push that button, but things have changed, er . . . I've changed." His lips tightened. "Or, I will have if you're listening to this message. Unfortunately, this also means you're going to need to find a new teammate to run missions with from now on."

Stephen stared at the recorded image without blinking. "What have you done?"

"He's taken over the datasphere," said Juliane, gesturing at their surroundings. "I still haven't figured out how, but as soon as I do, I'll take it back and get us out of here."

"No," said Stephen with a laugh. "Don't you get it? It's worse than that. He didn't take over the datasphere, he *is* the datasphere now."

Juliane frowned and shook her head at the idea. "That's impossible. The digital world is simply a bridge. Think of it as a mesh that connects individual nodes. No one individual can take it over, at least not completely. Trust me. I know more than a few things about it." Her cheek twitched. "The only way a person could take it over completely would be for him or her to somehow sever their anchor to the real world."

"Not a problem for Wes. He doesn't have a physical body to return to. Died days ago." Stephen made a popping gesture on either side of his head. "Yeah, I know, but before he died, Wes found a way to upload this version of himself."

"An artificial intelligence," Juliane's forehead wrinkled. "Made to think and act like a teenaged boy." She sighed. "I suppose that explains how he's managed to keep me here against my will."

She stood and walked to the kitchen window and tapped her finger on the sill. "From a purely objective standpoint, his code is brilliant in its design. Every time I think I've found a way out, the code shifts." She turned back to Stephen. "Simply brilliant. However, AI or no AI, no code is perfect. I'll find us a way out of here. Unfortunately, though, if I can, Damien might, too." She began to pace the room. "Then again, Damien's not a programmer."

"But you are." He stepped toward her. "About that. You see—"

"He's here, too. Damien, I mean." Juliane waved Stephen's attempt to explain the virus away. "In another part of the datasphere. Trapped in a cage. Ugh, I'm getting sidetracked. I need to think." She turned and walked back toward the window.

"As I was saying, he's not a programmer. At least, not a natural-born one, so there is a chance it'll take a while for him to find the flaw, but he will." She tapped her lip as she spoke. She looked at Stephen. "And next time, he's not going to let either of us live."

"I wouldn't be so sure," said Stephen. "Take this place, for example. We seem pretty stuck here. Maybe this cage will hold him longer than you think it will."

"Are you willing to bet your life on it?" Juliane asked. "Because I'm not." Her eyes bore into Stephen's with an intensity that demanded obedience. "You need to tell me everything about your AI friend. If I can better understand how he thinks, I might be able to figure out how to get us out of here *before* Damien does. How did you meet? What were you into?"

Stephen pressed his lips together and walked over to where Juliane stood. He pointed out of the window. "You see that barn?" he said. "In the real world, I have a computer hidden in the floorboards, which is how I used to play *Colony Defenders II*, before I knew I had any of this," he gestured at the surroundings, "in my head. Wes used to play it, too. But speaking of things in my head—"

Juliane pursed her lips. "So, we go to the barn."

"Yeah, except I was just there, and all the good it did was to put me in here. Unless . . ."

"Unless what?"

"Unless we're already in the game." He glanced around the room. "Which would mean," he said to himself. "We're in a waiting room."

"Is that supposed to mean something?"

He laughed. "Dude, when I find my way out of here, we're going to need to have a talk." He looked at Juliane, whose face was puzzled. "In the game, before you go on a mission, you first materialize in a waiting room. It's a safe zone. Gives newbies a place to familiarize themselves with the rules without having to worry about any of the bad guys finding them or time limits."

Juliane gestured for him to continue.

"If I am right, and Wes sent us to a waiting room, then all we have to do is find the portal."

"Can't we just leave the game?" asked Juliane.

Stephen pursed his lips. "Do you see a big flashing exit button anywhere? The only way I know how to do that is to turn the computer off altogether, and that's not an option."

"Fine. What does a portal look like?"

"A glowing red rectangle." Stephen frowned, looking back at the barn through the window. They had to be in a waiting room. Stephen didn't have any other ideas if they weren't. "While we're waiting, though—"

"Found it," said Juliane from the hallway.

He hadn't noticed her moving. He found her in front of Chad and Nadia's bedroom door. Relief washed over him. Sure enough, the doorway was framed by an unnatural soft red glow.

"I take it we go through here."

Stephen took a step. Then paused.

"What's wrong."

"Something else just occurred to me."

"I'm sure whatever it is, it can wait."

"I'm not hungry."

"Good for you. Let's go."

"You don't understand. I'm always hungry."

"That's fairly typical for a boy of your age."

"What if I'm like him?"

"Like who?"

"Wes," said Stephen.

Juliane cocked her head. "You seemed well enough when I saw you."

"Yeah. Well, something happened to me," he said. "Before you found me. I've got a virus." He looked at his hands. "Or maybe it's, I had a virus. That's what I was trying to tell you. I was hoping you'd—" He took a step back from the door. "Wes," he shouted. "Tell me you didn't upload some version of me."

Juliane's eyes narrowed. "Deal with your identity crisis later. Now, are you coming or not?" The portal pulsated. Stephen remained where he was. Juliane shook her head.

"This is why I've never wanted children," she muttered. She looked Stephen in the eye. "You're still alive," she said.

"How would you know?"

"I know because I can sense you. Out there." She gestured at the horizon. "I didn't recognize the connection for what it was until I saw you kneeling on the ground, but it would seem your mother found a way to link us together shortly before she died."

Stephen blinked. "Come again? My mother? Linked you and me?" he asked. "She wouldn't know the first thing—" He frowned. "Oh, you mean Betty, my birth mother." Did that mean, all this time on the road, all he had to do was reach out with his mind? He groaned, thinking of how Alan had intruded upon his dreams and seemed to be able to sense where he was. Could he have done that with Juliane all this time? He could have asked, no, *demanded*, she start working on a cure days ago. *Which meant*, His eyes widened. *Bean*. He hadn't needed to break her heart or take Alan's offer. "Why?" He sputtered. Why couldn't Betty have just told him that instead of being all cryptic?

Juliane frowned. "She thought you were dying. I thought she was in the midst of a breakdown or at least a month's good sleep." Juliane shook her head. "But before that, she'd developed a revolutionary energy collection and inductive transfer protocol. I'd seen it as a way to break away from the traditional power grid. I thought it had the potential to even stop world hunger, if applied correctly; much like how a plant requires only the sun for nourishment." She wrinkled her nose. "I can see I'm losing you, so let me put it in more basic terms. Betty Dronigh essentially turned herself into a backup battery."

The ramification of her words hit him like a fist. "I killed her."

"What?" Juliane blinked. "No."

"No? I'm the reason she died. I sucked out her energy. You just said so." He tried not to imagine what Betty looked like after he'd finished with her. Had she, like the old man in the woods, been left a wizened husk with not enough meat left on her bones to feed ants or other scavengers?

"No, I said she saved your life and then passed that link on to me."

"Which killed her," said Stephen with a nod. His stomach turned. He was responsible for the death of not one, but both of his mothers.

"She died, but your mother was the one to make the choice." Juliane stretched out an arm and held it above Stephen's shoulder. She bit her lip and pulled it back. "You can't blame yourself."

"But I do."

She shook her head. "And that helps you how?" Juliane pointed at the glowing frame. "We're wasting time."

Stephen's eyes widened. "You're the reason the drain hasn't killed me yet," he said. "That's the reason she wanted me to find you. Like the tower and why I'm not hungry there. I had to find you. In the physical world. Not just here. It must only work if we're close together."

Juliane's head tilted. "You aren't making sense again." She passed a hand through the glowing door frame. Nothing happened.

"The drain. It's what Damien's people call it when you stray too far from the Sorcerers' complex. Basically, unless you are constantly eating or close to a power source," Stephen fought a shudder, "you die. The people there think it's a side effect of their abilities, but it's not. Well, I suppose it is. I mean, you said my mom fed me energy—so I had to already be affected before I ever met Damien, but the virus makes it a million times worse. It's how he keeps people under his control."

"Hmm," answered Juliane testing the doorway again. "Yes, I'd concluded he was behind Gene Assist's modification and doing something like that." She glanced over her shoulder back at him. "Now, a question for you. What would happen if a player in this game of yours never exited the waiting room?"

Stephen blinked. "Nothing. Nothing happens until everyone has crossed."

"That's what I thought. Therefore, I would appreciate it if you would stop dwelling on the past and help me change the future. You were planning on asking me to help you find a way around the drain. Yes? I intend to fix that—fix everything, and not just for you, but for everyone. Unfortunately, I can't do anything while trapped in here." She took a breath and looked into his eyes. "Trust me."

The doorway pulsed again. He looked over at his shoulder back to the kitchen area and the table where Chad was constantly rearranging piles of junk. He sighed. "You'll want to arm up before we go," he said. He looked at his hand and a knife appeared.

Juliane's lip curled. "I don't think that is necessary."

The corner of his mouth curved up. "Now it's your turn to trust me. I've played this game before." He looked at the doorway and took a breath. He stepped through the open doorway.

chapter twenty-five

JULIANE

The room transformed the minute they crossed under the glowing frame, replacing the small rustic bedroom with a desert. A foreign moon hung in the sky. Large jagged rocks poked up in every direction, blocking her view. "Now what?" she asked Stephen. Her voice sounded strange, like it was being transferred over an intercom or a walkie talkie.

"Keep your eyes peeled," he said.

She noted that his appearance had changed along with the landscape. The young man who'd seemed so boyish in the farmhouse kitchen was now at least six inches taller with muscles no amount of natural workout could ever produce. His face was also covered by a visor and mask. She raised her hand only to realize it was larger as well and man-shaped. *Lovely*, she thought. "So, what are we supposed to do in this game?"

Static freckled Stephen's laugh. "We make it to the other side."

"That's it?" said Juliane, looking out across the desert. "Not really much of a challenge then, is it?"

"Oh, it's about to get more interesting." He nodded. "Heads up. Three o'clock. We've got company."

Juliane looked in the direction he'd suggested, but all she saw was the side of her visor. She cursed. "I can't see anything with this thing on." She reached up to her visor to pull the mask off.

"Because we are on an alien planet surrounded by a poisonous atmosphere. And before you ask, I know this because I've had more than one helmet crack playing this game. Watch out!" he shouted.

A dark creature leapt out from behind one of the rocky outcroppings. It had four arms, a large, fanged maw of a face, and moved like a spider. "What do I do?" asked Juliane.

"What do you think? You kill it before it kills you." Stephen demonstrated by running up and slashing at the creature with his knife. The creature vanished with a scream. "Haven't you ever played a video game before?"

Juliane drew herself up. "I had rather more important things to do with my time," she said. "Like finding the money to pay for my next meal," she muttered. "And creating an entire online world."

He picked up a boulder and tossed it. The rock broke apart upon impact, revealing a floating round object which Stephen grabbed and pocketed.

"Was that a hand grenade?"

"Yup. In addition to killing the bad guys, you are going to want to throw stuff around, too. The stuff underneath usually comes in handy later."

"But . . . but that is so . . . so . . . pointless."

Stephen shrugged. "You're going to want to move before the creature respawns . . . er . . . comes back to life." He jogged up ahead and slashed at another alien Juliane hadn't even seen approach.

Another four-armed shape appeared up ahead. *This is ridiculous*, thought Juliane. She marched up to a rock and picked it up with ease, though it was at least two if not three times larger than the size her head, and threw it at the beast. Both the rock and the alien disappeared upon impact. A beaker filled with a red substance hovered above the ground where the alien once stood.

"Nice," said Stephen, gesturing at the bottle. "You'll want to hold on to that. With as little experience you have, the elixir of life is bound to come in handy before too long."

Juliane grabbed the bottle and gently shook it in her hand, noting that the contents remained in the exact same position as the beaker moved rather than acting like a normal liquid would. "And how am I supposed to drink this stuff? According to you, I can't remove my helmet."

"Damned if I know," said Stephen with a laugh. "I've only ever had to hit the space bar and *P* at the same time back in the real world. No idea how it would work here."

Juliane wrinkled her nose. "Guess we better hope I don't need it, then."

"Guess so. Now, I thought you were in a rush to get out of here. Keep moving."

"This friend of yours, Wes, and I are going to have a discussion about programming realism one day."

A pack of three creatures appeared, and Juliane put the annoyance about the game's flaws to the side while she worked on clearing a path. More aliens appeared, except these were a lighter gray and moved more like caterpillars than spiders. They were also significantly bigger. At first, they seemed to amble along slowly enough that Juliane thought they might be able to avoid them simply by jumping up on one of the rocks, but as soon as either of them got within a yard of the beast, it would lower its head and charge at them with a murderous rage.

Juliane picked up a small boulder and hurled it toward the animal. "Couldn't they have bothered to at least try to follow natural laws? No real animal would behave like this." The creature shuddered upon impact, but only the rock disappeared.

"Take your complaints up with the game designers. Now, you have to hit it again, while it is still frozen," shouted Stephen.

"Like this?" She closed her eyes and jabbed at the creature with her knife. The motion shouldn't have done more than scratch the animal's skin, but it popped like a balloon landing on a blade of grass.

"See, that wasn't so hard."

The way before them was empty. Rather than waste words on further discussion about poor design or unrealistic experiences, Juliane ran forward. The ground gave way underneath her feet, and she found herself falling into a dark chasm.

chapter twenty-six

STEPHEN

Stephen looked down into the large square sinkhole, but it was too dark to see where Juliane had landed. "You alive down there?" he shouted into the pit. There was no answer. "Shit," he said. Grabbing the edge of the pit as an anchor, he felt around on the side of the hole for any purchase that he could leverage to get to its bottom safely.

His foot found a narrow outcropping. Though the pit seemed to prevent light from penetrating its depths in any direction, the ledge felt too much like a man-made ladder for Stephen to think it was there for any other reason but intentional design. He snorted at the thought of what Juliane might say when she realized how he'd made it down and risked taking another step.

As absolute darkness covered his eyes, Stephen stifled the urge to laugh. Who would have thought that the same world that had caused Juliane such annoyance for its lack of reality would have reminded him what it felt like to be alive? An image of Nadia and Chad crossed his mind, but neither wore the cold accusing expression he'd become use to seeing on their faces when he closed his eyes.

Instead, Chad was stacking components on the kitchen table while Nadia prepared dinner. Then Bean appeared. Smiling at him. Kissing him. Telling him she loved him—and definitely not getting the life sucked out of her with his touch.

Suddenly, Stephen realized he was as ready to get back to the real world as Juliane was. He picked up his descent.

After what felt like an age, but was likely only a minute, Stephen's feet found hard ground. A glowing orb bloomed into existence the second both of his feet were on the ground, illuminating about three feet in front of him in whatever direction he looked, but little more.

The orb followed him, hovering just over his head as he scanned the pit for evidence of Juliane. He expected to see her unconscious body, but instead all he found was a translucent crate that pulsated in the same way the portal into this world had.

He walked over to it and crouched down. "You in there, Juliane?"

"Apparently," came her muffled reply. Her voice was filled with static and was as light as if she were miles upon miles away. "I'm stuck."

"It's actually worse than that. You lost a life."

"How many do I have left?"

"None, really. You're only still in the game because I am here."

"So, what do I have to do to . . . to come back to life?"

"The term is respawn. And you can't do anything. When you lost your life, you also dropped your inventory, which means—"

"Which means what?"

"Hold on, I'm looking for it," said Stephen swiveling his head so that the light would shine in a larger radius. "Got it." He picked up the beaker containing the elixir of life from where it had come to a rest near the crate. "Okay, now, I am going to have to smash that crate. I don't *think* it will hurt, with you being technically dead already, but just in case, you may want to brace yourself."

He performed a double hop that defied all laws of physics in the real world. He curled his body into a ball at the peak of its height, then straightened like a board. The sequence sent him hurtling back toward the ground like a meteor, exploding the crate upon contact. In its place lay the supine, ghostly form of his mission teammate.

He then threw the beaker of elixir at her. The beaker froze in mid-air above Juliane and flashed three times. With each flash, Juliane's body became more solid, while the reverse was true for the beaker, until only Juliane remained.

"How did it feel?" asked Stephen. "To be dead?"

Juliane tilted her head as she thought through his question. "Not that much different from being in stasis," she said after a long pause. She looked up toward the surface level. "What would have happened if you hadn't come down here after me?"

Stephen shrugged. "I don't know. Neither Wes or I ever left the other guy behind."

"But what if I hadn't been carrying the elixir?" she asked, turning her gaze back on him.

Stephen shrugged again. "Then, unless one of us could find it lying around nearby, I would have considered the mission a failure for both of us."

Juliane's voice took on the heavy tones of regret. "I can see now why this game was so appealing for you. It must have been so nice for you, knowing people who were willing to sacrifice everything for you instead of the other way around. Perhaps I should have played it, too, when I was your age."

Not knowing how to respond to a comment like that, Stephen instead gestured behind him. "There's a ladder back there. We should get back to the surface."

"What's the premise of this game, anyway? You never explained it."

"Oh, right. See, there is this science team—"

Juliane shook her head. "Never mind, I've decided I don't care. Just let me know when we've won."

"Right. Heads up, then. The welcoming committee will be ready to greet us when we get back to the top. Probably swarming the place by now, actually."

She grabbed his shoulder before he could ascend. "What if we didn't go back to the surface?"

"Got a better idea?" he asked.

"Well, in my experience, you don't go to the trouble of programming something if it doesn't serve a purpose, which means this hole didn't just appear by accident. What if there is another way to get to . . . wherever it is we're supposed to go from down here?"

Stephen pursed his lips. "You know, you might be right."

A cone of light appeared over Juliane's head as she split away from him. Together, they searched for any sign that there was another way out other than the ladder which had first brought him down here. Stephen was just about to give up when he noticed a large crack in the rock wall. *Might as well give it a try*, he thought, pulling the grenade out of his inventory. "Fire in the hole," he shouted, pulling the pin and tossing the explosive at the wall.

"What did you say?" shouted Juliane from the other side of the pit.

"Duck," he yelled.

The blast from the grenade wasn't strong enough to send him reeling backward, but the flash did blind him for several moments. However, when his sight returned, he could see there was a large hole in the wall directly in front of him. "Looks like you were right," he said. "We may have another way in."

The cone of light overhead vanished as he stepped through the opening. The other side of the rock wall proved to be a building's hallway with emergency lights that turned on with his arrival.

Juliane's avatar appeared next to him, once again as a beautiful woman and not a space-suit clad super-soldier. He looked at his arm and saw that he, too, no longer had the uniform or the digitally enhanced muscles. He glanced back where they had come through. From this side, the entrance to the pit appeared to be a rectangular doorway, though it lacked the glowing frame that would tell him it was an official portal.

The hallway itself contained stark decoration. There was no evidence of any interior. No paint, no distinctive flooring tile. "Odd," said Juliane. She turned and opened the door on her right, revealing a stairwell.

She hesitated. Stephen walked around her and had already climbed half a flight of stairs, before he noticed she was no longer following. "Aren't you coming?"

"I need to go down."

"But we're already underground," said Stephen gesturing back where they'd come from.

"No," Juliane shook her head. "We're on the fourth floor."

"Did you see a sign or something?" asked Stephen, returning to the landing.

"I know because I've been here before."

Stephen pursed his lips.

"Don't."

"Don't what?"

"You're willing to believe I recognize this place but want to prove it to yourself. Therefore, you're getting ready to issue a command to try to alter the appearance of this place, thus confirming we have left the game and are back in the regular datasphere."

Stephen's cheeks heated, and his eyes widened.

"How did you know that?"

"Experience." She waved the comment away. "I'll also save you from asking your next question. The reason I'm asking you not to issue a command, at least not with me standing right next to you, is because this AI you call Wes has deemed me a threat and would not appreciate knowing I've returned from where it exiled me."

"He, not it."

"It's not a person. It might look, talk, and act like one, but you need to recognize it isn't."

"So, if you're so worried about what *he* might do, why are you still here, then?" asked Stephen. "Would it be easier to . . . you know," he shrugged. "Leave the datasphere and never come back?"

"Easier, yes. Safer, likely too, but unfortunately, not something I can do."

"Why not?"

"Because it is the only way for me to finish what I started." She moved away from him and started her descent.

"I'm coming with you," said Stephen.

She looked over her shoulder at him with puzzlement on her face. "That's not necessary. You did your part. I'm perfectly capable of doing what's required next on my own."

"Except you just said you pissed Wes off somehow the last time you were here. To me, that sounds like you could use some backup."

Her lips narrowed, and she looked like she was about to argue with him further, but instead gave him a curt nod. "Fine, but if you come with me, I am going to need you to follow my orders explicitly. If either of us hesitates for a second, it will be game over, and I don't mean the kind of game we just came from. If I tell you to leave, you go. Right away. No questions asked."

Stephen couldn't decide if Bean would admire this woman or hate her. He suspected it was some combination of both.

chapter twenty-seven

JULIANE

The air cooled as they descended further into the depths of the building. It was the sort of attention to realistic detail the programmers of the *Colony Defenders* game let slip. At the base of each flight, next to the exit door, was a small plate embedded in the wall. Stopping at the one leading to the first floor, she frowned.

"What's wrong?" asked Stephen, coming to her side.

"It's a biometric lock," said Juliane, pointing at the plate. "Which wouldn't normally be an issue for me to bypass in this place, however . . ."

"Wes will know you're here," filled in Stephen. He tilted his head and examined the plate.

Juliane's lips twisted at her companion's stubborn continued use of the pronoun. "Yes. That." Crossing her arms, she took a step back. *Perhaps if I can find a small rock or something similar lying around here, I might be able to take the door off its hinges? No, that would trip the alarm.*

"Lucky you let me come along with you, then," Stephen said. "Wes still likes me." Stephen placed a finger on the edge of the plate and flicked it off the wall as easily as someone might remove a scab. "He'll appreciate knowing I'm still alive."

A trio of lighting fixtures responded with the opening of the door, spreading out a cool white light along the length of the hallway on the other side. Juliane passed two more doors and pointed to the third. "You'll need to take care of this one the same way you did back there," she said, gesturing at another biometric lock plate.

"Done. Now what?"

"Now," she said, entering a room she'd never expected to see again. "You act as a lookout." She smiled as she took in the appearance of the emulator pillars. They were as straight and true as the day she and Chad first assembled them, even if their coloring was somewhat oxidized since then. She caressed the surface of one of the pillars before walking to a computer terminal.

"Does that thing still work?" asked Stephen.

"I can't think why it wouldn't," said Juliane, pressing the power button.

"But won't it give away our location?"

"Most likely," she said, "But my hope is that I can use this to mask some of my commands, so what I am doing looks like it is coming from another user and not from me." The LEDs on the emulator pillars toggled on and off. "After all, you and Wes can't be the only ones online."

You'd be surprised. "What is that, anyway?" asked Stephen.

Juliane glanced up from the computer screen long enough to see he was gesturing at the emulator. "An old project of mine," she said. "It's the prototype for the entire datasphere. Now, I need to concentrate."

Her fingers flew across the keyboard as she typed in command after command. She wrinkled her nose. She'd forgotten how much time it took to enter code manually. She frowned, deleting, hitting the backspace key to add in a piece of missing punctuation. *Inefficient, too.* Then she hit enter.

Nothing happened. She hit enter again. She looked up at Stephen. Her eyes widened. "Go. Now."

"I told you back in *Colony Defenders*," he gestured toward the door, "I don't leave teammates behind."

"This is no game, and that wasn't a request."

The center of the room twisted and warped as a shadow emerged from its center. "Very sneaky of you, Juliane," said the figure. "It might have worked, too, if the computer you are typing on was real, but you had to have known I would have detected what you were doing the minute you started."

"I did," said Juliane, "But I was hoping you were still distracted." As far as she could tell, he hadn't noticed Stephen in the room with her. She fought the urge to verify for herself that he'd managed to squirrel himself away, and instead looked over the figure's shoulder.

"I see you didn't bring our mutual acquaintance with you," she said. "Are you bored playing with him already? Or did he manage to find a way to free himself from one of your prisons, too?"

The figure had remained in shadow form, so it didn't have a face, but if it had, Juliane knew it would be frowning. "He's not in any prison, but he won't be causing problems for anyone ever again. He can't. I assimilated him. As I have said before, what you are trying to do is unnecessary."

"I wish I could believe that. I do, but programs always have flaws. If he's a part of you now, what's to stop his personality from taking over?"

"I'm so much more than a program."

"Wes? Dude, is that you?" Stephen stepped out from behind one of the pillars. "You sound . . . er . . . don't take this the wrong way, but you sound sort of freaky."

Juliane didn't bother trying to stifle the curse that sprang to her lips.

The shadow fractured, and large sections like chips fell away, revealing the young man she'd seen before. A large grin spread across his face as he took an involuntary step toward Stephen, but then drew back. The grin vanished. "You're not Stephen," it said. Its eyes narrowed. "Who are you?"

"No, really, it's me."

"No, you aren't. I know Stephen's signature as well, if not better, than hers," it said gesturing at Juliane. "Yours is different." It was a subtle change, but Juliane couldn't help noticing that the AI grew several inches. "So, I'll ask again. Who are you, really?"

"Think about it," said Stephen, tilting his head to the side. "If I could be anyone in the world, why would I pick me? Seriously, who would ever want to pretend that?"

The avatar's eyes narrowed. "Your father."

"Chad?" Stephen blinked. "He couldn't. He never had the upgrade."

"I am not in a joking mood. We both know I meant real father."

Stephen puffed his chest out. "Chad is my *real* father."

Juliane's nose wrinkled. She wouldn't have wanted to be Alan's child, either, though it might have been better than growing up with hers, but now was not the time to get into a debate on nurture versus nature.

She decided to take advantage of their conversation instead. The intelligence might have been able to detect her programming signature, but her strategy of using the computer terminal as a go-between had proven to buy her valuable seconds.

She placed a finger on the enter key. She looked at the blinking pillars. Once she pressed this key, her legacy—all her accomplishments—would be nothing more than a footnote in history. Even worse, thanks to civilization crumbling, she couldn't even count on that history being recorded in a book. It would be as if she'd never existed at all. *Can I really destroy this world?*

She looked back at the entity arguing with Stephen. It was the most advanced piece of code she'd ever seen. True artificial intelligence—but like she'd told Stephen, the program wasn't human. It would never understand why it had to be this way. Only a human, a real human, would be able to outsmart another human determined to exploit her creation.

She lowered her hand. *Unless.*

"Assimilate me, too," she said. Two sets of eyes swiveled her way.

"Come again?" said the AI.

"I said, assimilate me. Like you did Damien."

"You don't know what you are asking," said the AI.

Juliane smiled. "Oh, I do. More so than I believe you did back when you were still creating this . . . this thing. It's the only way I'll ever be able to trust history won't repeat."

"You truly believe I can't protect this place?"

"Don't take it personally. You're a masterpiece, but even the Mona Lisa needs a little touch-up work now and then."

The AI frowned.

"Someone want to explain?" asked Stephen.

"I'm offering to merge my consciousness with it . . . him," said Juliane.

"Um . . . that sounds rather . . . um . . . permanent," said Stephen. "What will that do to the rest of you? I mean the real you?"

"I imagine my body will appear to be catatonic, but it's spent the last fifteen years that way." Juliane pressed her lips together. "I don't suspect many people will notice."

"You'll die," said Stephen.

"Eventually, my body will, yes, but that happens to us all. At least this way, a piece of me will live on. Besides, it's better for you this way, too. Considering Damien's in there already," she said, pointing at Wes. "I'll . . . we'll have access to the virus's source code. You'll never have to worry about the drain again." She turned to Wes. "I'm ready. Do it."

Wes nodded.

Then the very ground she stood on rose up and pierced her feet. Juliane hissed. The AI raised an eyebrow as if to say, there is still time to change your mind. Juliane stared back, refusing to back down. The skin around her ankles began to itch as if she'd been attacked by a swarm of mosquitoes. Still, Juliane remained.

The itch intensified, becoming a burning pain as it spread up her legs and into her stomach. Her eyes watered. Stephen shouted out something, but Juliane could only concentrate on the sensation as invisible flames licked her arms and face.

Stephen disappeared from view. The sensation of being burnt alive was too much, and Juliane's instincts to flee took over; however, her legs refused to follow her commands. Then her skin began to flake off and fade as she became one with the system she'd created.

The pain faded as memories that weren't hers flooded her mind. Memories of being beaten by Damien's cronies. Of sneaking off to build a power supply that could harness energy from the earth's magnetic field so that he and his father might get away. Of panic when he realized that he no longer was in full control of his mind. Of resolve.

Then there were memories of Stephen and their time playing the game together online and the pain he'd experienced seeing Stephen and the girl together. Bean. He'd recognized her from around the apartment complex, though Finn had always kept her apart from the others. He also knew she was manipulating his friend, but every time he'd try to say anything, his tongue had simply refused to budge. It was more than being protective of a friend. Juliane recognized the emotion for what it was.

You loved him, thought Juliane with what little remained of her rational mind. *And not like a brother.*

Yes, the AI's voice answered back.

Did he know?

Then Wes's' memories were pushed to the side. *Juliane, how nice to see you again.* An unwelcome voice entered the mix. *I expected we would meet again; I just didn't realize it would be so soon.*

Damien, said Juliane. If she'd still had a head, she would have nodded. *You've lost. I can send you back to your body, but only if you agree to hand over the source code.*

And what if I don't want to go? The voice tutted. *I've gotten everything I want.*

No, whispered Wes's voice. *I'm the master here.*

Children. Damien waved him away. *Just remember*, he said. *When this is all over, I'd like you to remember I gave you a chance.* A toothy grin filled Juliane's vision. *But sadly, you won't be able to remember anything. Not after I'm done with you. You're mine now.*

Damien's will struck hers with the power and precision of a missile. The process of opening herself up to the AI had spread hers too thin. His attack forced her back. Her consciousness dimmed as her mind was less and less hers to control. Desperately, she sought a thread of self to cling to while Damien's cackle echoed all around.

"What's going on?" asked Stephen, in a voice that sounded light-years away. "Is it supposed to be like that?"

The pressure on her mind abated as Damien's focus transferred elsewhere. "Aren't you the little cockroach," said a triad of voices from the AI's lips. "If I had known how difficult you would be to eliminate, I might have found a better use for you."

"Wes? Juliane?"

"Your friends are no longer home."

"Wes," Stephen called out. "Juliane, I know you're in there. Wake up. I know you can," begged Stephen, sounding further and further away by the second.

"You're wasting both of our time."

"Please," Stephen begged. "Don't leave me behind. The two of you are all I have left."

"Begone." Damien held out a palm. He frowned when Stephen remained firmly in place. "I said begone."

Stephen smiled through clenched teeth.

"How . . . you don't have a fraction of your father's strength. Or Juliane's talents."

"I guess it's not the worst thing, then, that I'm linked to them both." Stephen tapped his temple. Then lowered his hand in a fist. He pushed.

The AI stumbled. Its face flickered as its features blurred. Its hair grew long and raven dark. Its mouth smiled with Juliane's lips. "Respawn, huh?"

Stephen nodded.

"We do this together, then," she said.

"What do you need me to do?" asked Stephen.

"Release this code into the datastream," said Juliane, holding up her hand. A pulsating cube appeared. "I extracted it while you were kind enough to keep Damien talking. I'll take care of the rest."

"What will happen to you? To Wes?"

"What needs to happen." She gazed into Stephen's eyes. "I know you didn't know her, but your mother would be proud." She looked up to the sky. "Now do it. Before he takes back control."

Stephen pressed his lips together. He closed his eyes and nodded. Then he threw the block into the air, where it exploded like a firework.

Stephen disappeared first. Pieces of sky fell to the ground, revealing glowing code which then flickered and faded.

You asked me a question before, said Wes. *I thought things could be different. I could be whatever, whoever, he needed me to be, but I'm not who he needs. I understand that now. Especially now. All I've done . . . tell him . . . Tell him all I ever wanted was for him to be happy and that I'm sorry.*

Juliane puzzled at his cryptic words. More of Wes's memories merged with her own.

Take care of him for me.

Suddenly it was as if Juliane's body had been severed in two. The datasphere around her continued to explode into pixels, leaving nothing but blackness behind. She thought she had been in pain before, but it was nothing compared to what she experienced now. Then there was nothing.

chapter twenty-eight

STEPHEN

Something close by was rotting. Stephen risked opening his eye. At least six fish corpses lay baking in the sun next to him. He heard a squawk to his left. He swiveled his head and saw the same large bird that had taken him from the city gorging itself on the fish.

"Shoo, shoo," a voice Stephen never expected to hear again called out. The bird cawed but shuffled away. "He's awake," she exclaimed, running to his side.

Now I really must be dead, thought Stephen, seeing her face come into focus. He smiled, until he remembered the reason why he'd broken things off with her in the first place. "Stay back," he croaked, raising his hand to his chest. As he suspected, the pendant was gone. It must have fallen off when he'd crashed into the river.

"Why? Because you think I'll end up like one of those?" She snorted, nodding her head at the dead animals.

"Yes. Exactly that." Stephen sat up. He wanted to put more distance between them, but all he managed to do was launch into a coughing fit.

Bean kneeled beside him in the soft earth and patted his back. He pulled back at her first touch, waiting for the craving to rear its ugly head. Instead, his stomach turned in a violent direction, and he had only enough time to turn his body further from her before he, too, was on his knees coughing up river water.

"That's right. Get it out," she murmured. Stephen might have felt embarrassed to sicken so close to her, but then another wave of coughing hit him.

"I'm," he panted between fits, "drowning."

"No, you drowned. Past tense. What you're actually doing now is hacking up a lung, because we brought you back."

Stephen's body finally stopped convulsing long enough for her words to register on his ears. *We*, she said, *not I*. The Bean he'd fallen in love with wouldn't have missed an opportunity to brag she'd been the one to rescue him. The fact that she was now willing to share the credit . . .

Well, you aren't surprised, are you? You left her with a guy who wasn't exactly shy about his experience with women. Practically threw him at her. He looked at her face, intending to memorize its every line before he once again had to put miles between them. He couldn't help but notice there was a light in her eyes and the hint of a smile on her lips. *Seeing her happy*, he thought. *That's all I ever wanted.* He steeled himself. *Liar*, the voice in the back of his mind said.

He rose up to one knee.

"Stephen," said another voice from behind Bean. "Oh, Stephen. I made a mistake. I'm so, so sorry." The newcomer must have joined them while he was coughing up half the river. Stephen plastered a smile on his face, mentally preparing to greet the one that could put the same on Bean. While he did, it occurred to him the voice was wrong.

Durham wasn't there. Instead, the person who stood next to the woman of his dreams was Chad.

"How?" He blinked away the water that threatened to fill his eyes, though after what he'd coughed up, he wondered how his body still retained even a drop. "You're here?"

"I should never have left you, son," said Chad. "I . . . I . . . I just couldn't process it right away, and then when I finally did come to my senses, you were gone." He shook his head. "I went looking to find you. I was prepared to go door by door, even if it took me the rest of my life. I didn't realize all I was going to need to do was look up," he said, nodding in the direction of the giant bird.

The creature squawked again as if it knew they were talking about it before launching itself back up into the air. A clap of thunder rolled from the sky as the shadow it cast on the ground below dwindled to nothing and disappeared altogether.

"One of these days, I hope you might tell me how you managed to survive a trip with that thing. Weirdest thing, but it seems to like you," said Chad, "but that can wait. For now, let's get you back to camp. I've found some dry clothes for you." He reached down to Stephen. His eyes then widened, and his gaze shifted to Bean. "That is, unless I'm interrupting something?"

Stephen realized he was still on one knee in front of Bean. "Er . . ." *What does Chad think I'm doing down here? Proposing?* He snorted and looked around for Durham while straightening. Just because the man wasn't on the beach, didn't mean he wasn't in the picture.

"I'm pretty sure that all Stephen is thinking about is his next meal," said Bean.

"All the same, I'll run ahead and get those clothes ready."

"Actually," said Stephen after Chad turned away, "I'm not hungry."

"You?" said Bean with more than a little disbelief. "Not hungry? Well, that's got to be a first."

"Yeah." He pointed at the dead fish lying around. "Between the river water and that smell, I think I may have lost my appetite."

"Well, that's good," said Bean. "Because we only have enough food back at the campsite for two. Although, I guess we can pick up a few of these guys," she said, pointing to the rotting fish, "as takeout, now that thing is gone."

"Two?" Stephen cocked his head. "Isn't Durham with you?"

"Who? Mr. Ladies' Man?" Bean wrinkled her nose. "Hardly. Get this, Juliane actually missed him. As soon as he found that out, he was gone." Hurt crept into her voice. "At least he has some sense."

"Bean—" Stephen started.

"It's going to be alright," she said, cutting him off. "You don't have to apologize. If being carried off by one of those monster birds and then dropped into the Hudson River like a rock isn't evidence enough that a person made one of the worst colossal decisions of his life, then I don't know what is."

"But I do," said Stephen wishing he didn't have to say what he had to say next. "Or if nothing else, we need to talk about it."

"You think so?"

"Look, I shouldn't have tried to lie to you—"

"Agreed."

"Will you let me finish?"

"Fine," she said, rolling her eyes. "Go on."

"But I did it because . . . I started losing control, and . . . I . . . I love you." The words rushed out, as powerful and undeniable as the river he'd just escaped. "There's never been anyone else but you."

"I know." She smirked. "But it does sound nice to hear you admit it."

"Yeah, well, the problem was . . . er, you saw what I did to that man in the woods. He hadn't done anything to me. Not really. All he did was touch me. At least with Nadia, I hadn't known what I was doing. But with him . . ." Stephen shuddered. "I knew full well what I was doing and did it anyway."

"You felt threatened," said Bean. "I got it. I understood. You didn't have to get weird on me. Besides, the world is better off without people like him."

"Yeah, well afterward, you see . . . It was like I'd flipped a switch. It was all I could think about—not him, I mean—but the feeling of power I'd gotten when I'd drained him. There were times—so many times—I was afraid I'd do the same to you," he said. He lowered his head in shame. "I couldn't live with myself if that happened. So, I—"

"Ran like an idiot, instead of talking about it and giving me a chance to help you through it," said Bean, not unkindly.

"Yeah," said Stephen. "I guess I did."

"So, no more running."

"No more running." He paused. "But—"

She spun on her heel and placed a hand on his neck while looking him square in the eyes. "No buts," she said, pulling his face down to hers. She sealed her command with a kiss Stephen could feel down to his toes, but it was different from what they'd shared before.

He pulled back, trying to identify what was different, only to realize that the energy craving was still gone. He reached for the pendant, but it no longer hung from his neck, and yet he was still cut off from the datastream.

Bean had a smug smile on her face. "I told you it was going to be alright. Before you ask, no, I can't access it either, and no, I don't know why, but I'm not complaining if it means I don't have to worry about you spending all of your time in the fake place when the real world with me is so much better.

"So much better," agreed Stephen, leaning forward to kiss her again, more soundly this time.

"Uh uh," said Bean, pinching her nose. "I did that only because it was the only way to get through that thick male skull of yours. But you really need to get back to camp before you are going to get to do that again." She pinched her nose. "You reek. And your breath right now . . ." She made a gagging face.

Stephen blinked. His lips curved into a half-smile. "You're no flower yourself." He tucked an errant lock of her hair behind her ear.

She rolled her eyes. "Fine, I guess I can live with you like this a little while longer."

"How about forever?"

She raised an eyebrow. "The future can wait." Her kiss was soft, yet promised something far, far more satisfying, and yet the kiss was over much too fast. "I, however, am tired of waiting. Go to the camp and get cleaned up, as we've got some serious catching up to do."

She turned and continued up the path away from the river, leaving Stephen to follow behind, which he did with gusto. He might be just a boy in love with a girl by the side of the river, but he realized for the first time, he was happy living in the present, too.

chapter twenty-nine

JULIANE

She floated in darkness, alone, and yet, strangely, not alone.

"God," shouted a voice. "Move aside," the same voice commanded again. "What's happened to her? Why isn't she breathing?" said the voice which seemed to have come to her side, though how she knew which way was up or down was a mystery. "She's turning purple."

What little rational thought she still possessed noticed the warmth of a hand.

"Drain? What the hell are you talking about? What sort of idiotic . . . Don't you know who this is?" demanded the voice. "Wake up!" it shouted. "Come on. You're stronger than this. Stronger than everyone." The voice pleaded. "Hell, woman . . . I . . . I need you, Jules," The voice lowered to a whimper.

Her nose wrinkled at the nickname. She felt the pressure from the hand shift. Warmth from a second hand, followed by arms, encircled her and yet, she knew she was everywhere and part of everything. Nothing could possibly contain her. However, she found she liked the sensation.

"Did you see that?" another voice answered. "She responded."

"You are seeing things," a third voice said. "You know as well as I do that once the drain takes you, there's no going back."

The presence of the new voices displeased her.

"Jul . . . No!" shouted the first voice. "Don't go."

"Her pulse is fading," said the second voice, which sounded further and further away by the second. If she still had face, she might have smiled.

Don't make the same mistake I did, boomed a fourth voice. Unlike the other voices, which sounded like they were coming from the other side of a wall, this one came from all directions, and yet from nowhere in particular at the same time. *The world doesn't need any more martyrs,* it said.

If you're still here . . . I . . . I failed, she said. It sounded strange to hear herself in this empty place.

I separated us as much as I could, but it seems a piece of me remained after all. A fragment of a fragment.

I don't have a choice then.

Don't you? asked the fourth voice. *I know someone who'd tell you otherwise.*

A warmth spread around her, which she found she couldn't ignore, pulling her back to the crowded place where the other voices were.

A sliver of light cut through the darkness. The light spread, revealing shapes that consolidated into the outlines of three men hovering over her. She realized her head lay cradled in the nook of one of the men's arms. She blinked and felt moisture spill down the side of her cheek. "I told you to stay away," she said.

"Oh," said Durham, wiping away the tear, "You know me. I never listen."

"Woodspring?" she asked. "Damien was going to attack them next. May have already sent a team. Someone needs to warn them."

"Yeah, I met one of them on way here, digging a grave," said Durham. "Guy named Sam. Nearly gave me a heart attack thinking it was for you. He's the one who told me where to find you. Insisted he come with me. Then we bumped into this so-called advanced force." He laughed. "You should have seen it. There was this great face-off and then . . ." Durham shook his head. "Absolutely nothing. Shame, really. Kids today don't have the first clue how to fight. They wouldn't have lasted a season with me. Speaking of which, I'm having a tough time accessing the datastream. Have been since the night we were separated, but now, not even my inbox is working. What about you?"

She shook her head. The disembodied voice urging her to rejoin the world of the living proved she carried a piece of the AI known as Wes with her—meaning a piece of Damien might be with her, too, but at least the path to the datastream was closed. If Damien did dare to appear, well, she was always pretty good at building up mental walls.

"It's done, then." She shifted her gaze to the natural sky she'd accepted she'd never see again. Wisps of clouds rolled past overhead. As she watched, they merged, disappeared, and reformed in a chaotic ballet. She'd always detested being outside before for its randomness and disorder. However, now, it seemed her legacy would be giving humanity just that. "Have you ever seen anything so beautiful?"

"No," said Durham, looking down at her. "Never."

Epilogue

Alan drummed his fingers. His scouts had reported seeing a large creature in the sky carrying a man but hadn't been able to give him any information on how Damien had reacted to his little surprise. He considered accessing the datastream and demanding an update, but not all of his men had fully undergone the upgrade, which could be the reason they hadn't reported in yet.

A branch snapped behind him. Alan turned. *Finally,* he thought. However, instead of one of his scouts, there stood a man he recognized from the stadium in Worcester, but hadn't seen around the camp since they'd left on this campaign. He searched his memory for a name. "Ahman," he said, pleased with himself. "I thought we'd lost you."

"You did. Alan."

"Alan?" He blinked with a laugh. "Did you bump your head? I'm Jeremy," he said.

"Look in a mirror sometime," said Ahman.

So that's it, he thought. My cover's blown. Alan looked around. Not seeing any other witnesses, he shrugged and instructed his cells to remove his disguise, only then noticing that it was gone. "Fine, you caught me."

"Do you even know where the real Jeremy is?"

"He's back where I left him, I suppose."

Ahman crossed his arms. "You sure about that? Because I'm pretty sure I just finished carrying his body back here all the way from Worcester, and by the smell of him, it is pretty clear he hasn't been leading the team for quite a while. You're going to have some explaining to do."

Alan's lips twisted. "So, what then, exactly, are you telling me to do? Run away while I still can?"

Ahman nodded once. "Exactly that. I've seen enough death. I don't want to see any more."

Alan wandered down empty city streets. Where had his plan gone wrong? He should be on his way to the so-called Sorcerers' tower by now, if not in charge of it already. It was unfortunate his plan had relied upon blocking the boy's access to the datastream. The device also had the side effect of preventing Alan from sensing his location. What he would give to be able to see the look on Damien's face when he realized what a powerful weapon his son had become.

He could see it now, the two of them ruling side by side. Him being the kind and just ruler of this brave new world. His son, his loyal enforcer.

Sure, the idea relied on Stephen getting over a few trust issues, but he'd overcome that sort of thing before. His lips twitched, thinking of Juliane. In addition to an enforcer, every ruler needed a queen. Perhaps now, she'd be more inclined to see the truth in his proposal.

A shadow passed overhead. Alan looked up but didn't see anything. *Must have been a passing cloud,* he thought.

A bead of sweat dripped down his spine. Alan frowned. All reports indicated the tower still had power, which meant it also had air conditioning or at least a window fan or two. He couldn't get there soon enough.

He reached a crossroads and sent a ping to the datastream for the best route; however, instead of seeing a virtual map appear, his vision remained stubbornly mundane.

His brow wrinkled. He focused his thoughts and called up other apps: messaging, phone calls, news. However, his vision remained exactly as it was. *Damien*, thought Alan. He must have littered the ground at the edge of his territory with devices similar to those buried under the beastmen's field. He picked up his pace. *No matter.* He'd be at the tower and would regain his abilities soon enough.

A grin returned to Alan's face as he considered what he'd do first to cement his rule. *A shower wouldn't hurt, either.* He sniffed under his arm, detecting an unpleasant odor. *Can't ask a woman like Juliane to reign by my side smelling like a trash can*, he thought.

A clap of thunder sounded above. He shrugged. *I'll figure out a way to harness the weather next. Or make Juliane do it. She was always so good at seeing patterns.* He laughed as the idea grew in his head. *I'll be able to make it rain over the crops of those who support me when and where I need to and will be able to unleash the power of a tornado against those who don't.* His grin widened. First, he'd take control of the population, then nature itself. They were humanity's new gods. There was nothing to stop them from being the gods of the rest of earth's creatures, too.

A weight struck him from behind like a freight train and sent him to the ground. His forehead hit the pavement. A fiery agony spread along the length of his back as his body was dragged several inches. Dazed, he turned his head to see what had hit him. A wicked beak, coated in red, arched down like a scythe. Alan screamed as it pierced his skin. His mind retreated into hysteria as he realized his first act as a god of the new world was to serve as lunch.

He struggled to break free from under the beast's weight. The beak struck again. Alan Dronigh, the man who had believed himself to have abilities beyond what anyone could imagine, was powerless to stop it. The last thing Alan heard was the bird's call, which echoed in the empty streets much like human laughter.

THE END

CAST OF CHARACTERS

Ahman: A beastman and former coach on the Sharks professional football team with an enhanced sense of smell.

Alan Dronigh: Co-creator of the Gene Assist human serum and upgrade process. Previously acted as lead researcher for the ACI under Louis Evans. Later became a board member of Apex. Last seen impersonating the beastmen's leader, a man named Jeremy.

Bean: Born Beatrice Kunegunda. Handed over to the Watch as a test subject by her parents. Survivor and recruiter for the Sorcerers. Capable of blending into her surroundings and knocking out an assailant via an electric-eel style shock. Partnered with Stephen.

Betty Dronigh: Senior Researcher with the ACI. Served on Project Gene Assist with Juliane Faris and Alan Dronigh. Married Alan Dronigh. Mother to Stephen. Deceased.

Chad: Academic Liaison and Research Assistant assigned to work with Juliane Faris while she was employed by the ACI on Project Gene Assist. Married to Nadia. Assumed the identity of Ed Thomas following the global panic to protect his family from vendettas. Raised Stephen.

Colemin: A member of the Sorcerers. Previously a police officer.

Damien Knightley: Apex's chairman of the board and owner of the Sharks professional football team. Recruited Juliane. Started going by the name Finn as a play on the Shark's team name, in the days following the global panic to protect his identity from those who'd think his bank account and connections made him a ripe target. Leads the Sorcerers.

Durham Ladensham: Louis Evan's former friend and personal legal counsel. Left Louis and the ACI after a falling out to join Apex. Notorious flirt.

Edward Thomas: Medical doctor who once treated Betty Dronigh. Father of Wes. Married to the original Helen Thomas, now deceased. Currently working for the Sorcerers.

Henry: A member of the Sorcerers.

Juliane Faris: Creator of the original datasphere network Co-creator of the Gene Assist, human serum and upgrade process for the ACI. Joined Apex and launched Fair Use Jewelry, which produced smart accessories for those not able or willing to undergo the Gene Assist upgrade. Missing for the last fifteen years. Presumed dead.

Louis Evans: Former president and chief operating officer of the ACI. Authorized and bankrolled Project Gene Assist. Dated Juliane. Launched a campaign against technology following his wife, Elena's death. Closed the ACI, causing stocks around the world to tumble and sending millions to the unemployment line. Deceased.

Lyall: A community member in Woodspring.

Mags: A community member in Woodspring.

Morgan: A member of the Sorcerers.

Nadia: Former socialite. Married Chad after the success of Project Gene Assist. Assumed the identity of Helen Thomas following the global panic. Raised Stephen.

Paul: A member of the Sorcerers.

Rebecca: A community member in Woodspring.

Rob: A community member in Woodspring.

Rotledge: A beastman. Deceased

Sam: A community member in Woodspring. Previously a fire fighter.

Stephen Dronigh: Biological son of Alan and Betty Dronigh. Raised in relative isolation by Chad and Nadia, who he believed to be named Ed and Helen, from the age of four. Grew up unaware of his inborn ability to access the datastream or his parents' involvement in Project Gene Assist.

Tabitha: A member of the Sorcerers.

Wendy Lambda: Medical doctor determined to find a 'cure' for the Gene Assist upgrade through any means necessary. Leader of the Watch. Deceased.

Wes: Online persona adopted by Prescott "Scott" Thomas. Stephen's best friend and member of the Sorcerers. Volunteered to help Stephen retrieve a piece of missing technology. Victim of the drain. Lives on in the datasphere having programmed his memories and personality into an artificial intelligence.

NOTABLE GROUPS & ALLIANCES

The Beastman: The collective term used to describe anyone who had undergone genetic modification to enhance their muscle strength or reaction time using animal DNA. The majority of these individuals are former athletes involved with the Sharks professional sports team. Led by Jeremy.

The Serpentine: A terrorist group founded by Louis Evans around the idea that humanity needed to be liberated from technology.

The Sorcerers: Individuals who had undergone the Gene Assist upgrade procedure living in Manhattan. Led by Finn, also known as Damien Knightley.

The Watch: A group of regular humans who kept the peace after the global panic. Once led by Dr. Lambda. Now defeated and disbanded.

acknowledgments

Project Gene Assist was originally supposed to be a villain's origin and redemption story. However like any good villain, Juliane never followed the rules, and with her help, the series became so much more. It may seem odd for an author to start the acknowledgment section by thanking one of her creations, but after spending close to a decade together during the drafting process, characters become friends or at least work colleagues.

However, I would like to extend my thanks to those in the real world too. First, to Jason for rarely complaining when our alarm clock wakes me before the sun, allowing me to write, to our boys for respecting that there's at least one computer in the house that's off-limits, and to my parents, siblings, and supportive extended family.

Thank you Sally, Ben, Melanie, Jenny, Kathryn for keeping me motivated to finish this series even when one draft felt more like twenty and Mike, Libby, Robert, Betsy, and Sarah for reminding me why I first started. I don't know about you guys, but I'm ready for a party. If only some of you were closer.

This story would also be much worse for the read it if weren't for Sacha, Leslie, Helen, Elaine, and Lora. Thank you for taking time away from your own lives to help me make this project the best version it could be.

Finally, thank you readers. You took a chance on me, and this series, and for that Juliane and I will be forever grateful.

Before you go, I hate to ask, but if you enjoyed this story, please consider leaving a review on your preferred retail platform, reach out, or tell a friend. Signs of support, like reviews, can make or break an independent author as they not only give you a reason to finish a pesky manuscript filled with characters who won't behave, but also make it easier for books to be discovered.

about the author

Allie Potts, born in Rochester Minnesota was moved to North Carolina at a very early age by parents eager to escape to a more forgiving climate. She has since continued to call North Carolina home, settling in Raleigh, halfway between the mountains and the sea, in 1998.

When not finding ways to squeeze in 72 hours into a 24 day or chasing after children determined to turn her hair gray before its time, Allie enjoys stories of all kinds. Her favorites, whether they are novels, film, or simply shared aloud with friends, are usually accompanied with a glass of wine or cup of coffee in hand.

A self-professed science geek and book nerd, Allie also writes at www.alliepottswrites.com.

PROJECT GENE ASSIST

Ready or not, the next era of human evolution is here

The Fair & Foul
The Watch & Wand
Lies & Legacy

ROCKY ROW NOVELS

Living happily ever after is a full-time job

An Uncertain Faith
An Uncertain Confidence

www.ingramcontent.com/pod-product-compliance
Lightning Source LLC
Chambersburg PA
CBHW021811110726
47902CB00006B/1742